MW01482538

Author's Note

Ryerson is the most important work to me that I have ever written. Some people maintain that a piece of the writer always goes into their work, and nothing is ever truly "fiction." That may be true, however, none of it reflects just one experience or person, and was instead gathered and inspired by various people and experiences. Ryerson is, and always will be, a work of fiction, that I think everyone will find a little piece of themselves in. Each character has a piece of me, and everyone who has inspired me, in them. I owe so much, to so many, and would like to take the opportunity to thank them.

This is for my parents, who have stood by me, showing their unconditional love and support, and bestowed in me a set of morals unparalleled. Thank you.

This is for my brother, who was the first to read Ryerson, and has always been brutally honest about all my work. Thank you.

This is for Rick T, Pat O'C, Louise S, Jan D, Wendy K, George M, and Maureen R. You instilled a passion for learning in me and so many others I am certain. Whether you were my teacher or mentor, you guided me every step of the way. I will forever remember the lessons learned from great teachers. Thank you.

This is for Pauline, truly an angel, who will forever be in my heart as someone who showed me unconditional love and taught me so much about life and spirit. Thank you.

This is for the dear friends whom I grew up with, Amy, Dan, Nicole, Matt, Miguel, Lisa, and Chris. Sometimes you don't realize just how much people mean to you until you've lost touch. You each inspired me in your own way. Thank you.

This is for the three greatest friends I could ever have, Jonathon, Eric and John. The three of you have always been my rock, and my confidants. Thank you.

This is for my Grandparents. Perhaps my memories of you aren't strong but nonetheless I feel every day as though you guide me in strange and mysterious ways. Thank you.

Lastly this is for my Sarah, my love, my soul mate, my partner, my wife. You are my eternal partner and my world is never complete without you by my side. I am forever grateful to you for everything. Thank you.

Chapter 1

There are always some memories from your childhood that stay with you throughout your entire life. Whereas some things you forget by dinnertime, other things such as sights, smells, voices, feelings, they haunt you...or in some cases visit you for the rest of your life. Sometimes you feel something deep inside you that just sends you back to another time and place. Quite often the person that I remember the most when I am hit with those feelings is my Grandfather.

Sometimes I smell or see something on the street or in a restaurant or office, and it immediately makes me think of my Grandfather. Strangely enough, I can't put my finger on why it reminds me of him. Occasionally it makes my stomach sink, and I reminisce of old times lost. Although now, years later I can't remember a lot about him; I still miss him.

My Grandfather passed away when I was ten. He was my father's Dad, and everyone in our neighbourhood knew him. He was the only Grandparent I ever knew. My mother's parents passed away when I was just a baby, and my father's mother died when he was extremely young. However, my Dad was lucky because Grandpa was about the greatest Mom and Dad a kid could have. In one swift motion, Grandpa could bake a cake and throw a fastball that would put any player to shame.

In saying all this, my story certainly does not begin or end with my Grandfather, but it certainly gives you an idea as to just how influential my family is to me. We were always extremely close. I guess you could say that, from what I have seen and heard from friends and co-workers, I am the only living human being who did not have a...what they call..."dysfunctional family."

I was born on a chilly July afternoon in 1949, and I certainly could go into a "David Copperfield" type birth story but it was pretty uneventful. I am an only child and never missed having siblings. I had a mother, and a father who loved each other as much as they loved me. I was not spoiled, and I was certainly not made to go without. I think I was an attractive kid, with my mother's deep green eyes, and my father's wavy, thick, dark hair. We lived on a little street in a small suburban town called Medford, Ontario. Our neighbourhood was known as "The Ryerson Neighbourhood."

Douglas Ryerson was a successful banker at the turn of the

century. He built the first home on the street and many others after that. He struck it big in Real Estate and continued to live in the very first house he built, until his death in the late sixties. His house was enormous. It was a big old style, Elizabethan mansion. Old Man Ryerson was friendly enough, and everyone knew him, but for different reasons than my Grandfather was well known. Ryerson was the type of guy you waved to, tossed him his newspaper, and said "Good morning Mr. Ryerson," because it was polite to do so.

Generally speaking, he would wave back or nod, but my friends and I always thought he looked at everyone as though they were guilty of something serious. Ryerson Street was about ten houses long and came to a dead-end. There were only houses on one side of the street because the other side, across from my house, was a park...appropriately named Ryerson Park. Medford was a town of about 4,000, so pretty much every street was ten houses long with a park nearby.

Even still, our street was special. Our house was the second last one from the end. It was a good old red brick with green shutters and my father bought it right after the war. It was my parents' first and last house. They were not big on change, and I thank them for it now because I loved the house I grew up in. I can not even imagine how different my life might have been, if they had made me leave Ryerson. On our left, in the last house on the street, was my Grandfather's house until he passed away. So I had two great yards to play in and lots of space for baseball, which we frequently used my yard for, even though we had the park right across the road.

My two best friends since...well, since forever...lived right up the street. Brian was three houses up, and Michael, well he didn't come into my life until later on, but he didn't live far away. This was my neighbourhood. This was Ryerson in little suburban Medford, Ontario. This was also thirty years ago.

TORONTO, AUGUST 1990

My name is David Emerson. I grew up in Medford Ontario, and eventually I left to pursue a career in fine arts, which changed to Law, and then to a History Major and then finally I graduated with a degree in advertising. So, I work for an ad firm in Toronto. I do all right. From a cute kid, I grew into what I consider to be a pretty good-looking guy. My dark hair from childhood lightened slightly, but it's still dark and wavy with a few streaks of grey starting to show through. My green eyes never changed, and I keep myself in decent shape.

If you asked me up to this point to talk about my life, I think I would have refused. I would have cited that nothing of any interest has happened to me and that I was just an average "Joe" going through life like everyone else. I was perfectly immortal with no thought to the ultimate future.

I can't honestly say that one particular event sparked my, what society would call, mid-life crisis. I don't call it that at all. I think each one of us reach a particular age when we suddenly see things so much clearer. Life suddenly becomes reality and things that were previously unimportant become shatteringly clear. Unfortunately for the majority of the human race this little "awakening" does not happen following puberty or even during puberty but years and years after when much of our life is behind us…hence the term, mid-Life crisis.

In my twenties I used to dread the thought of being caught in the monotony of "mid-life." Having the same routines day in and day out and living your life void of all spontaneity. Even so, twenty years later here I was, up at six, enjoying my coffee out on my balcony watching the sun come up, going to work, coming home and falling asleep in front of the television. This had become my routine over the last several months.

It was a Tuesday when I came home early from work, mostly because I had put in a lot of hours and I needed the rest. I just wanted to relax, catch the Jays game on Television and maybe see a movie later. I had only been resting for an hour when the phone rang. Casually I looked over to my end table where the cordless phone sat. It rang twice before I actually made the attempt at getting up to answer it. Suddenly I could feel my mind race. It's a stunning thing, our privately telepathic minds. It's almost as though the phone has different rings for the message on the other end because it never fails, when its bad news, you sense it as it rings. One of my greatest fears since childhood was that tone the phone seemed to have when it was bad news. It's like when the phone rings in the middle of the night; your first instinct is a feeling of dread. However, this wasn't the middle of the night, it was barely three in the afternoon, but that feeling still overwhelmed me.

I stared at the phone my stomach sinking with each ring. I got up off the couch, set my drink on the coffee table and slowly lifted the receiver. "Hello?" The sound on the other side was a muffled voice and, in the background, there was the unmistakable sound of tears and several people talking. There was a long pause before someone spoke. His voice was quiet and broken. "Davey, its John." It took me a minute before I realized who it was. John was my cousin from my Father's side. I had not been exceptionally close with my Uncle Howard, but John and I had spent a lot of time together. We had not spoken since Christmas, both of us tied up in our jobs. "Davey, I'm sorry to have to call you like this..."

"What is it John, is Mom okay?" I asked, but inside I knew the answer.

"Well, yes, your Mom is okay."

That left only one alternative. "What happened, John?"

"It's your Dad, David, he had a stroke just a couple hours ago, they're telling us that he's not going to make it, and we best get the family together."

I swallowed hard. The room was spinning, and nothing seemed like reality. My Dad was my hero, my best friend, and my whole world. None of this made sense until much later on but now I believe that sons are reflections of their fathers, which is why when a father dies, it shakes the son's world to the very core because ultimately it's foreshadowing their own death. Of course, none of this occurred to me at that moment. All I could think of was that my Dad had been struck down in his prime. Truth be told, my Dad hadn't been in his prime for years; he was sixty-nine years old. He was far from a spring chicken but, in my mind, he was as young as I had ever known him to be. I tried to shake myself back into reality and focus on what was going on...my Dad was still alive and, for the time being, that's all that mattered.

"Can you make it here?" he asked.

"John, I'm on my way. Tell Mom I'm coming. Don't let anyone leave until I get there. I'll be there as soon as I can."

"When are you leaving?"

"Right now, I'll take a flight from the airport."

"Do you want me to meet you?" John asked.

"No just wait for me there," I said, getting annoyed that he was holding me up. I was now standing in my bedroom, with the phone tucked under my chin, cramming my wardrobe into a small carry-on bag. I hung up the phone and grabbed everything I thought I needed. I didn't have the time to think about what I had forgotten.

Benefits of working for an ad company included getting flights to anywhere...fast. I called my office and explained everything. Before I knew it, my friend and partner was telling me the plane, he had managed to book for me, was leaving in a half-hour. I was in Medford by late that evening. I took a cab from the small airport where they landed the plane. Airplanes used to bother me, but I even got used to the little twin engine pipers I always took from Toronto to Medford to visit my parents.

The cab pulled into the empty airport, and I got in the back. The driver smiled and greeted me. Small town cabs are kind of like being picked up by your friends, everyone knows everyone, and you get the same driver every time. In Toronto, sometimes it's comforting to know that you can call the cab driver any damn thing you want, and he either won't understand you or you'll never have to see him again. "Ryerson Park, please." The driver nodded and headed out to the highway. I checked my watch for the first time since getting off the flight. "9:26 PM." I rolled my eyes and rested my head back. I couldn't believe how late it was. What if I were too late? What if I miss the chance to say goodbye to my father? What if I did get there on time, would he pull through for me?

"You're Gary Emerson's boy?" the driver asked.

I nodded looking in the rear view mirror. "Yes."

"Back for a visit?" he asked.

I took a deep breath. "Remember he doesn't know, it's not his fault," I thought to myself. "My Dad had a stroke this morning. He's in pretty bad shape I guess. I'm just going there now."

I could actually see the driver's eyes sadden. "Oh son, I'm sorry I had no idea."

"I understand, it's no problem. But you understand my rush?"

"Certainly, I'll get you there young fella." Young fella? This of course did not occur to me either until well after that. Why was a man probably only ten years older than I was calling me a young fella? I was forty-one years old. I looked out my window as we began to pass the familiar buildings of my childhood. I saw the old corner stores, the dress shop, the hobby train shop, the little ice cream place, the pet store, as usual remarkably little had changed. There was the odd new store, but it was easily overlooked compared to the stores that had been here thirty years or more. Medford seemed to be frozen in time, and that was undoubtedly part of what made the little town so remarkable. The more things changed, the more they stayed the same.

The driver took several side streets before turning onto Ryerson. The park was shadowed in the moonlight with trees around the outskirts. My mind flashed to the many, many years spent in that park, running, smiling, laughing, and utterly immortal.

It seemed as though, even at this late hour, every light on the street was on. I could see our house in the distance. It was lit up more than any other was. The driver pulled up out front my old home. "David, don't worry about the fare. You just take care of that Pa of yours and let me know how he is."

"Thank you..." I replied, searching for the man's name.

"Larry," the driver said, extending his hand. "Larry Fitzsimmons, I played golf with your Dad."

"Thank you Larry," I replied, taking his hand in mine and at the same time giving him his cab fare. Larry nodded and took the money without mentioning it. I climbed from the cab with my hastily packed suitcase in one hand. I stood before the old turn of the century house looking up at what used to be my bedroom window. The front porch had just gotten another new coat of white paint, and the deep green shutters were starting to chip. The house still loomed over me. I had not been by to visit since Christmas, however, I called my parents three times a week faithfully. Not because I had to but mostly because homesickness in the big city would overtake me if I didn't hear they're strong parental voices. I had just talked to my Dad last night, just over twenty-four hours ago.

How astonishing is that, you talk to a person seemingly just moments before and now you wonder if you will ever speak to that person again. This made me suddenly realize that my fears of never saying goodbye were wrong; I did say goodbye to my Dad. That had been my last words to him. What were his to me?

"*I better let you go Dad; we both have a busy day tomorrow.*" That's right; Dad was going to see about getting new tires on his car.

"*You take care son, call us Thursday and we'll argue more about those Jays.*"

"*Alright Dad, give Mom a kiss for me. Goodnight.*"

"*Goodnight son.*"

"*Hey Pop?*"

"*Yeah Davey?*"

"I *love you.*"

"*Hey back at you my boy, I love you too.*"

My arms broke out in goose bumps as his voice echoed in my head, and throbbed through my brain. "*I love you too.... back at you my boy...my boy...my boy.*" I couldn't go without hearing his voice ever again. How could I?

Not realizing it, I dropped my suitcase to the sidewalk with a quiet thud. The front door opened and I was flooded with light from the porch. "Davey? Is that you?" My eyes adjusted to the new light.

"Yeah John it's me." I replied. My eyes searched the front of the house and continued up to each window. Most of the lights were on but there was one dark window on the right side. I sat there staring up at my old bedroom.

Chapter 2

July 1959

It was raining, the kind of rain that hits the ground and then flies back up at you. I sat in my bedroom window staring out at the gray, dull looking park where my birthday was supposed to be. I can still hear the sound of that rain hitting the cement outside and our gutter on the house. It banged like someone dropping pans in mother's kitchen. A shadow crept over my shoulder as I stared out into the rain pouting, my hands firmly planted on my cheeks. "That's really quite a nice little shower out there isn't it?" my father's voice said. I said nothing back to him.

"Aren't you going to get ready for your party?" he asked.

"What party, how can I have my stupid party when it's raining? If I can't have it in the park, I'm not having it at all; I just will stay nine."

My father walked across the room, the floorboards creaking under the pressure. He sat on my bed, a few feet behind me and ran his fingers through my hair. I crossed my arms and tears welled in my eyes. It was always harder to be manly when Dad was tousling my hair.

"So why don't you go downstairs and get your boots, and your rain jacket, and you and me, and Brian will go out to the garage and have a great party in there. It's not the park, but its outside, and I think you'll like what's in there."

"Brian went home cause Mom said that the party would have to be another day," I replied.

My mother had now joined the parade in my room and was standing in the doorway. "Davey, listen to your father, go get your boots on and go with him to the shed."

I scowled and then quickly hid it when I saw my mother's glance. "Yes Ma'am," I replied.

I walked downstairs...actually stomped downstairs, making it clear to everyone I was still not happy, and got my rubber boots on. They were caked with mud from the last frog catching expedition Brian and I had been on. Brian and I often walked to the nearby farmer's field and got ourselves stuck in the mud and eventually Dad would have to come and pull us out, sometimes leaving a boot or two behind.

This was a regular occurrence at least three times a week. I pulled my rain jacket from its peg and slipped it on over my head. Dad was coming down the stairs too, also in his boots. We walked to the back door and Dad opened it. Together we hurried from the back of the house out to his garage.

The garage was Dad's special spot. Not even Mom bugged him about cleaning up the garage and it needed it sometimes. Once in awhile, if Dad wasn't welding or doing something else a little dangerous, he would let Brian and I come in and look around. Dad had drawers and drawers of every bit of useless junk you could think of. I swear some of it you wouldn't even know what it was. He had drawers of rubber bands, and pencils, and writing ledgers, and little hand-carved soldiers, and things he had stuck together with wire, and glue, or sometimes just things he slammed together until they stuck. He had ashtrays, and penholders and weird looking foam things. To this day, I still have some of that stuff lying around, and still don't know what most of it is good for.

Brian and I spent many, many summer nights playing in Dad's garage and I know we still didn't get to the bottom of all his junk. We used to sit underneath one of his homemade counters surrounding the garage and get out the many little plastic and metal soldiers and play for hours. Mom called Dad a packrat; he never threw out anything. So when Dad opened that garage door on that rainy afternoon of my tenth birthday, you'll understand my shock.

Brian, my best friend, who was eight at the time, was sitting in a chair on the far side of the room. Dad's drawers and shelves were gone from this one corner of the room where Brian was sitting, and there were balloons and streamers and a big yellow card with red letters that said "HaPpy BIrtHDaY DaviT" (obviously done by Brian with great pride.) "Dad where is your stuff?" I asked pulling his hand.

Dad looked down at me and smiled. "Oh I decided to stop making your mother angry and get rid of some of the older junk. The stuff that I really didn't even know what it was. Then I took out the extra shelves and drawers and gave them to Henry down at the store, he said he could use the extra storage."

"So what are you gonna put over there now?" I asked, pointing in Brian's direction.

"The question is what are you going to put over there now? It's your space; I'll help you build whatever it is you want. I made a couple of chairs for you and Brian and a table as well, and we'll go down to the Hardware store and get you some tools to work with. Maybe you and I can start making some things together."

"Wow!" I exclaimed, running over to Brian. When I think back now the space was no bigger than the average persons bathroom but for two kids, who's only fort was what we could manage to make out of our mother's bed linen before she caught us, it was perfection. Not only because it was inside, and dry, but because now all of a sudden I had my own workspace right next to my Dad's. Mom brought the cake and drinks, and some hot dogs out to us, as Dad, Brian, and I sat at my new table in the garage and played Checkers. Brian and I always won Checkers against my Dad, always.

PRESENT AUGUST 1990

"Dave, come on in. Your Mom wants to see you," John repeated.

I nodded and picked up my suitcase off the sidewalk and headed for the front door. John stepped aside as I walked into the hallway. I set my suitcase down and looked at him. He had been crying too. He nodded towards the other room.

I walked around the corner and stood in the doorway between the hallway and the living room. Two of my aunts, one was my mother's sister, the other was my father's, were both crying and holding my mother. My mother looked astoundingly old. When you haven't seen someone for a long time you notice small things about them that most people don't realize. If I had seen my mother every day for the past six months I probably would have thought she looked great. I would have said she hasn't aged at all in the last year.

Standing here looking at her through the eyes of someone who hadn't been here, she was old, old and worn. My mother to me will always be the woman who used to hum the tune of the Battle Hymn Republic in the kitchen while she baked double chocolate cookies. I used to come from outside, or wherever I was, to sit on the floor in the kitchen and just listen to her hum. She had long dark hair and her eyes were such a brilliant green. She used to look down at me on the kitchen floor and say…"now if you'd put a sponge in one hand and a bucket in the other, you'd be that much more productive." Then she'd smile and brush my cheek with her hand.

Now, my mother was barely a shell of that vibrant, young woman. Her hair was a brilliant gray and her eyes had darkened and turned a color that was simply unrecognizable. But she was still the same woman, and I missed her. She wiped her eyes and looked at me standing in the doorway.

"Oh my baby," she cried, and tears begin to stream down her cheeks again.

"I missed you Mom," I said, and took her into my arms. She squeezed me close and for that minute I was able to be ten again. She looked at me and smiled through all those tears.

"Dad isn't doing well baby, he's not going...he's not..." she trailed off and fell into my arms again. I couldn't stop any sort of emotion at that moment. The whole situation suddenly and fiercely hit me like a wave of water. My father was dying. I began to cry and my aunts and cousin put their arms on us as we stood in the living room where I had spent days and months and years with my father.

Chapter 3

August 1959

  Running into the house was a bad habit that no one seemed to ever think they could break me of, especially when it involved suppertime. It was exhausting playing baseball for three hours between lunch and dinnertime. My mother would walk out onto the front porch, her favourite blue and white dishtowel in her hand, the towels that matched our best china, and she would call my name. *"Davey, dinner time."* Usually, it would come at the best of times, some time after our friend Bobby had just slid past Brian on third and Brian was ready to "tell his Mom" because he swears Bobby was tagged long before that touch on base. But it didn't matter anymore because it was time to eat. It was an incredibly hot day in August when I got the familiar dinner call and bolted from the field tossing my glove to Brian. He liked my dinnertime too because it meant he got to use my glove. I ran through the field and across the dead-end road to my house. Mom had already gone back inside to serve the food. Dad would be sitting at the kitchen table reading the newspaper, his shirt covered in sawdust from his latest wood project. His glasses would be pushed to the end of his nose and he would be whistling some little tune. That was only if tax cuts were in the works. Otherwise he would be shaking his head at how an Irish Catholic President would certainly be different for the United States, and how unfortunate it was that John Diefenbaker put an end to great liberal rule. He later changed his mind and ended up voting for Diefenbaker in '63, not that it did any good. My Dad was not always a die-hard liberal; he went with whoever he thought best represented the country.

  I ran towards my front porch and inside the front door. I could smell Mom's delicious meal just yards away and it made me run faster. I think that is the point when my sneaker decided to revolt. It had enough abuse and was ready to fight back. I felt my foot hit the small step leading into the living room, and it was too late to stop, I was going down for the count...hard! My shoe actually flew off my foot as I came down towards the floor. Unfortunately, between the carpet and I was the stair banister leading to the upper floor. My face collided into the banister, with nothing between them to slow the fall, or pad the break. I could feel pain flashing through me, my gums pinched into my teeth and a warmth that could only be thick, heavy blood washed over my face. I bounced off the banister and fell sideways onto the floor beside the stairs. You could count off three seconds before shock was gone and pain was inevitable. My screams were shrill and cut through the air. I heard a dish smash to the ground in the other room and my mother gasp, "oh my gosh."

Footsteps were pounding towards me under my bleeding head. I don't know if it was black washing over me in the form of unconsciousness or whether it was actually just blood, but it hurt. My hands lay at my side as I rolled on the ground screaming. "David," I heard my father say with a fear in his voice I had never heard before. He rushed to my side and immediately, without hesitation, scooped me up into his arms. He rushed me from the front foyer into the kitchen and grabbed Mom's favourite dishcloths. I remember being bent over my father's strong arms. My mother stood beside him crying out..."David, David, baby are you all right?"

The dishcloth hit my face and my screams doubled. The pain was excruciating. In my head I think I honestly wondered if my face was still there. "David, please hold still," my father begged, still with a tone of fear in his voice as he ran the warm dish cloth over my face. I could suddenly breathe better as he caught the blood on the towel. It only enabled me to scream louder.

"Diane, bring the car around alright?" my Dad said, still holding the cloth to my head.

"Gary...I...no...can't..."

My father turned his head to face my mother. "Honey, we need to get David to the hospital, he's going to be fine. Now please, go get the car." I heard my mother coughing back sobs and then rushing towards where my accident had happened. The cloth stayed on my face, and I stayed close to my Dad's chest as we drove to the hospital.

I could hear his whispers as he lowered his lips to my ears, "my little man, you've certainly made a mark, but you're gonna be as good as new."

PRESENT AUGUST 1990

'My little man, you've certainly made a mark.'
I held my mother closely to me. Her small frame crumpled into my body as I held her. "Can we see him Mom, can we go see Dad?" I asked holding her back to look into her eyes. She nodded and

wiped her tears.

"We can see him anytime, David. I just want him to be alright," she cried.

"So do I, Mom, so do I." I took her into my arms and rubbed her back comfortingly.

"Your mother needs her rest; can you wait a little longer?" my Aunt asked, from behind us.

"No, I can't do that. I have to see him tonight," I replied, looking at my Aunt. "I can't miss the opportunity to..." I looked around at the faces surrounding me, "well I just have to see him tonight."

My Aunt nodded understandingly. "Mom, I think you should stay here with Aunt Susan, and I'll call you from the Hospital if anything has changed alright?" My Mom looked up at me and I tried to force a smile but I know it came out as a look of sadness. Tears were still streaming down her cheeks.

"How will I live without him?" she asked, and for that moment I was no longer her son and she wasn't even speaking to me but just to the powers-that-be. I motioned to my Aunt Susan to take her and she ushered my Mom to the couch to sit down.

"John," I said, motioning for him to come close to me. "Can you take me to the hospital?" I whispered.

"Absolutely David, let me get my coat."

Despite my Aunts' protest about waiting there was no way I was waiting any longer to see him. As long as they were giving immediate family access to my father's room in the tiny Intensive Care Ward of the local General Hospital, I would be there. John got his coat and his keys, and my Aunts took my mother to the back porch to get some air.

We got into John's car and it was almost eleven o'clock. We didn't speak to each other as John headed down the street towards the hospital. I knew he was glancing at me, looking for the words to say, but there was nothing to be said. Everyone sensed the inevitable and speeches and tears needed to be saved.

I walked through the sliding doors of the Hospital that opened as I approached them. The hospital halls were quiet as I made my way up the main corridor. Small hospitals after hours were like something from a horror movie, no sounds, no voices, and no personnel. It was as though some evil creature had eaten them all. I walked towards the front desk that was more of a small square window in the wall. John had stayed outside for a cigarette, and at my request. If I was to see my father, it would be alone. The hospital had not changed in thirty years or more. The furniture was up to date and the magazines a little newer but the same walls, the same paint, the same pictures, and the same smell met me as I walked down the halls.

August 1959 (several minutes after the accident)

I remember thinking how dizzy it was making me watching the ceiling lights flash above me as my father ran inside the front doors of the hospital, the dishcloth still placed strategically over my wound. The nurse at the front desk stood from her chair as my father rushed in with me in his arms and my mother trailing behind him. "Emily," he said calling the nurse by name, "my son, he needs....David....he needs a doctor, right away, please."

My cries of pain had subsided into coughs and the occasional moan. "May I take a look?" Emily Kenns asked. She motioned for my father to set me onto a stretcher in the hallway of the hospital. I have no doubt that, at six o'clock in the evening, there were other patients in the ER that night but of course I have no idea whether or not that was the case. I remember my Dad finally laying me down on the crisp, cool sheets of the hospital stretcher. She peeled back the dishcloth, which was sticking to my face already. My father still knelt beside me squeezing my hand in his.

"That is one nasty scratch you got there young David," she said looking down at me. She was a pretty nurse, young, with long blonde hair. The sight of my newly developed face didn't seem to phase her much, which either meant it wasn't that bad as the pain indicated or she was used to looking at things like this. My father's expression, on the other hand, told me it was likely the latter of the two.

"Alright, let's take him down to the examination room and see if we can't fix you up." She took the handles on the stretcher and pushed me towards the exam rooms. My father and mother were on either side of me and I was beginning to wish I had stayed at home to find out if Brian had actually tagged Bobby.

We banged through a set of swinging double doors and I could hear other voices in the room. "Doctor, could you take a look at this young man. He's got...," what followed was a jumble of words that was something like what I heard coming from the evening news when my Dad watched it as I was going up to bed. It was distant, and completely incomprehensible. The only word I heard that I understood was cut...which was used way more than once in her description of my accident. My mother's cries were comforting actually. It let me know she was still there, as two nurses and now a doctor stood over me. I heard the sound of tape being peeled off something, and then something banging around above my head. Light hit my face from the doctor's headlamp. He pulled his mask up over his mouth as he lowered his head only inches from my face. Next came the dull taste of gauze. I always figured that Peas, a vegetable I had not yet been forced to try, would taste something like gauze. It's a taste I don't think I could ever forget and never grew quite used to, despite my many trips to the Dentist.

I coughed twice and tried to open my left eye, which hurt more than I wanted it too. "Is my face gone?" I asked quite matter-of-factly.

The doctor smiled, although I couldn't actually see the smile through the mask. "No your face is still there, Davey. However, you're missing a couple of those little white teeth you might be fond of." The doctor then stood up and let the nurses attend to feeding me the gauze.

"Gary, Diane, he's going to be fine, there are no cuts to his head, and there are no serious bumps or bruises anywhere on the skull. He knocked out two or three teeth and cut up his lips and gums pretty good. A couple of stitches to the gums and he'll be better before you know it." My mother thanked him and I could hear him walking away from me which was actually a relief.

My father knelt beside me again and I looked over at him out of my right eye. My left eye still hurt too much to bother opening. My father was smiling now and the fear was gone. He was back to himself again and I was relieved. "Davey, you're gonna be okay. The doctor says in a few minutes he'll have your ugly mug right back into place." I tried a smile but that hurt worse than anything did. "How would you like some ice cream after? I'll go get us a great big bucket." I nodded and my Dad smiled and tousled my hair. "I love you son," he said and kissed my forehead.

Chapter 4

PRESENT AUGUST 1990

I looked inside the small, cramped, night office looking for the nurse. She was sitting off to the side reading some sort of romance novel. "Excuse me?" I said quietly. My voice was hoarse and my throat was dry. "Ma'am, I need to see my father."

The woman looked up. She didn't look familiar which actually gave me a feeling of relief. She was in her mid-forties and was well kept. She looked tired but not worn out, the benefits of being a small town nurse. "Sir, visiting hours are long over." Her voice was soft, and compassionate, very unlike some medical personnel that I had come across in the city.

"My father is Gary Emerson; he suffered a stroke this afternoon and is in your Intensive Care Ward. My mother told me that I could visit him any time tonight, by the Doctor's orders. My name is David, David Emerson."

"Oh Mr. Emerson, I'm sorry, of course, let me take you there." She walked away from the window and a door to my left opened. She began heading down the hallway that branched off from the main corridor. The side halls were dark, barely lit by the emergency lights overhead. Cutbacks meant that nightlights were not used. A large set of double doors sat in front of us as I hurried behind the nurse to keep in step with her.

She entered through the doors, and then turned sharply to the right through another single door marked "INTEN IVE C RE" in cheap, blue lettering that was peeled and cracked. The Ward was ominous and smelled the way a medical office usually smells. It was silent except for another nurse sitting at a desk in the centre of the ward scribbling on a notepad. I stopped to listen to the hum of the machinery and the steady *beep, beep, beep* of....someone's.....heart monitor.

I stopped just inside the ward and the nurse asked me to wait there. She walked over to the other nurse who didn't stop writing on her pad to greet us. They spoke in muffled tones at the desk and they glanced at me several times. I looked around the small Intensive Care Unit. Several different rooms were off the main area. Most of the doors to these rooms were closed except the very first which was left open, and was in view of the Nurse's desk. It would appear, although my senses were far from being in good shape, that the heart monitor noise was emanating from that room. My senses were so dulled, and my emotions rattled that it truly never crossed my naive mind that my father might be laying only feet away from me in that very room. The nurse who brought me to the ward walked back towards me.

"Mr. Emerson? Nurse Haskill will take you in to see your father, if you need anything before you leave, let me know."

"Pardon me?" I asked trying to focus. The nurse smiled a sympathetic half-grin.

"Come see me if you need anything, Mr. Emerson," she repeated.

I nodded and the first nurse disappeared back into the hallway. Nurse Haskill approached me slowly. She was a much, older, heavy-set nurse with years of worry creased into her face. "Mr. Emerson, if you'd like to come with me, your father is in the other room."

Again, I simply nodded and could barely lift my feet to follow her into the very room I had been looking at. "Not to upset you in any way, but I always like to prepare family...your father is very sick and he will be very pale, and look very different. Do you understand this?" she asked.

"Yes of course, I understand." I replied. Of course I had not heard anything she had said. She nodded and stepped aside ushering me into the room. I can't say I actually remember moving my feet by voluntary action but somehow, something kept me moving as I entered the room. The heart monitor was deafening now...*beep....beep....beep*...and if I had been more aware of my surroundings I may have covered my ears. But it would not have made a difference; the sound echoed in my head, *beep....beep....beep*.

I walked through the door, and the nurse pulled back the sky blue curtain that surrounded my father's bed. There was an overhead light above him that illuminated the room just enough to see. My eyes scanned the room. The shadowy form of a crumpled man ruffled the pale blue hospital blankets marked MGH on the seam. My eyes searched the sheets as I walked towards the side of the bed. Medical equipment clogged the far side of the room, all of them whirling, and shining and of course the steady... *beep....beep....beep*. My eyes fixated on the face of the man I had known my entire life. The man who held me when I scraped my knee, or crashed my face into the banister, yelled at me when I broke the car window, talked me through every major teenage disaster, dragged me to my room when I refused to clean up my mess, and always, always, loved me unconditionally. He lay before me, silently, his face was pale white, white like snow. His face had added character in the form of a clear plastic tube running from his nostrils to the whirling, machine on his right. My whole life just froze in that instant. I felt my mouth open in shock staring down at my father.

His eyes were closed. If I tilted my head just right, I could tell he was looking at me through slits, waiting for me to try and squirt him with water or shaving cream. Then, when I got close, he would jump from the bed before I got him, and get me twice as bad. I knelt beside the bed and slowly, very slowly took his wrinkled, cold hand in mine and pressed it to my face. There was no life in his magic fingertips. There were no quarters behind my ears, there was no carved toys left in those worn hands. They sat lifeless in mine.

A tear came without warning and sobs followed, sobs that drowned out the horrible death machine...*beep....beep....beep*. A sob escaped from my mouth and I lowered my head into his hand. "Dad," I cried, "oh God, Dad." The hospital halls took my sobs and carried them through the empty hallways. "I love you Dad."

Chapter 5

"Amazing Grace, how sweet the sound, that saved a wretch like me...," that song, even before my father died, or my Grandfather, or anyone else I had lost, haunted me. Perhaps songs, books, and people that show truth scare us. That song sent shivers down my spine every time I heard it. We lost my father that night, just after I said my final goodbye.

The shock still overwhelmed me. All around me, at the funeral, people sobbed, hardly to be noticed by me despite the fact that they cut through the air. The minister spoke of salvation, and how Gary was a man who feared God, and dealt with life like he did his death...peacefully. I stared at my father's face only feet away from me. His eyes were closed in a morbid and terrifying way and I had to look away, knowing they would never open again. My mother sat beside me overwhelmed with grief. John held her the way that perhaps only a son should during this time but my mind and heart just wasn't there the way she needed it to be.

In fact, I don't know that my mind was there at all. Physically, I sat in the pew, listening to the words and songs of my father's funeral but I don't think to this day that I could recount much else. My mind simply kept repeating the idea that my father was not coming back, he was gone. I looked around at the people sitting on either side of me, family, friends of my mother and father's that I hadn't seen in years. It was like I was behind glass looking at them from another room. I turned my eyes to the front of the church focusing on a large wooden cross hanging behind my father's casket.

"At this time, I would like to invite David Emerson, Gary's son, to the front to say a few words about his father." The minister was looking down at me and....smiling? Smiling? What a dick...how could he be smiling at me? The compassion and understanding and sadness in his smile were severely overlooked by me at the moment. I was suddenly jolted into my body by the revelation that this minister, who knew my father well, was smiling at me while my father lay there in his casket....dead.

I looked around me and suddenly realized that everyone was looking at me, and most of them were smiling? Had the whole damn town lost their minds? My father was dead. A man they all supposedly adored and they sit here in this church where they spoke with him every Sunday and Wednesday and the occasional Thursday evening...and they are laughing at me. They don't have any sympathy, they're probably glad he's gone, "good riddance to Gary Emerson," they whispered under their breath. They were horrible people. How could these people pretend to be my father's friends? They hate him, they hate me and my family, they don't understand, they don't understand what it's like to not have your father with you anymore.

Suddenly I was standing in front of these people, the pulpit in front of me. The minister stood several feet to my left, his head bowed in silent prayer, and the trails of tears still fresh on his face. The faces that looked at me from the pews were dark and saddened. They weren't the happy, vindictive crowd that my mind made them out to be only a moment ago. They looked at me for words of wisdom, for words that perhaps my father would say in this time of mourning. My father was gone, and in his place he had left me to feed these people with the words from his heart to my mouth.

"Alone but not quite alone, I face an empty chair. Yet somehow in the silence, I know that he is there. With me for so many years, and now no longer here with me, and yet in some unusual way he keeps me company. That poem kept surfacing when I was looking for something to say about my father," I began speaking. "My father, was not a man of action, he didn't change the world, he didn't run for office, or heal the sick, he wasn't a man who was set in his ways. And still my father...," I cleared my throat and looked down at the podium. "My father..."

I looked over at my Dad, "...my father was brilliant, caring, decent, moral, and a beautiful human being. He believed in love, and trust, and honesty. Perhaps he didn't leave us money or material things but he did leave me something that I won't ever lose and that's how to be a real man." Whatever I had written down as a guideline began to leave me as I began to tell them about my father. They all knew Gary Emerson, they probably knew Gary Emerson better than I did, but the one person they could not possibly know about, like I did, was my Dad.

SEPTEMBER 1959

I don't think I will ever know why Dad walked me to school that day. It was my first day of the fourth grade, and Brian was long gone to school. Dad had unfortunately discovered my hiding place underneath the front steps on his way to the garage. I scrunched up against the house and held my breath as I heard him talking to my Mom and then I could hear his heavy steps on the cement porch.

My shoes, once again getting me in trouble, were sticking out from the side of the porch. I heard my Dad pause on the step and chuckle. He put his metal toolbox, the one with his name on the side in black marker, down on the cement and sat down on the middle step.

"Boy, if the hooky police catch you under our porch, I'd be afraid that they'd take you to jail."

I stuck my head out from under the porch and looked over the side at my father. "There is no hooky police," I replied, instantly scared to death of them.

"Nope, there isn't, but if I catch you missing school you'll wish there was," he replied, seriously, but smiling.

I crawled out from under the porch. "Dad, you don't know Miss Hairy Perry...she's awful, she makes kids shovel dirt when they're bad. Last year, Brian's brother had to refill the whole sandbox because he forgot his homework."

"Miss who?" my Dad said, obviously missing the point of my story.

"Hairy Perry..." I replied. My father nodded and appeared thoughtful for several moments before he spoke again.

"Well it sounds to me like you've got Miss....Perry....in the best way." I climbed out from underneath our porch.

"What do you mean?" I asked sitting down on the step beside my Dad. He put his arm around me and squeezed my shoulders.

"Well, you of all people don't have to be worried about her because you have her secret."

"What secret, that she tortures children?" I asked.

My Dad laughed. "No, if she made Brian's brother do that because he forgot his homework than you'll never have to shovel dirt."

"Why?" I asked.

"Don't forget your homework," he replied matter-of-factly. Then with that he stood up and began to walk down the front sidewalk. He turned to me as he reached the end of the walkway and smiled. "Come on, I'll walk you to school before Hairy Perry marks you late."

I smiled back and ran to my father's side. We began to walk towards the small middle school not more than a block or two from my house. My father reached down and dropped his arm around my shoulder. "So...son..."

"Yeah Dad?"

"Why do they call her Hairy Perry?"

Chapter 6

"...it's funny the things that people say to you that you remember for a lifetime, especially Dads. The only time I ever went to a racetrack was with my Dad and my Uncle Howard." The people of the church seemed to have stopped mourning quite so vocally. It was truly as though my words soothed them. As I stood there talking about my Dad and all the clever things he did for me, and the way he used to make those annoying sounds with his tongue when he was getting angry but didn't want to say anything, it was as though my father appeared to them through me and comforted them. Seeing this comforted me.

"My Dad's friends, some of you here today, tell me that my Dad loved the track. I don't know if my Mom and I knew that or not." There was a chuckle throughout the church and I looked down at my Mom and she smiled. I continued. "I was almost twenty-one when he finally took me to the track. I loved watching those beautiful horses race around. It wasn't nearly as fun though as watching my Dad with my Uncle Howard as they looked through their grotesquely large and embarrassing binoculars." I made circles with my hands and put them at my eyes mockingly. The crowed chuckled again.

"My Uncle Howard would yell 'Come on you sons of b...' and my Dad would elbow him, and he'd finish his sentence with 'bad ponies.' My Dad, as you all know, was very calm and usually quite laid back. Perhaps that's why the track intrigued him so much because it brought out a certain monster in him known as the competitive spirit. He'd yell and cheer and elbow my Uncle...and he'd shout and do this ridiculous dance when his horse won." I cleared my throat again. "The dance he did when his horse lost was even worse." The crowd chuckled again and my mother laughed in spite of herself.

"Then that one day...after two hours of races...he said the magic words and handed me a two-dollar bill. 'Wanna bet?' he asked me. I nodded, and we slowly made our way, with Uncle Howard, to the betting booths. I kept staring at the two-dollar bill like it was magic, this money would soon be in the saddle of a beautiful horse. 'Who do you like to win my boy?' he asked me at the booth, passing me a list of the horses."

"The list had eight horses and all kinds of stats that meant nothing to me whatsoever. I think if you asked Dad or my Uncle Howard they had no idea either." My Uncle Howard smiled and winked at me from his front row seat in the church. His tears had subsided to a look of reminiscence on his face. "I walked to the booth with my Dad beside me. 'I want Angel's Delight to win.' My father smiled at me and nodded. The lady behind the booth hadn't smiled since the early sixties by the looks of her. She stared down at my two-dollar bill like it was poison. My Dad stepped in and pushed the money across the counter at her. 'Two on Angel's Delight to win.' She nodded and handed me back a slip, which said something like what my father had said."

"We returned to our seats and my whole outlook on the racing situation had changed. Suddenly my heart pounded and my hands were sweaty and the small ticket in my hand was bunched up and soaked in my sweat. My mouth was dry as I stared at the countdown clock till Post Time. It was exhilarating! The horses got into their places and waited...and waited...and waited...and finally BANG, the horses jolted from the starting block. Angel's Delight bounced from the gate and surged into second place just inches behind Mommy's Mare.., 'GO!' I yelled suddenly jumping from my seat. My Dad looked over at me and smiled."

"Angel's Delight did pull into first on the second lap...for about four and a half seconds before dropping down to fourth in the homestretch and coming across the finish in fifth. Devil's Own flew across the finish line in first...he was my Uncle and father's choice to win. My Uncle shouted in joy and my father didn't do much at all. He just smiled and looked at his winning ticket in his hand. He looked over at me staring down at my useless waste of two dollars. He chuckled and patted me on the back. I looked over at him and I said..., 'I knew...I knew I should have gone with Devil's Own.' Dad looked over at me and squeezed my shoulders. As he walked towards the exit, with my Uncle Howard, he said something that my whole life I will never forget because I knew even then that what he meant was not just for the race we had just seen but for my entire life. He said to me, 'Son, it's always easier to pick the horse, once the race is over.'"

I had said my part, it wasn't anything near what I had planned on saying but by the looks on everyone's face including that of my mother, I knew it didn't matter. I had given them a glimpse of something that I thought they could not possibly understand, the love I had for my father.

I looked at each one of their faces and for the first time I realized that perhaps I hadn't given my family and friends a fair chance. It was true that, to me, he had been my father, a title that was significant to me and me only. But each one of these people had a different way of knowing my father., friend, co-worker, neighbour...and each one came with it's own share of stories, and memories and...love for my Dad. I looked at each one of the people below me in the church pews. Tears began to build up in my eyes as I saw the look of loss in each one of their faces. They looked like I felt and it comforted me to know that I wasn't alone at all. My eyes fell across the front row where my mother sat. She gave me a heartfelt smile, and I smiled back at her. I looked up and down the aisles at each person until my eyes stopped on a familiar face. His face had aged, I mean, I hadn't seen him in over a year, just distant phone conversations and hurried post cards. I didn't think he had come. I didn't even know if he knew my father had passed away. But sometime during the funeral he had come in quietly and seated himself in the very back row of the church. It was Brian, my best friend, my soul mate, since forever.

I honestly wish I could recount the day that Brian and I met. I know, only that we were two, and my mother brought his mother some sort of traditional "welcome to the neighbourhood," greeting gift. From that day on, as my mother always said, Brian and I were inseparable, which was convenient for him since I turned out to be a slightly bigger kid than Brian, and a little more broad shouldered, and gutsy. Brian was the type of kid that the other kids just couldn't help but pick on for whatever reason. He had blond hair, dark blue eyes, and was scrawny. He just never seemed to fit into his own skin growing up. I never saw anything wrong with him, he was my best friend, case closed. Our friendship may have benefited him for protection from the bigger kids...or smaller kids...or any kids...but it benefited me even more. Brian was my rock. He was always there for me, and today on the most devastating day of my life, there he was once again, nodding supportively.

I cleared my throat and stepped down from the podium. The ceremony continued and everyone shed tears. I sat in my seat beside my mother, staring at my father's final resting place. Inside the casket was my father's lifeless body. The only father I would ever have.

There are only a few things in life that can't ever be replaced. A father is definitely one of them

I didn't cry throughout the sermon. I didn't feel the need to. My mind was still elsewhere, but now I was being flooded with thoughts and memories, and mostly just my father's voice. It was as though he was taking a final opportunity to recap everything he had taught me. Before I knew it, people were standing. The Church was silent and the minister was making his way to the back of the church to shake people's hands. I heard nothing of what went on between my final eulogy to my father and this moment but it didn't bother me because I felt as though sitting there, the closest to my father I would ever be again...was enough for me. I ushered my mother to the front door and we stood beside the minister as our friends, family and neighbours made their way towards us.

I shook hands of people I didn't recognize anymore, it had been so long. Most of them were people who I had known well but they had simply aged. They called me by name, their hugs were sincere and loving and yet if I saw them elsewhere then this church I wouldn't have been able to identify them as friends. I looked up the line of faces waiting to offer their sympathies to us. Brian was not in the line. Brian was sitting in the front row of the church, his head in his hands. The line seemed to last forever, and I started to feel my hand cramping from all the shaking. I waited anxiously for the last person to pass me by.

I turned away from the front doors and walked down the middle aisle towards my best friend. I slid into the row behind him and sat down. I reached forward and put my hand on his shoulder. His head lifted and he turned to face me. I leaned forward. "Hi," he said.

"Hey."

His eyes were wet with tears. Brian's father had died three days before he was born. He was raised with my Dad being like a father to him. I hadn't thought how incredibly hard this must be on him. "You...uh...you look good," I said smiling at him.

"Thanks, you too." We both chuckled, mostly at ourselves. Here were two best friends barely able to make small talk. It had been almost five years since we had spent any significant time together. Although brief letters and phone calls kept us in touch, it wasn't enough to pretend we were still inseparable.

"Do you want to go outside and talk?" I asked him. He

nodded and we both stood. Together side by side, saying nothing, we walked away from my father.

September 1961

It was the best fall day. You know the kind...the wind is like spring meets summer with a teaspoon of winter. Crisp and clean, and the leaves are crunching underneath your feet, and you just want to lay back in them and look up at the blue sky. I had stayed behind in school later than usual to help the coach clean out the equipment room in the gym. Brian had decided to not wait because he wanted to get home and ride his bike. I swung my backpack over my head playfully, breathing deeply and thinking about Samantha Morrison's breasts that we had almost actually seen today during Gym glass when she took a nosedive into the mud. Needless to say this train of thought meant quite simply that I was twelve.

I approached Ryerson Park and I could see my house on the other side. I could also see several kids standing around the playground equipment directly across the road from my house. My pace quickened as I approached the crowd. I could almost tell from the children's stance and shouts that only one possible thing could have brought together a crowd like that....a fight...or more appropriately a beating. As I got closer I could see between the legs of some of the kids. Brian on the ground, blood running down his face from his nostrils. Some other kid, who I couldn't recognize from the sneakers or the fists that occasionally were coming down on Brian's head, was sitting on top of Brian.

I threw my bag to the grass and bombed towards the crowd. As I got closer I began to yell out so the crowd would let me through. "Hey, get off him." I ran through the screaming kids and hit the attacker broadside, sending him sprawling onto the grass. The other kids liked this added excitement and cheered me on.

Hitting Brian's attacker the way I did, I felt it too, because it sent me sprawling not far from him. He was on his feet too quickly and Brian was rolling over onto his stomach and holding his bleeding nose. I scrambled to my feet in time to take a blow to my nose from this equally tall, and same sized kid as me. He had dark black hair, even darker than mine, and a very unique complexion and the bluest eyes you have ever seen. They were piercing and bright. I took a step back and then hurled towards him, arms waving. This kid was not from this neighbourhood. Not only because of how he looked but he could actually fight. He didn't learn his moves from watching Pro-Wrestling. I was just a Gorgeous George wanna-be...this kid could actually scrap. Ultimately, I knew two good moves that had worked so far up to this point. I knew the tackle which consisted of bending over and ramming anything in sight until you hit the ground, and I knew the grapple, grab your opponent and pull them, shake them, throw them, basically scrap.

The kids were now cheering...not for either one of us...but just for the continuity of a fight. Then there was someone else coming towards us...I could feel him coming, as my first blow finally caught this little punk's cheek. The kids were silent, they were parting the crowd and I could sense his presence and it was not happy. The scruff of my neck was grabbed and I flew back from the fight into the air. My father held me firmly several feet from the ground. We were small kids but even if we weren't, my father was a big man.

"What do you think you're doing David?" he demanded, setting me down. The other boy stood up and was standing several feet in front of me, his arms crossed firmly across his chest, his blue eyes staring right through me.

"He was beating up Brian, Dad. He made him bleed."

Dad looked over my shoulder at Brian who was now standing to my left, but slowly making his way behind my father. His nose was still bleeding but it was slowing now and he had a noticeable bruise above his left eye. "Brian what happened?" my father asked, turning away from me and kneeling in front of him.

"He hit me. Then I fell down and he got on me and was hitting me really hard," Brian said, trying not to choke on his words. His eyes were teary but he was desperately trying to stay strong.

My father stood up, towering over all of us. "What's your name son?" he asked the mystery boy.

"My name is Michael Finn," he said. The kids still hanging around, who hadn't left for dinner, began to murmur and laugh. I kind of stopped and listened closely. He had said his name, and yet it was almost hard to hear him. It was almost as though he wasn't speaking English but he was...it was just covered under the strangest and thickest accent I had ever heard.

"Michael Finn...oh geez...you're Paul Finn's boy. You just moved in up the road there right?" my father asked him. Michael nodded. "You're not making a very good impression here, Michael. How come you're picking on kids smaller than you are?"

"He said I sounded like a head-hunter, and he said I was probably from the jungles of some country." My Dad turned to Brian again.

"Brian, now you definitely know better than to judge someone by the way they talk or look. Michael is from Australia, a continent that is a very, very long ways from here. Imagine how he must feel being so far away from his home."

My father had a way of making someone see the error of their ways very quickly. Brian nodded, looking down at the dirt. "And Michael, around this neighbourhood we talk things out before we start beating on our neighbours, alright?" Michael nodded. "Alright son, let's go, dinner's ready. Brian, come on to our place and I'll get you cleaned up before your mother sees you. She'll have a fit."

Brian walked a few steps behind us as my Dad and I walked together towards my house. "Dad, are you gonna give me heck too?" I asked finally. Dad looked at me and smiled. He rested his arm around my shoulders.

"Davey, your whole life, you're going to come across situations like the one you just saw and not just on the playground. Usually you'll find that, if you stop and think, you can always find a smart way to deal with it." I nodded and lowered my head. I was going to get heck and a lot of it. My Dad cleared his throat. "And then there will be times, that will come up, when someone you care about is being hurt or in trouble...and when that time comes and you have three seconds to weigh out your options...you just may have to jump in there and kick some ass." I looked up at my Dad and he smiled and winked at me. It was not only the first time that my father had actually used an inappropriate slang term with me, but I felt it was my first piece of adult advice. He was giving it to me straight, no editing, no cushion, and just straight talk. And even though I knew that my Dad hated seeing me fight, and hated violence, somehow I felt that he was proud of me that day because I had defended Brian in my own way. Besides I was a boy, and a few good scraps were part of the job description.

Chapter 7

Brian and I decided to avoid the lunch after the funeral. Everyone was meeting at the local "Hall" to have a lunch and "talk time" with family and friends. Instead we chose to walk along the old river where we used to fish and swim and hang out when the summer got really, really hot.

Brian told me about his job, he was management in a communications firm out west. He made decent money but a lot of it went to his mother who was very ill. Brian's mother no longer lived on Ryerson, or even in Medford. Instead several years ago, when she got a bad case of Alzheimer's, Brian moved her out to a very good and a very expensive care home in British Columbia.

"So...what about you? Still talking about Brewers and how it's the beer that will make you proud?" he asked.

"Yes, still doing advertising but the Brewer account is not with us anymore. I'm focusing right now on a Shampoo that doubles as a tub cleaner."

"What? Are you serious? You're kidding me..."

We both laughed. "Hey, people will market anything." We walked further up the river, the waters flowing south behind us. We were silent for a few minutes. I knew we were both thinking about Dad.

"Did you get to see him...before he died I mean?" Brian asked.

"Barely," I said.

"I'm sorry," he replied.

"You know, I keep asking myself what would be easier, if he had been sick and we could have at least seen it coming and emotionally prepared for this, or if it's easier this way."

"It's not possible David, I mean, I'm not emotionally prepared to see my mother die but it's only a matter of time. And, at the same time, when my brother died in that accident, no one could prepare themselves for that either."

We turned around and began to walk back towards Ryerson Park. "So are you staying in town?" Brian asked.

"I'm going to stay for awhile and make sure that Mom is okay. I don't know if she'll ever be okay though, you know. I'll stay as long as I have to. I took an indefinite leave of absence from work," I explained. Brian nodded. "What about you," I asked him. "Are you going to stick around?"

"I don't know. I should get back, I mean Mom is out there, and my work, and I really can't afford to miss a lot of time from work." He paused and looked towards his old house in the distance. The family that had bought his old home had painted it and added a deck and windows and gardens and such but underneath it was still his home. "Now that I'm here, with you, and seeing everyone, and I just think I'd like to take some time here."

"Well you're welcome to stay at the house with Mom and I. You can have our old spare room," I said, smiling.

"I might stay for a little while. Hey, have you talked to Michael?" Brian asked.

"No, I tried calling him in Boston at the number his office gave me but no answer. Maybe I'll try again tomorrow." We didn't say much else as we walked back to my place. It wasn't an uncomfortable silence, we were just taking in everything. We got to my house and went inside. The first thing that greeted us was the smell of cookies being baked. My Aunt was in the kitchen in her apron baking several sheets of cookies. She always cooked when she needed to relieve stress. It was getting late; Brian and I had walked the river for close to three hours. The funeral was long over and both of us just felt relieved to have each other.

"Oh David, good you're home. Your mother is asleep and I thought she could use the rest; I'll just make up some dinner for you and Brian. I nodded and Brian and I sat down at the kitchen table. My Aunt searched the pantry for some dinner ingredients. When she came back out she snapped her fingers in my direction. "I almost forgot, you'd never believe what I found in the closet when I was looking for your mother's jacket."

I shrugged. She walked to the closet and rummaged through it, pulling out a dusty old black ball mitt. It was my baseball glove, my pride and joy for so many years. My Grandpa had bought that for me from a Cubs game down in Chicago. My Dad spent hours just breaking it in with oil and tossing the ball in to it, so that it would be worked in. Brian smiled and I stood up. I took it from my Aunt and held it up. I slid it down over my hand and showed it to Brian. "Still fits," I said, smiling. The glove brought back so many memories of days and nights spent out in the baseball field at Ryerson Park. I could hear us shouting and laughing and just spending so much time being the happiest we could be. Of course you never know when it's happening that they are the greatest days of your life.

"So are you goin to stand there all day and look at it, or are we goin to play some damn baseball?" said a heavy accent from the doorway. Sometime since we had come in, someone had followed behind us. I turned around to face the voice and Brian jumped up from the table. Standing in the doorway in a very expensive Armani Suit was Michael Finn. He had a baseball in his left hand and a flask in the other. He tossed the baseball to me. "Batter's up baby, I bet I can still whoop you both."

As the sun sank into the sky, and our dinner was put on hold, Brian, Michael and I added another two hours to our time spent in that dusty old diamond . We could still crank that baseball far into the outfield. I hadn't hit a ball in that field since I was twenty years old. Brian was still the fastest pitcher outside the majors. Michael's vein in his temple still flared when Brian sent three fast balls flying past him. "Ohhhhhh Strike Three Crocodile Dundee, you're out!" Brian yelled. Michael laughed sarcastically and then went straight faced as he threw the bat and chased Brian around the field.

"You better move back there Finn...this one's going right over your head," I yelled towards the outfield as Brian wound up his pitch.

"Move back? Why so I can lie down and go to sleep while you strike out?" Michael retorted. The bat cracked as it connected and the ball bee lined for Michael. He snapped it out of the air and into his glove. "HA!" he cried out.

"Lucky catch."

Michael stepped up to bat. For five years, he was the only one in Ryerson who could consistently put a baseball through nearly any one of the windows of the houses on the street. That was a homerun and then some. "Alright, here I go, my infamous Ryerson homerun," Michael said, aiming the bat at the houses across the road.

"Have you got your bifocals in old man?" Brian asked.

"Hey up yours, Parker, pitch the ball," Michael retorted. Brian sent the first ball flying past the plate. Michael tossed it back to him. "Okay, now this is it," Michael repeated. Brian wound up and pitched another one but this time Michael's bat connected...hard.

"Going, going, going..." I called.

"Towards that car..." Brian replied.

"Oh no," we all said at the same time. The ball landed square in the middle of Mrs. Havisham's hood.

"Well shit, that never happened before," Michael replied, matter-of-factly.

Mrs. Havisham was coming out on her porch to investigate the noise. We all waved at her and she frowned in her direction. "Run, run now," I said. Three forty year old men running away from an eighty-five year old lady. We headed back to my house and dropped off our baseball equipment and then headed out to walk the familiar streets.

An hour later we sat in the local bar. It had changed names several times but it was still Murphy's to us. Even as kids, we came in here to see our Dads. We used to spend hours on the love machine in the corner that had all the lights and noises and used to say words we didn't understand. We'd annoy our Dads' for nickels until finally they'd give us some and we'd go back to the machine. Now we sat in our fathers' favourite booth in the corner of the bar, a pitcher of beer in front of us.

"To your father, Gary Emerson, a man like none I ever met," Michael said, raising his glass.

"To Gary," Brian agreed.

Our glasses clinked and we took a long drink. "So what's the news fellas...still employed I assume? You seeing anyone Brian?" Michael asked, taking another drink and then quickly chasing the beer with the flask he had at my house.

"Well I never got married," Brian replied to the question.

"I figured that, you're gay," Michael said.

"I meant in a relationship."

Michael smirked and waved his glass in Brian's direction.

"What about you ladies man, are you married?" Brian asked Michael.

"Sometimes," Michael replied. "Twice actually, but not currently. Both times their fault naturally."

"Naturally," Brian replied, smiling.

"How about you Davey boy? How's the wife?" Michael said, nudging me with his glass.

"What?" I asked, snapping back from my day dreaming. I had

been drifting in thought with the conversation.

"Wife…Sara, the old ball and chain,?"

"Uh…oh she's good, we're great," I replied.

"I always knew you'd be the first to go Davey. I mean, I wasn't about to settle down any time soon and Brian well….he still can't get married until it's legal…but you, I always knew you'd find the perfect girl and settle down."

I cleared my throat. "Yep, definitely found the right girl," I said, taking a drink from my glass.

"I think we thought you might have left Ms. Right behind," Michael replied, smiling and lifting his glass.

"Aw… the beautiful, and vivacious, and incredibly sexy Kathy Carmichael," Brian said, clinking his glass against Michael's.

"Kathy…Kathy…was twenty years ago…," I said, smiling at my friends.

"Kathy was the love of your life, David. You guys were like Bonnie and Clyde," Michael said.

"Lucy and Ricky," Brian added.

"Snow White and Prince Charming."

"Bert and Ernie," Brian chimed in. Michael looked at Brian, and Brian shrugged.

"You had to go there didn't you," he said. Brian laughed.

"I miss Kathy sometimes. I mean, even years later, I hear a song we danced too, or a smell that reminds me of her perfume. She meant a lot to me," I said.

Michael uncapped his flask, his beer having been long consumed, and took a long drink, emptying the flask too. "She still lives here you know," he said, sticking his flask inside his jacket pocket. Brian looked at Michael with disbelief.

"Kathy? Kathy Carmichael still lives here in Medford," Brian asked. Michael nodded and bobbed his thin eyebrows provocatively, glancing in my direction. I shook my head at his gesture.

"I figured she would have gone south, hit California and went for that dream occupation in Marine Biology," I said.

"Nope, actually, she did go south, moved to Florida until her father got crippled in a car accident. She moved back here about ten years ago and hasn't left since," Michael explained.

"I knew about the car accident," I said, "but…uh…how do you know so much about Kathy? You just got into town a few hours ago."

"Well let me tell you...I'm driving into town just before three, and I drive right past this little diner on the outskirts of town, Ranch Diner. It's the same place my Dad used to take me every Thursday when my Mother worked late. It was the only place in town, he said, that you could get a real dog's eye and great mystery bags that tasted just like Aussie home cookin.'"

I looked at Michael curiously. "Dog's eye and what?"

"Oh it's like a meat pie and sausage...don't ask...you don't want to know what went in them where I came from...anyway, so I swing in there and see how the old place is doing and I see a closed sign in the window. Then the front door opens and I'm staring up at this gorgeous set of legs. Naturally, as I make my way up the rest of her...it's none other than Miss Kathy Carmichael."

"Has she still got that great rack she had in High School?" Brian blurted out.

"Brian...focus...and you're gay remember, start acting like it," Michael replied.

"Right sorry."

"So I roll down my window and call out to her. 'Kathy,' I say. She comes up to the window and looks in. Doesn't recognize me from a Koala in a tree...sorry...something my Grandmother used to say, anyway...I say to her...'it's Michael, Michael Finn from Ryerson High.' She recognizes me and I offer her a lift into town...I even know where she's living now. She's renting a place a few blocks from here over on Fifth Street. So she gave me a rundown of her life, and where she's been and how she ended up back in our beloved little never-never land."

"Wow, sounds like you've had an interesting ride into town," Brian smirked.

I just looked at Michael and nodded. Kathy...Kathy really had been my first love, maybe my true love.

Chapter 8

I don't really know if I ever actually enjoyed football. Understand that, nowadays, the padding and extra cushion they give a high School kid for protection is about a 300% improvement over what we had. Our padding consisted of some sort of foam, which was about as thick as a worn out pillow. When we got sacked, you felt it. I was a good sized kid, starting to form a pretty good rack of muscles on me and it still hurt when those guys hit you from every which angle.

But being sixteen, and in High School, and desperate to fly with the in-crowd made Football an absolute necessity. Plus Michael made it clear that High School football, in Australia anyways, meant instant dates on the weekend. Michael was good at football; he had the speed, the skill, and the arm to actually play this game.

I suppose with practice, and a little enthusiasm, I could make people believe that this was my game too but baseball was my game and football was a little more than foreign to me. There I was anyway, on the High School football team. It was the first game of the playoffs, and it was a home game. The other team appeared bigger, faster, and very much better than our own team. Fortunately, it was never usually in the Coach's game plan to have me get the ball. I was used more as an annoying distraction and certainly that I could do.

We huddled out into the field for our fourth down, in the third Quarter. It would have to be a decent play to make the forty-five yards for touchdown. Michael nodded at me and motioned behind him at our enthusiastic cheerleaders. They were fifteen of the most beautiful girls in our school. I knew some of them, even dated a few mostly because Michael took out their friends. It was natural to double date back then. Both my parents and Michael's parents didn't approve of us "group dating" at sixteen much less dating on our own or even doubles. We huddled down and Michael pulled his rubber mouthpiece from under his lip. "Where did those cats come from?" he asked the group of well-battered players. "Those aren't our sheilas, I don't recognize half of them."

"Sophomores, Finn, now can we focus on at least scoring one touchdown tonight," Bobby Gallagher insisted. He was the team captain and usually quite serious about his football career. "Alright, now everyone listen up, we have to take them by surprise, and right now it's like they are reading our every move. Finn, you're gonna be the distraction this time. Go up right field, far right field and fake like you're preparing for a pass. Emerson..."

Emerson? Did he just say Emerson...that was me...that was my name...Bobby Gallagher did NOT use my name when discussing important plays that the entire season of High School football hinged on.

"Emerson?"

"Yeah?" I said, snapping back to reality.

"You go straight up middle field, I know it's not your usual play which is why they won't expect it. I think they'll try and cover Finn and Ryan if they go up the outer field. That way, logically speaking, you'll have a clear run for the goal."

Logics? Logics? He was actually working the word "logically" into a football play. This wasn't about logics, this was about man's primordial lust to bash each other's brains in. This was the civilized replacement for war...they threw a ball into it, ironically shaped like sort of deathly harsh projectile, and gave us helmets, but in reality we just wanted to kill each other. Logic had nothing to do with it.

"You're using David for this play?" Michael asked. I was wondering the same thing. "What do you think this is, bush week?" Michael added. None of us understood what that meant. But it was obvious that no one understood why Bobby had decided I would be playing the pinnacle role in this play.

We broke our huddle and took our places on the field. I stood completely out of my area, immediately to the left of Bobby. He scanned the field expertly looking for all his options and investigating the other team's formation all in one sweep. He looked over at me, and nodded, silently re-assuring me it would work.

He began to call his play, screaming out our numbers. Mine was in there somewhere...32...32...32...it echoed in my head. 32...the age I would likely never live to see if this play did not work. I would likely end my short pathetic life beneath the 200-pound frame of that guy...right there...

The ball snapped...and I ran...I ran like I've never ran before. I pretended I was running the bases at the World Series, rounding first, heading for second, the third base coach waving me through. I ran down the field, glancing back, and ready for the pass.

Bobby's arm cocked back and fired the horrible little spiralling piece of pig down the field at me. It was an incredible throw, almost poetic. It turned and turned heading right for me. Of course so was the entire opposite team. The ball reached my hands just as three of the largest teenage boys I had ever seen reached my body. I clutched that ball, about ten yards from the end zone. The boys hit me every which way and I was flattened hard into the mud. I felt my body crunch and the air in my lungs run for dear life out of my body.

The boys got up slapping each other a high five for their kill. I laid there, the ball clutched in my hands tight against my chest. I heard my brothers, my team-mates, approaching to check my vital signs. I was staring into the beautiful blue sky.

Michael knelt beside me and slapped my helmet. "Good-on-ya mate, you really got nailed though."

Other people approached my side. There was a crowd gathering around my body. I was looking into Michael's face when I heard the voice that changed my life forever. "Are you alright?" she asked. She leaned over me and ran a wet towel across my forehead. I turned away from Michael and looked into her eyes. She was beautiful, she was more than beautiful...she was hot.

It wasn't just the fact that she had a killer body, I mean, I was sixteen, and every girl had a killer body. Her eyes were like a smouldering brown that I had never seen. I couldn't have been any more instantly in love if I had just bumped into Julie Christie. Suddenly football made complete sense. She was wearing a cheerleader's uniform, which consisted of the only short skirts ever allowed to grace the halls of Ryerson High.

She looked down at me. I opened my mouth to speak but nothing was coming out. Fortunately for me, my lack of speech could be blamed on my injury. Michael offered me his hand and he pulled me to my feet. I stood there, slightly dizzy. Seeing that I wasn't dead after all, the crowd began to disperse. I held my head and watched her walk back towards the bleachers where the cheerleaders were taking a break. "Like that one huh?" Michael said, slapping my back.

"Who is she?" I asked. Mostly, this was a rhetorical question. I was expressing a feeling of amazement...like...who is that girl...kind of thing. Obviously Australia is not up on rhetorical questions.

"HEY!" Michael yelled.

I looked over at him in shock, who was he yelling at? "Hey, Blonde girl?" My dream girl turned around and looked at us, shielding her eyes from the sun. "My friend wants to know your name, he thinks you're just cool," Michael yelled. The other guys were looking now. Suddenly I wished I had died on the ground.

She smiled. "Kathy," she replied. Then she turned her attention back to her friends. I stood there my mouth gaping that he had done that to me.

"There ya go, Mate," he said, winking at me and then running across the field to get a drink.

Kathy. Kathy Carmichael. The object of misplaced lust filled teenage fantasies. Fortunately for me, she became more than that...not that the first part wasn't fun too.

April 1965

It doesn't take a teenage boy long to figure out where the object of his affection spends most of her time. And when that love interest happens to be the most popular girl in school...in actuality, in the whole town of Medford....it's even easier.

So it suddenly became a more convenient way to walk home with Brian and Michael, to go past the malt shop on Main Street where Kathy worked, and hung out with her friends. It didn't take Michael and Brian long to realize that I was completely infatuated with Miss Carmichael.

The day that our relationship changed from infatuation to friendship was perhaps the greatest day of my entire teenage existence. It's just one of those things that you remember for the rest of your natural life, even if it also happens to be one of the most embarrassing moments of your life. It was a Friday, the sun was out, the air smelled of spring. The weekend was ahead of us. All I could think of was seeing Kathy in the hallway at school. Her locker was around the corner from mine and I could stand at the end of the hall and just look down at her. Its funny how at any other time of life something like that would be considered creepy and...well illegal...but in High School...it's teenage angst.

Michael and Brian were shoving each other around and pretending to shoot each other and figure out who was the bigger Gunsmoke fan. I didn't say much of anything, I kept to myself and stared at the sidewalk. As we approached the little malt shop on the corner, Brian nudged me. I looked over at him. Michael and he had both stopped walking. They were smiling at each other mischievously and looking at me. Brian nodded up the road. "Look who's directly in our path."

I looked up the sidewalk and there she was, her hair blowing in the wind. It was the kind of moment where everything else stops...you know, freeze frame, and in your mind the music playing is...*Pretty Woman*...or wait...maybe *Stop In The Name Of Love*... On second thought, *Pretty Woman* works better. She was beautiful. Her smile, her eyes...her...everything else...

She was wearing her school sweater and the greatest poodle skirt. Man, I miss those skirts. She was laughing and talking to her friends outside the shop. "Okay...Davey, it's time you did something about this Kathy Carmichael problem. Now I've got..." Michael stopped and reached into his coat pockets. "I've got a nickel...and some gum. Brian, I need some cash."

"I've got a dollar," Brian replied, producing it from his pocket.

Michael's eyes widened. "You've got a dollar? Where did you get a dollar?"

"I dunno, it's been in my pocket for awhile."

"We coulda got like ten comics with that," Michael replied. He nabbed the dollar from Brian's hand shooting him a dirty stare. Then he focused his attention back at me. "Now the three of us are gonna go into that shop, order some sodas, and you're going to talk to Kathy. Maybe even get her to go out with you."

"Michael, I can't do that, alright. I'm not you."

"Hey that insults me. Trust me, you're a reasonably sexy man," Michael said smiling. I smirked at him. Michael pulled out his comb and began to fix my already perfectly styled, slightly long Beatles cut. "Hey trust me, you are. Isn't he Brian?" he asked.

Brian was not impressed.

Both of them were looking at me waiting for the go ahead. I had planned to speak to her every day for the past month since I first saw her and now the opportunity was in front of me and I wanted to turn and run. Finally I gave in.

"Alright let's go," I said, still very reluctant. Michael smiled proudly. "But let me do this my way. I don't want your help or advice on this, thank you very much," I said, pointing my finger at Michael.

"Hey it's all you cat, it's all you." Kathy was heading inside for her Friday night shift. Her friends headed in the opposite direction. The three of us walked inside the shop. There were kids everywhere. There was no way I would ever get to talk to Kathy with all these people in here. One girl in the corner was on roller skates, and was demonstrating to her friends the art of spinning while drinking a coke. The jukebox in the corner was blaring the King of Rock and Roll singing about a Hound Dog. I scanned the crowd and finally...there she was...at the end of the counter, serving a large float to Bobby Gallagher. Bobby was obviously entertaining her with some sort of witty story because she was laughing like he was the funniest thing since Ed Sullivan.

"Let's sit over here," Brian said, motioning to a booth not far from the counter. My eyes never left her as the three of us made our way to the seats. We sat down and I watched as Kathy made her way towards us. Michael smiled at me encouragingly. Several kids were now jiving to Elvis and his ballad.

"Hey boys, what can I get ya'll today?" she asked. She chewed her gum delicately like an angel. I was speechless.

"Well, Brian and I, we're gonna have two cokes," Michael said.

"And how about you David?" she said. Wait what did she say? She said David...she called me by name, my actual name, she KNEW my name. My eyes looked up and met hers. She was smiling at me, pen in hand ready to take my order. My whole insides froze. In my head I could hear "*Pretty Woman*" playing again.

"David...," Brian elbowed me out of my coma. "What are you gonna get?" he asked, smiling at my expense. They were both enjoying my embarrassment. Everyone seemed to be looking at me. The pressure was too great, I couldn't handle this.

"I...I uh...I uh I uh..." it's true no word of a lie; I used the word "Uh" three times in one sentence. Not to mention more I's than Mississippi. My throat was dry, and my body was paralyzed in fear. It was too late I was stuck here now. There was no escaping...it would be a quiet, dry mouthed, romantic death. "...Orange..." I managed to finally get out.

I saw Brian look at me curiously. Kathy smiled, and nodded. I imagine she must have wondered when I had completely lost all motor control. Then again, until just that moment, I didn't even know she knew I existed. She turned away from the table and my lungs began to function normally again. Brian leaned forward across the table. "You hate Orange Soda, the last time you had Orange Soda it made you vomit a very bad color of green."

"It was the only thing I could force out," I said, laying my forehead against the table in defeat.

"I have never seen such a poor display of courage. You are an insult to mankind," Michael joked.

The Jukebox began belting out another song by the Four Tops. The kids who had been swivelling their hips to Elvis were now making fun of the kids bobbing to the new song. Kathy was back faster than I would have liked. A good ten minutes...or ten days to recover from our first involvement would have been nice.

She set the drinks down in front of us on a red tray and smiled at me again. I don't know what my facial expression was but I'm sure it wasn't pretty. My face was still felt frozen from the first conversation...or lack thereof. She turned away from us...her skirt flowing ever so perfectly around those incredible legs. It happened again...the slow motion, the turning of her body, the background music playing "I Can't Help Myself" by the Four Tops. This time the music actually was playing...from the Jukebox.

"Go now, Davey, go now, talk to her."

I looked over at Michael, and then back to Kathy. It was time to make my move, it was time to get all my courage up and do this. It was now or never, do or die. The Four Tops would guide me through this. I would remember that song for a very long time. I stood up very slowly, unfortunately it wasn't slowly enough to prevent our tray of drinks from standing with me. The drinks toppled down off the tray into my lap. I tried to avoid most of the sodas but I only managed to knock the guy behind us down onto the table sending his soda flying across the table. And of course when soda falls, it is automatically drawn to the area of ones pants commonly saved for two-year-olds that can't hold their bladders. I stood beside our table, in the aftermath of my display. Brian was wide eyed, and covering his mouth, and Michael was holding his head shaking it.

Kathy turned and looked over at me. I stood there, soda running down my lap. The guy I knocked over was brushing himself off but not nearly as much had hit him. No soda had hit anyone except my lap. I could actually feel tears starting in my eyes.

She walked back towards the table and offered me a dry cloth. "Thanks," I managed to say and dropped the cloth down trying to hide my mistake. Every kid in the whole shop was staring at us; it seemed as though even the jukebox had stopped and was listening intently for my next blunder. However, the music hadn't stopped, it was still playing mockingly.

"If you didn't like the soda's you could have just told me," Kathy joked.

"Huh?" I said. I was like a human anti-dictionary...my vocabulary consisted of grunts and the occasional single syllable word.

She nodded at my mess. "Oh, well...I...I...".....yeah exactly, point proven. Hey if you saw this girl, you'd understand. Kathy laughed. I'll just go get something to clean this up.

"...out wanna with me?"

What's that you say Mr. Emerson? Who the hell knows.

"Pardon?" she said.

"Umm...would you like to go out with me? A movie maybe?" There that wasn't so hard...right!

"Sure I'd love to." She didn't even hesitate. A sixteen-year-old with a wet spot down his entire pant leg and she doesn't even take time to think about whether she might want to be seen with this moron.

"Great...how about tomorrow night," I blurted. Everything was going too quickly. I had to get this over with before my balloon burst and I was left with something else on me.

"Sure, here's my number." She reached out and took my hand. Probably a good thing my pants were already wet. My eyes widened as her soft hands touched mine. She pulled out a pen and very neatly wrote...KATHY 555-6075...followed by a little heart, with a face on it. She had to write Kathy beside it, which was kind of amusing. If that ink had been permanent, and she hadn't wrote her name, 50 years from that day on, when I was in an old age home, I would have been able to pin point who had grabbed my hand that day and written her number on it.

I smiled and nodded and Michael, Brian and I headed for the front door before any other mishaps. We hit the street outside the shop and I jumped into the air, following that with the loudest 'woo hoo' my pubescent cracking voice would allow. Hopefully she didn't witness my dance of joy that day or she may have changed her mind. Together the three of us walked towards home. "So tomorrow night huh?" Brian said. I nodded and smiled at him. "You know of course that Saturday nights are when you have to work for Mr. Jenkins."

"Oh I know, I realized as I was saying it that I was giving her the wrong day."

"Just so you know," Brian replied.

Chapter 9

The following week was full of heartache, renewal and closure. My mom and I spent a lot of hours sifting through Dad's things. We spent entire days together cleaning his garage and deciding what we both could and could not part with. I didn't want to part with any of it but Mom didn't have the room for it, and my apartment in the city didn't have a lot of storage space so I got rid of what I could. Still, there were just some things that I could not part with.

April 1960

My Father had worked in carpentry my entire life. When I was born he worked for a paper mill but in his spare time he made cupboards, and tables, and the occasional rocking chair. He never thought his work was worth much, and his designs were not fancy, by any means, but his work was sturdy and reliable and people liked that. By the time my Grandfather passed away in '59 my Dad worked on his furniture full time. My Grandfather encouraged my Dad to work on his carpentry and he took care of us financially. My Grandfather was a war hero. Dad rarely mentioned it and I don't recall if my Grandpa ever shared with me stories of his war days. I only knew that when Grandpa went into the service he put all his money into steel and paper mills and when he got out of the service he walked into some big returns and cashed in his shares. He always shared the lot of it with my Dad. We weren't rich, in fact, I wouldn't have even guessed us as being well off although I suppose we weren't hurting. My father would leave the house most mornings with his lunch, just like every other Dad, but his office was in his garage. He'd spend ten, maybe even twelve hours a day making whatever it is he made.

When Grandpa died, I remember Dad bringing over a glass case with grandpa's pistol in it, and his ribbons and his stars and his badges. Inside a separate glass case was a smaller medal. It was shaped like a star and had a bright ribbon on it, and was engraved with some writing that I don't recall exactly. I remember though that I thought this medal was quite intriguing. Brian and I used to sit in my living room and look at it as though we expected it to move. We both talked about how great it would be to pin it on and wear it around the neighbourhood but we knew what it meant to my Dad and that we weren't to touch it. I knew that it had meant a lot to Grandpa to. What we didn't understand, at the time, is what it truly meant.

Even still I honestly believed I was doing my Dad a favour when I overheard him talking to Mom in the kitchen about all my Grandpa's old stuff. My father had just finished doing the annual taxes, which was always a stressful time for him. He hated pouring over all that paperwork for two days straight and it was a relief for him and my Mom when it was all over. Dad was sitting at the kitchen table and Mom was making dinner behind him. Dad was joking about inflation of prices and how next year he'd claim the entire neighbourhood as dependants.

I was sitting in the living room working on my homework when I heard him mention my Grandfather's things. "Well if we have to pay the Government we can always auction off Dad's things," he said to my Mom. My Mom laughed and told him to "stop kidding." For some reason I took their conversation as meaning that they were in trouble...money wise. I called Brian over to my house and together we went top to bottom in my room collecting all my old toys and everything I could possibly find. We set all my old toys out on my front lawn and I had a Yard Sale. My goal was to help Mom and Dad, and "earn my keep."

Brian and I sat out there for hours, and at the end of the day we had only made four dollars. "This isn't enough," I said to Brian. Brian shrugged. "Wait, I have an idea," I replied and I ran inside the house. Dad and Mom were sitting out back on the porch. They had assumed most of the day that I was simply out side on the front lawn playing with Brian...and a lot of toys.

I came back outside with the medal in my hand. "You're gonna sell the medal?" Brian exclaimed, taking the small glass case in his hands and staring inside.

"Dad said he might have to get rid of this, so maybe I can do it for him?" I replied.

We set it gently down on the table. "How much are we going to sell it for?" Brian asked.

"I don't know what it's worth."

"Well you sold your cowboy gun and badge to Will for a dollar...this doesn't even have a gun," Brian replied. His reasoning made sense.

"How about fifty cents?" I asked.

"Sounds fair to me, I'd pay fifty cents."

"Well you can't buy it, it would be better if someone else bought it," I said.

My Mom finally came out front to get me around eight-'o clock that night. I gathered up the toys I hadn't sold and put them all back inside. Just minutes before she had come outside to bring me in I had sold my Grandfather's medal and several other small things to an older man from up the street, who had been out for his nightly walk. My father was sitting in his armchair reading the newspaper when I came downstairs from my room with the shoebox of money I had made in my hands. "Dad, this is for you."

My father looked up at me and set his paper down. He took off his glasses and leaned forward. "What's this?" he asked.

"I know you were doing your taxes and you have to pay people so I sold my toys and Grandpa's medals."

My father's eyes widened and my mother, who had been standing in the doorway, came and sat down behind me. "What do you mean David?" she asked.

"I sold some things so that we could pay the people."

My father stood from his chair and went to the mantle where the glass case used to be. Needless to say it was gone. My father put his hands on the mantle and his other hand on his forehead. "Son, where did you sell Grandpa's medal?"

I looked at both of my parents. They didn't seem happy. I didn't understand why they wouldn't be happy with seven dollars, that was a lot of money. "I sold Grandpa's medal to Mr. Roberts."

"Go upstairs David," my father said sternly. His voice was just a whisper.

"Dad, what's wrong?"

"You had no right to touch my things, and you had no right to sell that medal now go upstairs right now!" he said, his voice raising.

"Mom..." I began. She looked at me and shook her head.

"Go upstairs, David," she repeated. Slowly I walked upstairs to my bedroom and lay down on my bed. I could hear them downstairs talking, but too quietly to hear them clearly. Eventually I heard the front door close and I fell asleep before I heard it open again. I wasn't sure what time it was when I heard my name being called. My father was standing in my bedroom doorway.

"David?" he said quietly. I was awake now but I was facing the wall pretending to still be asleep. I didn't want him to be angry with me anymore. He came in my room anyway despite me ignoring him and sat beside me on my bed. He put his arm on my shoulder and shook me gently. I turned my head slightly towards him. "David, I'm not angry with you at all."

"You're not?" I said, turning over to face him. He shook his head.

"Not at all. I understand that you thought you were helping me." He cleared his throat and leaned back on my bed. "We're not in any trouble David. We have plenty of money and if we are ever in trouble, I want you to know that you'll always be taken care of. I promise you that you'll never go without what you need. God provides for us son, and He's never let us down. Do you understand?"

"Yes sir."

"Son, you have to promise me that you'll never take Grandpa's medal from this house. If you want to look at it, or you want to show it to your friends or even pin it on, just let me know and we'll work something out, okay?"

"Did you get it back?" I asked.

"Yeah, I did. Mr. Roberts had it ready to give back; he just wanted to try it on," my father replied, chuckling.

My Dad got up to leave but stopped before he got to the doorway. "Have I ever told you why Grandpa got that medal?" he asked.

"No," I said, sitting up.

"Grandpa was sent to a place in France during the war. While he was in Normandy his men came under heavy fire on the beaches. You know Grandpa stayed with a group of four men and gave them cover fire with his gun and protected them until a medic got to them. He saved their lives and then they gave him the medal."

"I didn't know that Grandpa saved people," I replied.

"This medal meant a lot to him and it means a lot to me and I know that someday I'll give it to you too son."

"Thanks Dad," I said.

"Night Davey, I love you."

Chapter 10

Present Day
LAST WEEK OF AUGUST 1990

I found the medal while Mom poured over the boxes in the garage. Dad had it packed away carefully with Grandpa's other things. I took it out gently and tucked it away in a box of my own so that I could take it home. I like to think that Dad had given it to me in his own way and his own time.

Brian stayed at the house with us too. He was our rock for a lot of those days. Mom spent a lot of time crying in the kitchen, or in her room, or just anywhere. I spent a lot of time on our front porch where Dad and I, and sometimes Brian spent a lot of time talking about nothing, or sometimes talking about things that were really significant but you never realize it until years later.

We begged Michael to stick around and finally after a lot of convincing he decided he would stay too. The three of us had a lot to catch up on. Although that first week after Dad died, there wasn't a lot of time to catch up. Finally we had the garage completely sorted and packed away. It was a beautiful, warm Saturday morning when I walked to Michael's Motel room on the other side of town. Medford was not big enough to consider "the other side of town" as a long walk. It takes fifteen minutes to walk through Medford from one side to the other. There was only one motel in town and it was on the outskirts. It was called "The Hilltop Motel," and it served to people who were mostly just passing through or lost.

I knocked on the door marked "#8" and waited. I knocked again and checked my watch. It was after ten, surely he must be up. "Just a minute," I heard from inside. He sounded annoyed. I heard coughing and a lot of gruff sounding throat clearing.

Michael opened the door and I smiled. "Aren't we just a vision of loveliness this morning," I said.

"Oh God, what a night," Michael replied, ushering me in.

"What did you do last night?" I asked, sitting on a plush chair. The motel room was an average costing, well decorated room.

"I have no idea," he said, pulling a cigarette from his jacket pocket and attempting to light it. His hands were shaky and he was still swaying and stumbling back and forth. I motioned him over and lit the cigarette for him. "You want one?" he asked, taking a deep drag.

"No, I quit a long time ago. I haven't smoked since college."

Michael went to his bedside table and began to dig around behind it. He finally produced a bottle of darkish looking liquor. He uncorked it and took a very large swallow. I flinched and shook my head.

"Man you must have had some night last night. Chasing away a hangover with booze means heavy partying," I said.

"Well...I don't know if there was a party, I don't know who was there, I don't know where I was..." Michael stopped, and looked at me, he shook the half drunken bottle in my direction, "I do know however, that there was booze."

"Of course," I replied. Michael took another several swallows from the bottle. "Hey do you think you should be drinking this early, seriously."

"Oh don't even worry about it, nothing clears the mind like a good stiff one in the morning. Where's Bri?"

"He went into Colpoy today to get some things, wire some cash home for his mom. I thought maybe you and I could drive out to the beach, see some old sites, and hike up to our old camping spot."

"Yeah, yeah sure why not. Just give me a few minutes to get looking presentable."

"A few minutes?" I teased.

"Hey believe me, I'm a master at making myself look like a million bucks in extremely short notice," Michael replied. He disappeared into the washroom and I shook my head at him. He was quite a guy.

I suppose that you're wondering how Michael and I went from two kids scrapping it out on the ground, to being best friends. Michael became someone both Brian and I could count on. Over the years, I realized that through Michael's rough exterior, and his snide remarks, and sometimes seemingly cruel responses to situations, that he was very protective of those he cared about. There was more than once Michael had been there when Brian or I needed him. He was someone that was very important to my life.

January 1962

I stood at the top of the stairs listening to the laughter and conversation below. My Mother and Father had invited our new neighbours Paul and Ellie Finn over for a night of dinner and socialization. Unfortunately for me that meant they would bring Michael. It had been several months since I had shoved Michael off Brian, and stopped him from pummelling my friend. We hadn't spoken much since, although we got stuck together in the same grade six class. In fact Michael sat two seats behind me. I tried to avoid him and he didn't bother me, so it all worked out.

Brian still feared him and wondered if he would be back one of these days to exact revenge for the fight he never finished. "David? David, come down and meet Mr. and Mrs. Finn," my mother called from the living room.

I knew it was only a matter of time before my mother made me do this. I slumped down the stairs slowly, pounding my feet on each stair making certain my mother knew I was not happy about this. I came around the post I had once ran my face into and looked into the living room. His parents looked normal enough. They both smiled at me. Michael's Dad was the complete opposite of what Michael was. He was quiet, and soft-spoken. Although his eyes were the same piercing blue that Michael's were.

His mother was a very attractive lady, young, sweet, and beautiful. Of course no one ever mentioned the fact that Mrs. Finn was hot, especially around Michael. It made him upset. Michael was there as I suspected. I had heard my mother offer to hang his coat in the closet a few minutes earlier. He was sitting on the floor between his mother and father. He was paying no attention to anyone in the room, including me but instead was intently examining his book on the floor in front of him.

"Hello, David, how are you?" Ellie Finn asked, offering her hand. It surprised me that she did not speak like Michael did. She did not have the strange accent, which was a cross between Christopher Lee and Sean Connery...which was appropriate because in Michael I saw a cross between a vampire, and a secret agent.

"I'm fine, thank you ma'am," I replied in my best manners.

"David, have you met our son Michael?" Paul Finn asked.

Paul spoke with the heavy Australian accent. My Dad looked at Paul and smiled. "Remember, Paul, our sons decided they were going to battle it out for Heavyweight championship of the world across the road in the park last fall?"

"Oh yes right, so you have met. Well perhaps this time you can meet on better terms, eh David?" Paul said. I scowled and looked at my mother. She gave me the long awaited nod of permission to leave the room. I retreated to the kitchen and much to my disappointment, shortly after that, Michael came in too and sat down at the table. He said nothing, and paid no attention to me. He opened his book that was more of a photo album of sorts.

I poured myself a glass of juice and sat down at the table across from him. I drank my juice and stared at him. He finally looked up at me. "Your mother sent me in here to get a glass of juice," he said matter-of-factly.

"Get one then," I replied defiantly.

"I'm a guest, you get me one," he fired back.

"Last glass," I replied swallowing back what was left of the juice.

"I'll have milk," he retorted.

My mother interrupted our battle of wits calling from the living room, "Davey, get Michael something to drink, alright?"

I scowled again and went to the cupboard; I poured him some milk and walked back towards the table, setting it down beside him. "Oh sorry mate, I can't drink milk, allergies you know," he replied, smiling.

I growled at him and grabbed the milk, returning it the bottle in the fridge. I sat down at the table again, sitting across from him with my arms folded. Michael sifted through his pages of...cards...yes they were baseball cards sealed into a photo album.

"What's that," I asked curiously.

"Candy..." Michael replied sarcastically and then pretended to eat and chew one of his cards.

"What I meant was...well...could I look at them? I have cards too."

"Yeah...I guess..." he replied reluctantly.

I walked to the other side of the table and looked down at his cards. They were very carefully organized into different teams and different players. My eyes widened. He had quite a collection. "Who's this?" I asked pointing to one of the pages, my finger just barely touching the sheet.

Michael growled at me and moved my finger off the page. "Are you kidding me? My Dad said you were a baseball fan...that's

Hank Aaron. It's his 1961 card...he had 120 RBI's this year." I shrugged and went to turn the page. "You're kidding me right, Hank Aaron, Hammerin Hank?"

"I'm not a Braves Fan..." I replied.

"You don't have any Hank Aaron cards?" Michael asked, still stunned.

"No," I replied, calmly.

"Well I'll give you this one then...no trade; you can have it, if it means you'll learn to know who Hammerin Hank is," Michael said, scrambling to get the card out. I smiled. Michael got the card out, and then stopped.

"How did you know he played for the Braves if you don't know who he is?" Michael asked.

"What do you mean?" I asked, innocently.

"You said you weren't a Braves fan, if you'd never heard of Hank Aaron how did you know he played for Milwaukee?" I laughed and slapped my hand on the table.

"Okay you got me; I just wanted his card. I've been trying to get it but instead I've ended up with five George Altman cards."

"Really...you have George Altman?"

"Five of them, Bats Left, Throws right, Chicago Cubs...yeah I've got him."

"Would you possibly consider giving one or two of him up?" Michael asked quietly.

Suddenly his demeaning tone had changed. "One moment," I said. I ran up the stairs to my bedroom and grabbed my box of cards from underneath my bed tucked into the bed frame. I ran back downstairs and dropped them on the table. I dug around in the box and pulled out my 1961 George Altman card. "Will you trade me for that Hank Aaron?"

"What...no way...Altman is no fair trade for Aaron," Michael replied.

"Five minutes ago you were gonna give him to me," I said.

"Well who wouldn't give someone a Hank Aaron card if they'd never heard of the guy but since I know you collect cards too, you know what he means to a good collection."

"Alright...what do you want for him," I asked.

"What else do you have in there?" he replied.

"Well I got Mickey Mantle...128 RBI's this year."

"Nah I've got his from '59."

"Well I don't really have any more doubles; I traded them off with Brian mostly."

"Got any cigarettes?" Michael asked.

"No, no cigarettes."

"Wanna take some from your Dad and then trade me. Three Cigarettes and Altman for my Hank Aaron."

"My Dad keeps his cigarettes in the car. All he has in the house is a cigar, and he only smokes them after Sunday dinner. Hey, I got some firecrackers that Brian got from a kid at school."

"Hmmm go on..."

"I can get matches, and the firecrackers, and four chocolate candies."

"And the Altman?"

"Yeah and the Altman," I said, hesitatingly.

"Alright, deal but I want the matches too."

"Agreed," I said and extended my hand. Michael looked at me carefully and then took my hand. We shook on our deal and I went back upstairs to get my little stick firecrackers that barely burnt brighter than a match head.

The matches were from my father's garage. I wasn't big on breaking the household rules but Brian dared me to nab a box of stick matches one day and they've been stuck under my mattress ever since. I pulled them out and got my Altman card and went back downstairs. Michael was waiting patiently with my Hank Aaron card. We made the swap, carefully, and very friendly like.

Hank Aaron, 1961, do you know what I did with that little beauty? I held onto it for almost two years. And then my primal male urge to be a rebel and give in to "peer pressure" got the better of me and I gave up 1961 Hammerin Hank. I gave it up to Bobby Gallagher who wanted it desperately. He was the biggest Milwaukee Braves fan in the history of Baseball.

September 1963

When I showed Bobby that card, his eyes went wide. He broke the carnal rule of baseball trading and didn't show his poker face. It was obvious to me and Brian and any other person watching that Bobby Gallagher would have traded his soul for Hammerin Hank.

"What have you got Bobby, and you best make it good, cause I like this card," I said smiling.

Brian nodded. If Michael had been there, he could have negotiated Bobby's brand new bike for me, but I wasn't quite the smooth talker that Michael was. Although I knew that I could get something decent by that look in his eyes. Bobby looked at that card like I looked at Kathy Carmichael some two years later. Well maybe a little different, but don't underestimate a teenage boy's love of a good baseball card, especially before he discovers the opposite sex.

"I have some smokes, and some booze," Bobby said.

"Booze?" Brian asked curiously. "What kind of booze?"

"The kind you drink," I whispered to him and Brian nodded.

"Come up in my tree house," Bobby said. Brian and I followed him up his ladder and into his tree house. Bobby went over to a wooden trunk in the corner and dug through it. In the very bottom of the trunk was literally a swallow of vodka in the bottom of a bottle, and a package of *Target Tobacco* complete with rolling papers in the side.

"Whoa," Brian exclaimed reaching for the bottle. Bobby pulled it back away from our grasp.

"No one touches until we make a deal. Do you guys know how to smoke?" Bobby asked smugly.

"We've smoked, Brian and I smoked a whole cigarette down by the river," I replied, grabbing the tobacco away from him. We'll trade," I said.

Bobby appeared thoughtful. The art of trade was such a fine little game between people so young. "Mickey Mantle, 1961 and the Hank Aaron '61," Bobby said.

"Both cards?" I replied unsure of the deal at hand.

"Do it, David!" Brian exclaimed. Truth is Brian and I had smoked a cigarette down by the river. We found it on the dirt path leading to the swimming hole. We picked it up, and lit it with some matches Brian had and we took one puff each and we both choked so badly that we threw the rest of the cigarette into the river. But we had never drank anything like vodka, ever in our lives.

"Alright, deal," I said. I didn't really think that it was a great idea. They were two of my favourite cards. Although I thought in the back of my mind that maybe I could save my allowance and any money I made and buy both cards back from Mr. Frank at the card shop. They would cost a lot...two years old...probably at least a buck each.

Bobby took the cards from my hands and then casually passed the vodka bottle across at me. "Want some matches?" he asked.

"Yes." Bobby dug into his pockets and pulled out a few matches. I took them and passed them to Brian who had stuck the tobacco in his pockets.

"Aren't you going to have a smoke?" Bobby asked. He was daring me; I could sense it in his voice.

"We're going to wait, Brian and I like to have our smoke while we're fishing."

"Yeah, really brings the fish out when we throw it into the water," Brian replied. I elbowed him to keep quiet. We left Bobby's house and headed down to our spot on the river where we fished and swam and sometimes camped out in our little tent that Brian had gotten for Christmas two years ago. We rolled the tobacco in the paper and each took one. We struck our matches together and lit the cigarettes. I must admit...and don't ever tell my children this...but for that moment it did make me feel like Sean Connery. The smoke billowing over my lips, holding it in my fingers...."*Shaken, not stirred.*" The feeling passed, as my stomach quickly became shaken and stirred.

Brian coughed and spat, and pounded his chest. I dropped the cigarette and lowered my head. It made my stomach turn and I didn't usually have a weak stomach. Brian held onto his cigarette and looked over at me. "Hey you alright?"

I shook my head. Brian grabbed the swallow of Vodka and passed it to me. "Maybe you need a drink?" he suggested. He meant well. I thought it made sense. I drank the last bit of the vile crap in that bottle and that was all it took. I bent over the river and my stomach came up all over the shore. Brian stood beside me with his mouth open watching the cigarette and booze take its toll.

Finally I fell back on the grass panting. Brian tossed his cigarette aside. "Well I think we should give up smoking and drinking," Brian said. I nodded in agreement but said nothing. It's funny to think that we should have learned our lesson from that experience but we repeated our mistakes a few times in our youth.

I also don't really know what Bobby Gallagher did with those cards I gave him, but I do know, I traded barfing all over the shoreline for two cards that eventually reached a net worth of about three grand...each.

Michael and I walked along the beach enjoying the late summer. Michael spent half the time looking into the crashing waves and the other half of the time looking at the women of all ages tanning on the beach. I don't know where he got his energy, sexual or otherwise. He was the same age as I was. Not that I wasn't interested, I just didn't have his exuberance.

"So Michael, are you married now or divorced. You said last week you were married twice."

"Happily divorced," he replied, smiling at me. His dark sunglasses covered his crystal blue eyes. He could tell by my expression that I wanted slightly more detail. "My second wife, she wanted a baby. She was twenty-eight, and with me going on thirty-nine..." he said.

"Forty-one," I corrected him.

"Close enough. Anyway there was no way I was going to have a baby into my forties. If I haven't sprouted any seeds yet, I'm not going to start at this point. She decided that she couldn't live with someone who didn't love children. Of course I never said I didn't love children, I just don't want any."

I nodded. "And your first marriage?"

"Shannon. Shannon was a beauty. We met during an earthquake in California when I was down there for business. Our office nearly toppled and she and I got trapped in the cafeteria on the fourth floor until the fireman came and rescued us. Of course by that time, we had...uh...gotten comfortable with each other...twice..." Michael said smiling to himself. I chuckled and shuffled the sand with my feet.

"You haven't changed a bit Michael Finn."

"Oh change is what you make of it Davey, I mean, no one truly changes, we just stay the same and the world around us changes. It's an illusion, kind of like a trick with mirrors you know." He looked at me as I stared out into the waves.

"Do you ever think you'll marry again?" I asked.

"I don't think it's for me, I don't seem to have much luck with women."

I looked at him and laughed. I had seen Michael through a few short relationships, barely more than a few dates. However, I had also seen Michael through his first love and I knew that when Michael Finn fell...he fell hard.

August 1966

It was the peak of a beautiful summer. My Dad was barbequing on our front lawn, and the three of us were playing ball in the park. Brian and I were up against Michael and then in the fifth inning one of us would trade and the Handicap would change. Michael didn't seem to mind the Handicap since he was up two runs.

It was early afternoon when a large yellow and red moving van turned the corner at the end of the street. The Hoffman's had rented their home for the summer while they went down South. I had gotten quite a good deal for mowing their lawn while they were away.

All three of us stopped playing and looked at the truck with a beat up old van following close behind. "Hey Dad, the new neighbours are here," I called over to my Dad. He waved his barbeque flipper in my direction and we walked towards the road. The van stopped and the truck pulled into the driveway. Brian, Michael, and I sat down on the curb and put our mitts beside us. The Van door opened and four kids, no older than nineteen, poured out of the back.

Three guys, one girl and the driver who was also a guy. They were all dressed.... well differently. The music blaring from the van was *The Byrds* telling us there was a season for everything. The guys were all dressed in long bell-bottoms and dirty T-shirts. Two of them wore red bandanas and round multi-colored sunglasses, that I don't imagine protected them from the sun at all.

Michael's jaw dropped and he stood up still looking in the direction of the van. Brian and I were chattering about the new neighbours' weird clothes. We both looked up at Michael who was mesmerized by the strangers. "What's wrong?" I asked him.

"Nothing, nothing is wrong at all," he responded rather slowly.

Michael's source of hypnotism was the quite stunning brunette who was unloading the van. She had hair beyond her waist with a blue bandana across her forehead. She was wearing suede bell-bottoms and her shirt said "Peace" across the front with a picture of a dove on the back. Michael took several steps towards her, still with his mouth gaping open. I wondered if this is how stupid I looked when I met Kathy.

The girl turned and noticed us sitting nearby on the curve. She smiled and waved and poked the other guys, pointing us out. They all waved at us and Michael lifted his hand but couldn't bring himself to wave or even lower his hand back down.

"She's unbelievable," Michael whispered.

We had never seen Michael take this much interest in any girl, let alone for this long. "Let's go talk to them," I said. I owed Michael an awkward and embarrassing meeting with the girl of his dreams. Together Brian and I dragged Michael towards the van. As we approached them, the girl and one of the guys stopped to greet us. "Hey man," the guy said nodding at us and looking down his glasses.

"Hey guys, do you live on this street?" the girl asked.

"Yes I live three houses down from you," I said smiling.

"Cool, we're like neighbours cat," the girl said in a voice that even made my heart skip a beat. "I'm Jamie, and this is Rich. The other guys are Tom, Nick, and John."

"I'm David and this is Brian," I said. Brian was pretty quiet, but he always was when he met new people.

"And what about you sexy? What's your name?" Jamie asked, nudging Michael with her hand. Michael looked at her in a daze.

"That's Michael," I said.

"Hey you guys wanna come over tonight for a little welcoming party we're gonna have. You can all come," said Rich, grabbing another box from the van.

"Sure we'd love to, what time?" I asked.

"Right after we unload all this," Jamie replied.

"We can help," Brian said, blurting out something for the first time. Jamie smiled and nodded and stepped aside. Brian and I pushed Michael towards the van and we took boxes in our arms. We spent the rest of the afternoon helping the neighbours get their new house organized. With the eight of us working on the boxes it only took three hours, and my Dad thought it was great that we were helping someone out for the afternoon.

Finally, when we had everything unloaded, everyone sat on the living room floor. While Brian, Michael and I shared a coke, Jamie was digging through a small plastic bag filled with papers, and lighters and all kinds of little gadgets. She also had a slightly smaller bag with what looked like grass inside of it. She pulled out the papers and the grass and began putting a little on the edge of the paper.

She rolled it quickly and expertly and was lighting it before we knew it. Rich told us that they were all students at University of Toronto and they came up here to study for the summer and just get away from the city and have some fun. Since I had only been to Toronto a couple of times in my life, it seemed very strange to me that city people would come here to get away.

Jamie took a deep breath of the rolled paper and passed it to Nick on her left. Brian watched them curiously. Michael watched Jamie lustfully. I noticed that after taking several drags of her makeshift cigarette she was watching Michael carefully and even winking at him occasionally. The party was on and Nick and John brought out a case of beer which I carefully avoided and encouraged Brian to do the same. I still remembered the last time Dad caught us drinking.

They didn't seem to mind that we didn't drink. Michael gladly took a beer and was on his third, not to mention that the last time the funny cigarette had been passed around he had tried it. Michael was completely relaxed compared to when he came inside a few hours earlier. Brian and I were just content to sit there and listen to all their stories about protesting outside hospitals and police stations and the Government buildings in Toronto. They seem to know so much for a bunch of eighteen year olds, only two years older than us. I realized much later in the evening that Michael and Jamie had disappeared into the other room and it was late, it was past ten and our parents would be getting very worried.

I stood up and went down the hallway quietly whispering "Michael!" There was no response. I heard music blaring from one of the rooms at the end of the hallway. I crept to the door and knocked softly. I didn't know where they were. I thought I heard Jamie laughing and Michael's voice so I turned the doorknob and walked in.

Jamie and Michael were on the bed wrapped around each other. Their lips were locked together and Jamie was in some state of undress that, to this day, I have blocked from my memory. Michael looked over his shoulder and jumped off the bed onto the floor. There was a metal tray beside the bed with butts from at least ten cigarettes, or the other stuff they had been smoking. Beer cans also littered the floor and the room was hazy with a cloud of smoke. Jamie laughed and pointed at me strangely.

Michael's head was rolling on his shoulders and he looked as though he'd been caught in the headlights of a truck. "Michael, we have to get home?" I said and then left the room as quickly as I had walked in. For the next week we didn't see Michael. Anytime we tried his house, he was with Jamie, and sometimes from our spot in the park we could see Michael out back with them, or inside the front window with her. It made us kind of angry that he ditched us for some weirdo blonde and Brian didn't even know half the story because I didn't tell him about their little activity I had walked in on.

Truth is...we were more than jealous and after a week or two, we were furious at Michael. We were bitter. One hot afternoon Brian and I stopped by Michael's house and he was actually home. He hadn't cut his hair since we met Jamie, he was wearing baggy clothes and stupid looking sunglasses that he said Rich gave him. He was in his garage with his guitar that he had gotten for Christmas two years ago and hadn't touched once, but there he was in his garage strumming away on it and banging out some twisted rendition of *"Louie, Louie."* He stopped playing when we came into the garage.

"Hey guys!" he called out, as though he had seen us every day for the past two weeks.

"What are you doing?" I asked him.

"I'm practicing to be in Jamie's band, she loves a rocker," he said, winking at us. With that he broke out once again into the chorus. Brian and I turned and walked away from him and he didn't even seem to notice. We had no idea why he was so enthralled with this girl. Even I hadn't dumped them for Kathy.

It was another week before Brian and I heard a knock at my front door when we were in my room putting together a model airplane. I went downstairs and answered it and Brian followed when he heard me say, "Michael!"

Michael was standing at the door in his weird outfit and scraggly hair. He looked like he'd actually been crying. "Come on in," I said. Michael said nothing as the three of us walked back up to my room. I sat down on the floor and Michael sat on my bed.

"What happened?" I asked.

"I went over to visit Jamie today, she told me to come around noon but I came by at ten to surprise her. Well she was still in bed...and she wasn't by herself. She was kissing that Rich guy when I went in there."

"Aw Geez, I'm really sorry Michael," I said and Brian agreed.

"The worst part is they both laughed at me when I asked her what she was doing and I thought she was my girl. She laughed at me?" he asked looking at us with tears in his eyes. "I really thought she was."

"Did she explain to you why she did that?" Brian asked.

"She just told me to 'chill' and it was no big deal and she thought I could handle hanging out with them like a 'big boy.' John told me downstairs before I left that Jamie does this with all the guys. I was nothing to her and I thought we had something."

Both Brian and I sat on either side of Michael on the bed and put our hands on his shoulders. "We're here for ya," Brian said, smiling at him.

"Yeah forget her, you don't need her, you got us," I replied. "We have to cheer you up," I said and walked over to my record player. I loved that old player with the scratchy needle and all the records I had to save up for. I grabbed the closest one and put it on. "Let's hear this great singing voice you've practiced up on, maybe we'll start our own band," I replied, as the music started.

"I'm not singing," Michael replied, adamantly.

"Come on Mikey," I said, dancing around to the music.

Brian and I stood up and began singing in front of him. The music began to pick up pace and Brian and I bounced around to it and sang about a girl that couldn't be trusted. Michael couldn't help but look at us and laugh. Finally he jumped up on my bed, grabbed one of my rolled up comic books and began singing into it like a microphone.

The three of us were so busy dancing around the room and bouncing from floor to bed that we didn't notice my mother standing in the doorway watching us. She just shook her head when we finally noticed and stopped our dance show.

Chapter 12

Present August 1990

Michael grabbed a rock from the beach and tossed it into the waves. Medford sat on one of the most beautiful bays in Canada, big and beautiful and it ran clear across the province. "So, how about you...where's the Missus? How come she isn't here?" Michael asked

"Well, actually...we're kind of separated," I replied.

Michael looked surprised; nothing caught him off guard. "You said in the restaurant...well you said you were both fine."

"I lied. Well...I hid the truth."

"Why?" Michael asked.

"You know, it's me. David Emerson, Mr. Together, perfect life, no mistakes, and living the great Canadian dream."

"There's no such thing David, and if you have to lie to your two best friends, I mean, you didn't need to do that. We're not going to judge you no matter what. Christ, do you think I'm perfect? I've been married twice, both to beautiful, intelligent women, and lost them both. I've been through three jobs, numerous dead end relationships and I haven't got a thing to show for it. David, Brian and I never expected you to be perfect. God, if you were perfect, neither of us would have ever been able to hang around with you, would have made us look even worse."

"I have a little girl too. Did you know that? Her name is Samantha. Sarah and I, we were completely happy for ten years. Even after Sam was born, it just seemed like my life couldn't have gotten any better. My parents loved Sara too; she was like the daughter they never had. She really wanted to be here for my Dad's funeral but things just didn't work out that way. She thought it better...with the way things are, not to be here."

"So you separated?"

"Yeah, we've been separated for almost six months. Things just started to slide awhile back, and we drifted apart and didn't even realize it. Before long we were strangers in the hallway. Then one night I came home from work, it was late, almost midnight, and I came home to burnt out candles, cold chicken and a note from Sara saying she was taking Sam and getting away for awhile, and that we both needed to weigh our priorities."

"Okay and Brian doesn't know about this?" Michael asked.

"No and honestly, right now, I just don't want him to know. I think he suspected something was wrong when we talked at Christmas. I wanted her to meet you guys. I told her about you, she probably knows you as well as I do."

"Oh, poor girl," Michael joked.

I smiled. "Brian should be back from Colpoy soon, should we all grab a bite to eat?"

"Yeah let's go somewhere, I need a drink. I'm starting to sober up and I'm not liking it much," Michael said and then laughed. I looked at him and then laughed along with him. "What do you say we all go to Sam's Restaurant? I bet old Sam still makes the best damn burgers in the whole country and probably still says so himself." I agreed and we walked back towards the car..

Later that evening Brian, Michael, and I walked the few blocks to downtown Medford and then cut down a side street towards the harbour. Sam's Restaurant was right down on the waterfront in an old shipyard building that Sam Jenkins had renovated himself. When we were kids it was the best spot in town. Sam had the finest lobster for the adults and the dignitaries that came to town, and at the same time he had the best pizza, burgers and fries for the kids.

When we weren't at the malt shop, it was off to Sam's to grab a bite to eat. In my case, on Saturdays, from the time I was thirteen years old, I worked for Sam loading his kitchen with all the necessary things and cleaning up around the restaurant. The entire time Sam never failed to impart his life-long wisdom on me. It was different than the kind of things my Dad told me because Sam gave it to me straight, no fatherly shield to sift out the "good stuff." Sam gave me advice on things that stuck with me my entire life. He was one of those people that, thirty years later, I think about at least once a day. We could see the old red brick building ahead of us. We walked up to the front door of the familiar place and I stopped and looked up at the sign above the door. "Sam's Place," it read. It was still the same chipped brown paint that it had been when I worked there. The yard around the building looked the same too, with the brown picket fence surrounding the far side of the building where Sam used to keep Mutsy, his Beagle Hound. Mutsy eventually got ambitious and somehow leapt over that picket fence and met his match in the form of a milk truck that conveniently lost it's handbrakes further on up the street.

"Remember that fence?" I asked, pointing to it. It had seen better days for sure but it was still standing. It used to be the ugliest off-white color you can imagine. It matched the off-white shutters on the gables of the upper floor of the restaurant. Brian, Michael, Kathy and I spent a lot of time in the summer of '66 painting those shutters and that little fence. That was before Mutsy met the Milkman.

Brian walked over to the fence and knelt beside it. "Good old Mutsy," he whispered. We all smiled. "Mutsy jumped his fence, on a windy July day..." Michael began and we all chimed in after him...."he never saw that milk truck comin, and got right into its way." We all laughed. We loved Mutsy but that was a little poem that Sam came up with in order to tell everyone his sad story about his beloved hound and the picket fence.

July 1966

We were all 17, and it was the hottest July I had ever seen. I mean, usually it got hot in August, but this was like Texas hot...or outback hot as Michael put it. Truth be told, Michael was born and raised in Metropolitan Sydney until he was 10, and never saw a foot of true Australian outback in his entire life.

Hot was usually a good thing in Medford, hot meant the girls at the beach were also hotter than ever. However, this summer would not be spent...entirely...looking at beautiful women. Besides, I had my own beautiful woman to worry about. Kathy Carmichael and I had been dating for almost a year (don't worry I'll get back to that before long.)

My father decided to occupy our summer by setting us up with a summer job. Usually summer meant that I only worked one night a week at Sam's Place. He didn't need me as much with his son home from school and the college kids back in town looking for work.

But Sam needed his picket fence painted, along with the shutters on the upper floor of the restaurant. He had the entire building re-bricked in the springtime and the white shutters and white fence looked ridiculous. It would be a good hard job for young strapping fellas like us, my father said.

Then it was time for me to beg Kathy to come and help us, or at least grab her Pom-Poms and come cheer us on. Reluctantly, she agreed, only because I begged with such enthusiasm. So there we were bright and early, paint buckets and brushes in hand, a ladder hauled over my shoulder and Kathy stepping lightly in her sandals and red shorts, carrying nothing more than a lunch pail with our sandwiches in it.

The four of us painted like we had never painted before. Okay, so not all of the paint made it to the fence. Brian spent the first hour trying to paint a skunk's stripe down Michael's bare back. "Brian, I swear, if one more drop of that paint touches my skin I'll make sure you get a bucket of it all through your pretty little hair."

"Oh I'm scared," Brian said laughing. Brian dipped his brush into the pail and crept up behind Michael. Michael was well prepared with his own bucket of paint hidden in front of him. He saw Brian's shadow and turned suddenly, tossing the paint bucket in Brian's direction. Brian was left standing there in a puddle of deep red paint, with his brush in hand. We all laughed. Kathy sat on a stump off to the side laughing at Brian dripping in paint. She hadn't lifted a single brush since we started. Michael and I both stood up and looked at each other and then over at Kathy.

"What are you laughing at?" I asked her, straight faced.

"Yeah, it's not funny, our friend Brian doesn't deserve to be laughed at," Michael replied.

"Maybe, Michael, she needs to get her hands a little dirty." We both smiled and walked towards her threateningly.

"Both of you get away from me. David, I mean it, you'll never kiss me again."

I stopped and shrugged. "I hear Carol-Ann Morrison is a great kisser."

Kathy's mouth dropped open and she stood up. "You're so in for it," she said. She grabbed a brush from our buckets and dipped it into the paint. She walked towards me and kissed me on the nose.

"I know you wouldn't," I replied.

"Carol-Ann huh?" she said. I nodded smiling. Kathy plopped the brush dripping with paint down on my forehead and ran it down my face. I clenched my eyes letting the paint run down my shirt. We chased each other around and in the middle of having the best time of our lives, we did manage to do a great job on the building. What an incredible summer we had painting that old place.

We finally convinced Kathy to get on the ladder in order to do the highest shutter since none of us were crazy about heights. I was concentrating on keeping all the paint supplies handy that we could possibly need when I noticed that Michael seemed to be enjoying holding the ladder for Kathy.

I walked from the fence over to where Michael was holding the ladder, as Kathy carefully painted the gables. "What are you doing?" I asked Michael.

"Nothing," he replied, smiling suspiciously.

I looked up the ladder. "I think you're trying to look up my girlfriend's shorts," I said accusingly.

"I would never...really..." Michael said, backing away from the ladder.

"I'll hold the ladder," I said. Michael shrugged and walked over to the fence. Casually I looked up the ladder. Hmm, you could see up her shorts after all.

Chapter 13

Brian peered through the front door. The sign in the window said closed but it was after five and that was usually when dinner was served at Sam's Place. Brian tried the door and found that it was open. Together the three of us walked into the place where I had spent so much of my youth. The smells and the scenery came flooding back. I missed Sam's, but some things had changed. Mostly was the fact that the chairs were all overturned on the tables. The restaurant was spotless, no customers, no chairs to sit in, and everything had been cleaned from top to bottom.

The lunch counter against the far wall still looked the same with twelve stools from one side of the wall to the other. The only difference was a bar with a liquor cabinet at one end, except, the liquor cabinet was empty. There was a man standing behind the counter writing on paper intensely. He was well dressed in a shirt and tie.

I cleared my throat and we walked across the restaurant floor. He looked up. "Hey, sorry guys we're closed," he replied.

"My name is David Emerson, and I'm a friend of Sam Jennings."

"What's your name?" the gentleman asked.

"David, David Emerson."

"Davey?" he said.

"Yes?"

"It's James, Jim Jennings, Sam's son."

James stepped out from behind the counter. I froze in my place and looked at this aging man before me. He looked like Sam had looked when I left twenty years ago. It was like Sam hadn't aged a single day only this was his son, the son who had been ten years older than we were.

"James, hi, my god, I haven't seen you in twenty years," I exclaimed.

"It's been a long time."

"So where is the old man? I've been dying to get one of his

burgers and then we see this place is all cleaned up. He isn't shutting the place down I hope," I said.

"Well..." there was a long pause and James looked away from us. "The thing is...David, my father passed away a few days ago. He heard that your Dad had passed away, and he wanted to go to the funeral but he was just very sick. I'm sorry. If I knew you were still in town I would have called. I just didn't think you needed to hear more bad news on top of your father passing," James explained.

"Sam is gone?" Brian said, as if speaking for all three of us.

I had been so wrapped up in worrying about my Mom and cleaning up my Dad's things that I hadn't take the time to find out that Sam had died. There was a long uncomfortable silence. James finally spoke. "I wish more than anything I could keep this place alive but I just can't. I have my own business up north, and I just can't afford the old girl. My Dad would be heartbroken watching these doors close after thirty-four years. I'm sorry guys," he said.

"Well I'm sorry to hear about Sam. I wish I had known. I would have been there if I..." I began. James nodded. He understood. "How is your brother taking this?" I asked.

"As well as can be expected. He's keeping himself very busy. He came back for Dad's funeral and then had to fly back out east. His family is out there and he wanted to get back and be with them. I'm going to visit him when I finalize the closing." James' brother Jonathan was only a few years younger than we were. He had helped run Sam's Place every summer for as long as I could remember. I hadn't seen him in just as long. Eventually we gave James our sympathies again and headed for the front door. As we walked out past the picket fence and past the sign that still read Sam's Place, I began to feel as though it was my father passing away all over again. Two men that changed my life, and shaped the way I grew up and still effect virtually every decision I make, and they were both gone within days of each other.

As we walked by that picket fence, I could see shadows of us years ago running around each other, without a care in the world. Our lives were so completely free and clear of all worries. Even the worries we did have then were so insignificant just because we had each other and I had my Dad at home waiting for me, and Sam waiting for me every Saturday. My whole life was flashing before my eyes, and I felt like I was speeding towards a waterfall in a bucket and everyone, just inches ahead of me, were dropping off the edge and my turn was not far off.

That night I walked downtown Medford alone, my mind racing over all the memories that I had with Sam and my father and just this town. Everything around me was opening my eyes. It made me feel my own mortality like I had never felt it before. It's amazing when I stopped to think that every moment that passed would be a moment I would never live again. Each moment was gone and moving on to the next so quickly. It was almost as if since my father passed I could feel just how fleeting life was. I could feel every minute speeding past me, and I was desperately just trying to clutch onto each moment. It brought a whole new meaning to "Carpe Diem." Seize the day...hmm someone could have told me that twenty years ago.

Seeing and being with Brian and Michael felt good, it was like a certain piece of my past was put back together even if it was only short termed. It had been almost three weeks since my father's passing. Michael had decided he would stay in town as long as Brian and I stayed. Brian took a leave of absence and much overdue vacation time and Michael said he could stay as long as he wanted to. We assumed that meant he was unemployed or not needed. He never indicated which it was. I knew Brian would have left a long time ago if I hadn't encouraged him to stay. Right now, I needed them both; I needed my best friends. Perhaps it was selfish for me to keep them here but I just couldn't let go of these moments we were re-living. I reached the outskirts of downtown Medford. The only thing down this far was the local Grocery Store, which had been owned by Nick Gianni since...forever. Things hadn't changed in that department; in fact he was outside locking up his front doors. I looked at my watch and realized it was almost 7 o' clock.

Brian had taken a nap after dinner and I decided I would go for a walk and clear my head, see how Medford had really changed. Across from Gianni's grocery store was a bar. This was something new for Medford. It was called "Mike's Tavern," and featured an old style decorative design on the outside. I peered into the windows and saw a few patrons sitting at the bar jeering and cheering at the Television set and some boxing match, or wrestling, whatever it was.

The front door of the Tavern opened and someone stumbled out, almost tripping forward. I looked over and realized it was Michael. "Michael?" I said. He looked over at me and waved his hand wearily. He was tanked.

"Hey David, I was going to call you and Brian, see if you wanted to go out tonight, have some fun, maybe drive over to Colpoy and get some real action," he said, leaning his back against the wall.

"Looks like you wore out your night already," I said, smiling.

"What? Nah, that's ridiculous," he said, slurring his words. "I was going to call you right now."

"Michael you're already just about at the end of your party rope."

"Believe me David, I know when I'm at the end of my night and this, my old friend, is not it. Now let's get some booze into us eh mate?"

"I don't think so, why don't we just go back to my place and relax on the back porch."

"Excellent idea, we'll grab a bottle of Jack on the way over there," Michael said, and began swaying up the sidewalk towards my place. I followed him, a few steps behind, waiting for him to fall backwards. We got back to my place around a half hour later. Michael had bought his bottle of Jack and enough to refill that little flask he liked to tuck inside his jeans.

Brian was already sitting on the back porch when we got there. An hour later, Brian and I had the same drink in our hands that we had when we sat down, and Michael was passed out in our lounge chair with an empty bottle of *Jack Daniel*'s fine whiskey in his hands. I looked over at him and shook my head. "Hey Brian, does it seem like maybe...Michael drinks a lot? Like I mean more than he even used to," I whispered.

"I don't think you need to whisper, he's not waking up for nuclear war and yes the guy is an insatiable drunk, he always has been," Brian said, chuckling, mostly to himself.

"No, but seriously, you don't think that he drinks too much," I said. "I mean since we've been back it seems we never see him without a drink in his hand or him tipping something up to his mouth."

"Look David, I think being here, in Medford, is like a vacation to Michael and, when a man has a Peter Pan complex like him, vacationing means getting completely smashed nightly."

I looked apprehensively towards Michael and nodded. "Yeah and morning, and noon," I whispered.

"What was that?" Brian asked taking a swallow of his own

drink and setting it down on the patio table between us.

"Nothing, forget it, you're probably right."

"I'm going to go to bed; hey you guys want to go to Colpoy with me tomorrow? I'm going there for an aerobics class, we can work out, have some fun," Brian asked.

"Yeah sure definitely, we'll leave early."

Brian nodded and patted me on the shoulder. I smiled at him and he made his way to bed.

I grabbed a fleece blanket from the other room and threw it over Michael. It was a beautiful night, he might appreciate the fresh air, and the sleep under the stars, not that he was in any condition to appreciate them. Plus if he decided to toss his nightly binge drink it would be better on the patio than on Mom's carpet.

I bent over and picked up the empty bottle. "I hope you're right Brian," I said and headed into the house.

The next day when Michael managed to pull himself together, the three of us drove the forty-five minutes to Colpoy in Michael's car. It had been a long time since I had been to the city of Colpoy. It had about 30,000 people and was the spot to go for any sort of adventure outside of Medford and without going to Toronto.

We blasted the radio like we were eighteen again, and laughed at all the old songs that we could manage to find on the so-called "oldies" station. They played the songs that we used to rush out to buy when they were the newest record.

"Hey check this out...you guys remember this song?" Brian said, reaching over and turning the volume up a notch. Michael and I listened intently and then we began to nod along with the music. Brian was bouncing in his seat to the tune. Michael looked over at Brian through his sunglasses and holding his hand to his mouth like a microphone he lip synced, in perfect harmony with the radio.

Brian smiled and I laughed. Brian did the same and lip synced the words back.

All three of us sat back and belted out the song, the old favourite, as we drove.

"So where are we going Brian?" Michael asked. His Sunglasses were wrapped tightly around his head to avoid the glare from the sun that was inflaming his headache even worse.

"It's an aerobics class that I signed up for. I used to take one back home three times a week and, if I'm going to hang around

Medford for a bit, than I thought I better get back into my workout routine."

Michael looked at me and it was hard to see his expression through the sunglasses but I knew he was giving me the, "this is not going to be fun" look. We got to the gym and parked the car. It was the kind of place that you'd see in a Rocky movie. A former firehouse style building with a gym upstairs and the workout rooms down below. Brian grabbed his bag from the back seat and we headed towards the front door. We walked up to the counter and Brian set his bag down.

"Brian Parker...for the nine-thirty class," he said to the guy behind the counter. Michael and I examined the man, who's nametag read "Trent, Gym Promoter." There was something...different about him...we looked at each other curiously.

The guy nodded and showed Brian the way to the class. He headed towards the stairway and we followed close behind. We got upstairs and stood outside the large double doors leading into the gym. Through the glass windows we could see everyone getting ready for the class, stretching, talking, and drinking water. Brian put his bag down and pulled out his sweats and weights. He put his wrist weights on and pulled the sweats on over his shorts.

"So are you guys going to join me or will you wait?" Brian asked.

"I think we'll just watch for now," I said. Michael nodded.

Brian shrugged and opened the door tossing his bag to the side of the gym. We walked in behind Brian. "Hey David, do you notice something very off about this place? There is definitely something crook in Muswellbrook," Michael said.

"Yeah, like everyone in this class...is...well they're..." I stuttered.

"They're all men." We looked around at all the guys stretching and getting ready for their work out. Michael suddenly slapped his hands together. "Oh shit," he blurted.

"What?" I asked.

"He tricked us into coming here." I looked at Michael confused. "David, this is a gay gym...everyone here is gay, the guy at the counter, all these guys in here...that little prick tricked us."

"Well he does always say we never do what he likes to do," I said, laughing.

"This is not funny, we're in a gay gym!" Michael exclaimed,

trying to whisper. A well built young man walked by Michael and looked over his shoulder at him.

"Hey there," he said, winking at Michael. Michael flashed him a very fake nervous grin.

"We are so leaving right now," Michael said.

"Oh lighten up, we might have fun," I said, smiling.

"Fun? Fun? My fun involves women. Now I've spent a lot of years accepting Brian's life choices but I am straight, completely straight and so are you...I think."

"Hey, I'm straight, doesn't mean we can't have a good time, he's our best friend. Remember we promised we'd support him since day one," I said.

"Yeah well that was a long time ago, maybe I thought he'd get over it. And besides supporting someone does not mean working out with gay men. I can support him from the straight gym."

I smiled at Michael's homophobic breakdown.

"This is not funny," Michael insisted. The leader of the aerobics class was getting everyone into formation. Brian fell into line as the instructor prepared to begin his class.

"Alright guys, let's really mix this one up, let's really get our blood flowing," he said. Everyone in the class threw their hands in the air, and the instructor hit the button on the stereo system.

Music pumped through the whole room and the men began to lift their arms to a very upbeat tune. Michael's face went red. I shrugged and began lifting my arms to the beat. Everyone began moving quickly to the song.

"David, what are you doing?" Michael demanded.

"Exercising, it's the same work out we do Mikey," I replied.

The intense music began to pick up and the exercises began to get faster.

I began to twist my hips as the instructor lead the group in different moves. Michael shook his head. "I'm gonna regret this," he said, and then stood beside me and started doing the moves too. Brian looked over his shoulders at us and smiled.

Chapter 14

February 1970

College was a whole different world than High School, or any other time of our lives. Michael ended up working for his Dad and traveling a lot, rather than going to college right away. He lived at home and drove the hour every day, back and forth, with his Dad.

Brian and I ended up going to community college in a nearby city. We decided to do one year of college just to make up our minds about where we wanted to go. The best part was we boarded together and in that time we learned a lot about each other, mostly because we started college right during our transition from children to adults. People change a lot in that short amount of time. I think I always sensed that Brian was gay, but it wasn't something that was understood, or something I could put a word on, or an explanation to. After all we grew up in the sixties...and Brian couldn't even put a word or an explanation to it, so how was anyone else expected too. It was just something unspoken that Brian did not feel the same way we did about girls. Although there were times when he added plenty of interesting commentary to our hormone fuelled conversations...but it was still something unspoken that made it obvious Brian had different tastes.

He never made comments about guys, he certainly never made any indication that he liked any specific guy, but still somehow I knew. But for eight years or more, we said nothing. Sometimes I wondered, in my own mind, if Brian even knew that he was gay. I found out in an unusual way that Brian did know...and in doing that, he also showed me a level of acceptance that I never knew existed.

Michael had the hardest time accepting the fact that Brian's sexuality was different than ours, and also no longer a secret, when Brian finally did come out. Michael did accept it, and never turned him away, and remained his best friend, as best as we did throughout our adult years. But I knew it was very hard for Michael. He wasn't used to diversity in any way let alone something such as homosexuality. I was proud of Michael the way he handled it eventually.

It was near the end of winter in our Junior Year when we all returned home for our March Break. March Break ironically fell in February but it was good to come home, do laundry, eat real food and see Michael again. Michael always moved with the times. You could not miss the current fad or trend when it came to seeing Michael. Every time we came home he'd be wearing something new, or listening to the hottest new bands.

This particular trip home was our longest break since leaving for school in September. Each of our three families all got together at Brian's house for a "welcome home" meal. Everyone was seated around Brian's mother's massive dining room table. We said our grace and everyone began to eat. The questions were fired at Brian and I from all parents at the table. How was school? Was it what you expected? Which class was giving you trouble? It was only a matter of time before the topic of conversation reached a more personal note.

"So are you guys dating anyone?" Michael's father asked.

"It's College Dad, never tie yourself down when you're swimming in a sea of hot, young fishes," Michael joked. Everyone else laughed.

"So is that a no from you both? How about you Brian?" my mother asked.

If I had not had a mouthful of my mother's famous mash potatoes I may have spoken up and prevented a turning point in everyone's life. "I'm gay," Brian said, matter-of-factly. He said it clear, loud, and sure of himself. There was no response. Someone to my right let their fork drop to their plate with a very loud clink, but besides that, there was dead silence. Brian was looking down at his plate. He looked up at everyone and then wiped his mouth and stood up. "In case anyone didn't get that last memo, I'm gay, now if you'll excuse me I'll be on the back porch." Brian turned and walked towards the back door.

"Brian," my father said sternly. Dad stood up and Brian stopped at the back door. When my father said your name in that tone...you stopped. "Please come back here and sit down," he instructed.

"I need some air," Brian said, slightly irritated.

"Brian Parker, you will come back here and sit down," my father said, raising his voice.

Brian turned around and came back towards the table. "Look

I don't want to hear any criticisms or opinions or anything else. I get enough of that from school. I didn't make this choice and I don't intend to sit around and let you all come down on me about this." I had no idea that Brian took any negative comments at school...of course I didn't know there was any reason for him to.

"Sit down," my father repeated sternly. Brian's mother said nothing. She only looked from her son to my father. Brian walked back to his chair but did not sit. There was another long silence before my father spoke again. "You have your nerve, suddenly dropping this on all of us, and then acting like we already knew and had given you some sort of reason to think that we hate you for it. None of us had any idea about this, I'm sorry. You have to excuse our shock but not everyone announces they are gay at the dinner table," my father said, sitting back down.

There was more silence. Brian still did not sit. "Mom?" Brian said. She said nothing. "Mom, I need you to be alright with this, I need you to accept me for who I am. I couldn't live with myself if you were disappointed in me."

Brian's mother looked at him with tears suddenly coming down her cheeks. "Brian...," she said. She stood up and walked over to him and together they wrapped their arms around each other. She held her son's face in her hands. "My whole life, since the day I held you in my arms I have not spent a single solitary second of your twenty-two years being disappointed. This day changes nothing. My son, the son I know is brave, and courageous and full of love and kindness, and if you think that something like that would change how I love you...then you don't know your own mother at all. You're my son, that is the only thing that will ever matter or effect the way I love you."

Brian began to cry too, and they embraced again tightly. Finally they parted and Brian looked at all of us. "I really need everyone to support me, you're all like my family and I don't want you to be uncomfortable with this or think that it changes anything."

"Are you seeing anyone?" I blurted out. I set my fork down and tried to cover my face with my napkin. That was the most stupid thing I could have ever said. I don't, to this very day, have any idea why I asked that.

Brian looked down at me, a deep look of wonder in his eyes. "Yes, I'm seeing a really great guy from one of my lit classes."

Suddenly everyone at the table was looking at me. They were all wondering how I could not have known this.

"You didn't know about this? You live with the guy?" Michael said, across the table. Michael sat in his chair, leaned slightly to the side, his napkin tossed across his food.

"How would I? I spend a lot of time with guys too, doesn't mean that I'm..." I stopped before I could go any further. The silence was still deafening.

Paul Finn cleared his throat. "Brian, I'd just like to say that you have a lot of courage talking to us all like this. Perhaps we could have used a little more preparation but all in all it took a lot of courage to do what you did here tonight. I don't speak for anyone else besides myself but it certainly does not change the way that I see you and I respect your way of life."

"Bull shit, I don't," Michael said, throwing the toothpick, he had been chewing on, down on his plate.

"Michael Finn!" his mother exclaimed.

Michael pushed his chair back and stood up. "We've been friends for a long time Brian, and I haven't known you to be anything but exactly the same as David and I."

"I think that's the point," I whispered.

"Shut up, David, this isn't the time for your self-righteous crap," Michael replied, pointing his finger at me.

My father held up his hand to silence us. "Alright, listen Michael, it's natural for us to react badly to something that we don't know a lot about. I assure you that Brian's choices, or lifestyle, does not make him any different from us."

"Forget this, you're all completely warped." Michael turned to face Brian, "I don't accept this and I don't support you, let's get one thing straight. Whenever you decided to fag it up, obviously you didn't care enough about any of us to let your best friends know...so forget you," Michael said, and then stormed from the room. Several minutes later the front door slammed.

Brian lowered his head. "He'll come around Bri," I said, putting my hand on Brian's shoulder.

Brian shrugged and sat back down. "I'm sorry everyone, perhaps my timing was off."

"No time like the present when it's matters of the heart," my mother said, speaking up for the first time and smiling at him. Brian smiled back at her. We went back to picking at our plates. I set my utensils down beside my plate and looked at Brian.

"This does not give you an excuse to dress better than I do when we go out," I said, straight faced.

Brian looked back at me. My father began to laugh and I smiled. Brian laughed out loud as we all began to talk again about other things. Michael did not come back to the table that night. Eventually we all went home and Brian spent most of the night, after his Mom went to bed, sitting on the front porch.

It was almost eleven that night when Brian saw someone coming up the sidewalk. He could tell from a distance that it was Michael. Michael stopped in front of Brian's house, where Brian sat on the porch.

"Hi," Brian said, into the darkness where Michael's shadow was. He nodded and walked closer to the steps. "Wanna sit down?" Brian asked, moving over on the step. Again, Michael nodded and he sat down. It was a very cool night, it hadn't snowed in a few days but the air was still crisp.

"I was.... I was completely out of line tonight," Michael said.

"I don't think so," Brian replied.

"I was, believe me."

"Was that an apology?"

"I guess." They sat in silence for several minutes.

"What if...what if I told you that it just kinda weirds me out. I mean...I'm just not comfortable with it, so I lashed out just to make up for not being comfortable," Michael explained. He took a joint from his coat pocket and rolled it tight in his fingers before lifting it to his mouth and lighting it.

"I'm fine with you not being comfortable with it...I can understand that completely. I just don't want you to see me any differently...as your friend."

"So you can live with me being tolerant but not completely understanding?" Michael asked, looking at Brian.

Brian nodded. "Yeah, I can definitely live with that. Maybe someday you'll learn to understand it more."

"I'll do my best, I promise," Michael said. Brian nodded at his friend.

Michael stood up and took a drag of his joint. The sweet smell of the plant filled the air. "I'm going home to finish my dope and go to bed."

"I'll talk to you tomorrow," Brian said.

"Yeah alright." Brian got off the step and headed towards his front door.

"Hey Brian?" Michael asked, stopping at the sidewalk and turning to face him. Brian turned around.

"Yeah?"

"Ricky Nelson or Donny Osmond?" Michael asked.

Brian smiled. "Donny, definitely."

"Really? I kind of like that rugged, sexy thing Nelson has going on," Michael replied.

"I like the pretty boys," Brian replied.

"Righto," Michael said, waving his hand, and walking towards his house Brian waved back and went into the house.

"That was fun wasn't it?" Brian asked, as he tossed his workout bag in the back of the car. Michael shot him a dirty stare. "I knew you guys wouldn't come if you thought it was a gay gym."

"Thought it was a gay gym?" Michael said. "Thought? It was a gay gym, completely."

"Yeah but it was still fun," I laughed.

"Don't encourage him," Michael replied getting in the car.

"Oh I'm sorry Finn, hey I'll make it up to you and buy you lunch," Brian said. "I know this great little Italian Restaurant."

"Brian, if it's a gay Italian Restaurant...I'm never speaking to you again."

"Hmmm...okay...how about Chinese," Brian joked. We pulled out of the parking lot and in search of lunch.

That day in Colpoy the three of us forgot all our personal problems, everything that might plague us outside of Medford, and we were just "us" again. Someone once told me that you'd be lucky in life to find one true "soul mate." It's commonly misunderstood that a "soul mate" is a person that you end up sharing your life with as a couple, married or otherwise. To me a "soul mate" is a person that you're drawn together with, for some cosmic, unexplainable reason, and from the moment you're brought together they complete you. It's beyond friendship, beyond love, beyond anything that we comprehend. I was fortunate enough in my life to have two friends of this nature. As we drove around Colpoy looking at some of the places we used to go to as teenagers, I'd look over at Michael and Brian and I had to smile. Here I was during some of the hardest days of my life, and my two best friends from childhood seemed to make things so much better.

Eventually the sun began to set and we decided it was time to head back home. On the drive back to Medford, Michael told us about his last few jobs and what was "wrong" with the world in his eyes. He imparted upon us "Michael Finn wisdom" about women and jobs and life in general. Brian talked about his mom, and how sick she had been in the last few months and how hard it was to watch her fading. I didn't really join in on the soul bearing conversation. For the time being, I just wanted to listen to them.

We were about four miles outside of Medford when Michael pointed at a building ahead of us. "Hey, let's go to Harwood's and get some coffee or something," he suggested. We all agreed that Harwood's coffee would hit the spot. Harwood's was a small restaurant on the outskirts of Medford. Henry Harwood had been there for many years, originally owned it in the fifties. They used to cater mostly to tired truck drivers, and weary travelers who got lost and ended up in Medford. Once in awhile our families used to go there for a meal, just for a change of pace.

They had great food and even better coffee if I remembered correctly. We parked the car and I got out. "Hey, isn't this where you said you picked Kathy up last week?" Brian said to Michael, before getting out of the car. Michael motioned for Brian to be quiet so that I wouldn't overhear Brian's revelation. I was about to get sucker punched with a surprise reunion. I was so caught up in reminiscing about Harwood's that it had completely slipped my mind that Michael had mentioned Kathy was working here.

Unsuspectingly I walked through the front door of the restaurant. They had re-decorated and the place looked completely different than the last time I had been in here. I don't know why I expected it to be the same, it had been fifteen years or more. The last time I was here was when Dad and I came for coffee on one of my visits.

The lunch counter where the truckers used to sit and tell their horror stories was gone. Now, it was a conventional diner with a sign telling me I had to wait to be seated. I heard the kitchen door swing open, creaking on its rusty hinges. I felt a breeze from a non-existent wind hit me. It was like I was sixteen again, and the whole world around me froze. There she was...an angel in running shoes. She walked towards me in slow motion, looking as beautiful as the first day I had met her. Her hair was still long, and blonde, although slightly darker than it had once been. Her eyes were still the deep, soulful brown that used to make me melt.

"Whoa, is that Kathy?" Brian whispered to Michael.

"That's our girl," Michael replied.

Her long blonde hair flowed over her shoulders just like it did when we were kids. She stopped in her tracks when she got a few feet away from me. She tilted her head ever so slightly and my heart stopped. I couldn't move, I couldn't think, I couldn't do anything except look into the eyes of the girl I once loved.

"David?" she said.

Wait, what did she say? She said David.... she called me by my name...my actual name, she KNEW my name. "David Emerson?" she said again.

"Kathy," I mostly whispered. She smiled and I could feel my legs begging to give way underneath me. I stepped forward and felt myself slipping into her arms. She wrapped her arms around me and we hugged. I looked at her and smiled. "You look incredible. I thought I was sixteen again."

She blushed and smiled. "You look good too," she replied. "Michael told me you were still in town. I was so sorry to hear about your Dad."

"Brian said he thought he saw you at the funeral?" I asked.

She looked embarrassed and nodded hesitantly. "I was at the funeral, I heard your speech, and it was beautiful. I had to leave afterwards. I had to work a double shift here and I didn't want anything to be awkward, you know," she said.

"How could anything be awkward with us, Kathy?" I asked, still smiling like an idiot.

"Yeah no awkwardness here. You look like you've got a coat hanger in your mouth," Michael said, breaking our babbling, and throwing his arm around me.

Kathy laughed. "Hi Michael."

"Hey blondie."

"Brian...hi," Kathy said walking past me and giving Brian a hug. "I can't believe you guys are back together again, spending time together."

"Yeah we all took some time off our busy lives and decided to hang out in Medford for awhile," Brian said. I still couldn't take my eyes away from her. She was stunning. It was ridiculous to think that a woman could still make a forty-year-old man behave exactly like he was a teenager, but it was true. I'm not sure I have ever had that feeling again. I didn't think it was possible to be launched back in time like that.

"I'll take a break and sit with you guys for awhile," she said, turning to me. I nodded and she disappeared back into the kitchen. I turned to Michael and glared at him without saying a word. He looked at me casually and waved.

"You ass, why didn't you remind me this is where Kathy worked...some preparation would have been nice," I whispered.

"Hey relax, it's good seeing her again isn't it. I wanted to surprise you."

"Surprise!" Brian chimed in, looking over Michael's shoulder with a ridiculous grin on his face. Michael matched the grin as Kathy came back and waved us over to a booth by the window. Michael and Brian quickly sat together on one side of the booth and I stepped aside so Kathy could slide in first. I sat down beside her and the other waitress took our orders.

"So what are you all doing with yourselves?" she asked.

"Well...I am running a very successful office down South," Michael replied. The waitress returned to our table with our coffees. Michael reached around in his jacket pocket and pulled out his metal flask. He uncapped it casually and dumped whatever was left into his black coffee. "It's a good job, I have a lot of people working for me." He took a large swallow of his coffee and barely flinched at the additive. "Which is why I could handle taking some time off and let someone else do the running for awhile."

Kathy nodded. She didn't seem to notice Michael's coffee routine. She turned and looked at Brian.

"I work in communications, nothing exciting, good money, high tech work," Brian said.

"And you Mr. Emerson are in advertising," Kathy said turning to face me.

I nodded. "How did you know that?"

"Your mother keeps me updated on the life that is David's," she replied.

She reached behind her head and began to twist her long hair into a perfect ponytail. I could smell her hair and it brought me back so long ago when I lived to smell her, to touch her, just to be near her. She looked at me with those big, deep, brown eyes and I began to think back to our time together.

April 1965

I still, to this day, have never forgotten asking Kathy out in the malt shop. Sure, it was embarrassing and it was a story that I don't particularly enjoy reliving, but in the end it meant that I had a date with the most beautiful girl on the planet. However, what Brian had said was true. I did work every Saturday night at Sam's Place. I had told Kathy that I'd pick her up on a day when I actually would be at work. Just the idea of going out with Kathy Carmichael had made reason completely invalid. The only thing in my mind was to pick a night to take her out, and get out of there before I lost control....again. Eventually, after the malt shop fiasco, I did call her, at Michael's insistence, and made our date for Sunday night instead. It was a school night but the movies were an hour earlier than they were any other day.

Kathy assured me she could go out on Sunday. Now the hard part would be getting past my Dad. Going out with anyone on Sunday nights was impossible, let alone on my first real date. I never considered it a big deal that my Mom and my Dad both requested that Sundays were days that I stayed inside, helped my Dad around the house, or spent time with Mom in the kitchen, or just doing homework. It was the kind of day that my parents had set aside for personal time, whether it be alone, or together as a family. My Grandfather started that tradition. He always told my Dad that everyone needs time to reflect and for my family that time was Sundays. This particular Sunday I had spent with my Mom helping with our meal, and then we all ate an early dinner and I retreated to my bedroom citing that I had homework to do. In fact I was plotting my escape for my big date. The clock said 5:00 PM when I made my way towards the front door, stepping ever so lightly down the old wooden stairs. They creaked like monsters anytime you had to step down them. It had been a pretty quiet day, with nothing exciting going on, which meant Mom was probably knitting a sweater on the couch and Dad was reading his newspaper or his book in his chair. The radio would be on, giving me enough cover to creep out.

I made it down the stairs and actually got my hand wrapped around the doorknob to the front door before I felt that powerful hand on my shoulder. Of course, for some reason, I hadn't heard him approaching at all. I jumped and whirled around. I hadn't changed my clothes at all since Church that morning. I was still wearing my best clothes, and my shirt and tie. My mother must have been suspicious of something by now since any other day I was stripping out of my church clothes before we even hit the front door.

My father looked at me and smiled. "Where ya going, son?" he asked.

"Brian wanted me to drop by and help him with some of his homework for tomorrow. If we don't have it done, Mrs. Baker really lets us have it."

"You're going to visit Brian?" my Dad asked, sitting on the stairs in front of me. I nodded swallowing the lump in my throat. Let the lies begin! "You're going to see Brian," Dad repeated, "in a tie and dress pants."

"I was just so...uh...uh...comfortable in them all day that I just might wear them to bed."

My father stood up again and moved his face close to mine. "Does Brian require you smell that good when you go to help him with his homework?" My throat felt like I hadn't drank anything in a year. My hands were sweating, and my pulse was racing.

"It's just a little of your cologne," I replied, trying to avoid eye contact.

"You smell like a young man going on a date...on a Sunday night," my father said, crossing his arms and looking at me. I finally caught my Father's eyes and I felt that lump in my throat drop through my body. I knew when I was beat and this was definitely the case.

"I'm going to the movies with Kathy Carmichael," I said, finally caving in.

"Did it have to be tonight David?" he asked. "You know your mother and I don't like you going out on Sundays. It's the one day a week that we get to keep you home."

"Well yes, I mean, I don't know. Please Dad I'll do anything to go tonight. I'm supposed to pick her up any minute. Please." My father looked at me with an expression that I couldn't read. He looked stern but not angry. He sighed a few times and ran his hands through his hair.

"Well if you asked her to go tonight, I guess you can't very well let her down. But tomorrow night you come home and you work with me in the yard...all night...until dinnertime," he said.

I opened my mouth to protest and then weighed the options in my head. "Alright, thanks Dad."

"Have fun, and be careful," he said. "Oh and son...get the girl some flowers." I nodded, and gave my Dad a hug.

I went to pick up my date. My Dad watched me walk down the street until I was gone. I was floating on air and had a skip in my step. He chuckled to himself and sat back down beside my mother, picking up his newspaper. My mother put her knitting down in her lap. "What was that all about?" she asked.

"It appears your son is in love," my father replied.

"In love?" she said.

He looked at her and smiled. "There's no mistaking that look, sweetheart."

I remember walking to Kathy's house, my heart pounding. That feeling of first love is just indescribable. But we all know it.

Medford was actually ideal for teenage dating. Nothing required a car...except for parking up on "The Ridge," but I hadn't had that pleasure, with the exception of Michael and I riding our bikes up there to watch the older kids make out. I had everything planned for our first date...movies, a burger at Sam's, and a romantic walk home. I only hoped I could manage to keep my verbal skills throughout the date.

I stopped by the park near Kathy's house and got the best early spring flowers I could find. I even smelled them carefully to make sure they smelled nice. I got to Kathy's house just before 5:30. I knocked on the door and took deep breaths. A man opened the door and scowled down at me. My heart fell into my shoes. He was twice my size, and built like a brick wall. He was unshaven, and looked very cranky that perhaps I had interrupted the greatest sleep of his entire life.

"Hello...sir...I'm...I....," I stammered.

He turned away from the screen door. "Kathy!" he hollered up the stairs.

"Coming Daddy," I heard her reply. A few seconds later, which felt like a few hours with this monstrous man staring at me, she came floating down the stairs. She was dressed in the most beautiful blue dress, with puffed sleeves, and her hair was pulled back into the greatest ponytail.

"I'll be home by nine Daddy," she said, giving him a kiss on the cheek as she came out the front door. She wrapped her arm through mine and pulled me away from the house.

"Take care, sir, have a nice...," my politeness was cut off by him slamming the door shut.

Kathy and I bounced our way towards the theatre. She was so energetic and exuberant. Just watching her talk and laugh, and bounce down the sidewalk, was making me exhausted. She was perfect. It only took us less than ten minutes to get to the theatre. Nowadays, when I say theatre, automatically the thought comes to mind of multiplexes. Twenty-one movies in a building that could shelter a small country, complete with restaurants, arcades, games, prizes, and a screen the size of the Sears Tower. But back in this day, there was no such thing. Certainly there were rumours of theatres in the big city that played more than one movie at a time, but Medford's theatre was a small building just off the downtown strip Kids lined up there all weekend to catch the serial of the week, or the latest movie that came through town.

Inside the theatre was a simple lobby with one door leading straight into the movie, where the screen was average sized, and the snack stand was one guy standing behind a popcorn machine, and dispensing glass bottles of coke. Kathy and I stood in line, her arm still looped through mine. I can't imagine how many times I almost tripped both of us because I couldn't concentrate on the line ahead of me. Instead I was watching this beautiful girl hanging onto my arm.

We got to the ticket taker, and hoarsely I whispered "two."

He took my dollar and a half and I nodded at him smiling. In my mind I was thinking..."Do you see who I am out with...this beautiful girl on my arm is Kathy Carmichael."

And in his mind, I could tell by his bored facial expression he was thinking, "Dude, I don't care who you're out with, I have to sit on this stool for the next hour watching idiots like you smile about their lady."

We stood in the line for cokes and popcorn and then filed into the theatre with the rest of the kids. So far I hadn't done anything overly damaging to my romantic reputation. If I kept up a good pattern, Kathy might even think that I was normal. I let Kathy choose where she wanted to sit. We made our way into the ripped, torn, red seats and sat down. My hands felt like they were taps of water, as I attempted to dry them on the armrests of the chair.

Kathy looked over at me and smiled an excited and vibrant smile. I smiled back more nervously than anything. I realized then that

I probably would not survive this date, my heart would either stop mid-movie or my hands would sweat so much that Kathy and I would both drown.

The movie we saw was a musical. There was an early showing of the latest Bond movie before this but I decided, despite Michael's opinion, that seeing *"Thunderball"* would probably not be the ideal date movie. First of all...girls didn't usually go for explosions, and a secret agent shooting to kill...and also, it was just a really bad idea to take a girl to see anything where the main character was sexier than you were.

The lights began to dim, which actually relieved me because it was now dark enough to not worry about how I looked, or what my facial expressions were doing to me. The movie began...a woman was spinning on top of a hilltop singing about the hills and how alive they were.

Kathy was immediately gripped to the screen. Normally I would have been thinking about what a long movie this was going to be and how much more interesting it would be to watch Sean Connery whooping some bad guy butt, or at the very least what fun it would be to see *"That Darn Cat."*

But it really didn't matter what we were watching, if the movie was even remotely interesting it couldn't have gripped my attention more than Kathy. Her eyes sparkled as she watched this beautiful Nun fall in love with the overbearing and loud sea captain.

To this day, I've probably seen that movie a thousand times, but as for that first time sitting in that theatre, I can't remember a single moment of the movie. I only looked at Kathy, her eyes bright, her nose crinkled ever so slightly when she laughed or smiled. I handed her the popcorn and her drink when she needed it, and I just watched her. It never occurred to me that I could actually reach out and hold her hand, or awkwardly attempt to slide my arm around the back of her neck...I was spared all the awkwardness at first because I wasn't thinking about any of that. Maybe this is common first date jitters but the only thing that mattered was that she was here, with me.

The other guys around me, half way through the movie, had already managed to uncomfortably slide their arms behind their date's heads and by now their arms would be going numb and falling asleep but they wouldn't dare move them because their arms were actually wrapped around a girl.

And when they stood up and went to grab their coat, their fingers would be numb and they'd be dropping everything on the floor....foolish men. I was spared all this horrible embarrassment...well for now anyway. Captain Von Trapp began singing a beautiful love song to his Maria.

Kathy looked over at me and smiled. "Why are you looking at me so curiously Mr. Emerson?" she asked. I blushed, and shrugged sheepishly.

"You're the prettiest girl I have ever seen," I just suddenly blurted. Kathy blushed now, and she smiled.

"And you are the sweetest guy..," she said. She reached over and took my hand and pulled my arm around her shoulders. WOW! This was....well it truly was...the most uncomfortable, excruciating, and absolutely perfect position I had ever been in. After that night I decided that the backs of theatre seats were specifically designed to hurt young adolescent boys' arms. The manufacturers had us in mind, and they knew that they should design a seat that would be impossible to get fresh with our dates. I made a mental note, as my arm sat around Kathy's shoulders, to design theatre seats with backs so low you could get your arm around your date. Kathy rested her head back against my arm and reached up and took my hand. Her warm hand slipped inside mine and my heart pounded and at the same time melted. It felt so good, her hand in mine. A cosmic experience. The pins and needles in my arm were already starting to pinch but I didn't care, she was holding my hand. Several more minutes and I wouldn't even be able to feel her holding my hand but right now it was perfection.

I tried shifting my body slightly so that perhaps my arm might not feel so badly misplaced but I had to shift in a way that she wouldn't think I was uncomfortable. I swung my legs over to the left and tried that. It was even worse, it was cramping my legs. I winced slightly as my knees squeezed together. Kathy's other hand dropped down on my knee before I could move out of the excruciating position. I froze...slowly my eyes dropped from the screen to my knee where Kathy's hand rested comfortably. The hills were alive...and I wasn't going to move an inch.

My arm was strung up over the back of the chair, my legs were cramped beneath the seat in front of me and I would probably need some sort of petroleum jelly to get out of this position but I wasn't moving for the entire world. I probably should have checked the running time on the film. My legs stopped circulating blood right around the time the children were signed on to sing at the festival

Kathy never moved her hand. It was almost as if she were trying to keep me cramped in that position. The pain was hardly noticeable compared to my sheer happiness having her in my arms. Finally...the family escaped over the mountain and the credits rolled. Kathy and every other girl in the room had tears in their eyes. She sat up and took her hand off my leg to get a tissue from her purse. I tried to move...nothing...my legs would actually not physically move. I was crippled, I knew it, and I would have to sit in here and watch this movie over and over again for the rest of my natural life.

Kathy stood up and stretched. She looked down at me sitting in the chair. "Can you bring my soda?" she asked me, pointing at the other side of me where her soda was. I nodded and smiled at her trying to hide my pain. She began to shuffle her way out of the row. Slowly I stood up, my legs ached and there was no blood in them, no doubt about that. I had never allowed my legs to go like this. I picked up Kathy's soda and shook my leg several times. I had to get everything circulating.

"Walk straight, walk straight, walk straight," I kept repeating to myself. "Here's your Soda..." I started to say as I stepped forward. My legs did not agree it was time to go. My left one buckled and I fell to the theatre floor between the seats and Kathy's soda went spewing across the aisle. Kids in the back laughed, and pointed and Kathy turned to see what had happened and rushed to my side. What exactly did this girl do to me to make me fall so hard?

Chapter 16

It had been several hours since we left Harwood's restaurant. Kathy and I sat on two swings in Ryerson Park later on that night. The three of us had waited for her to get done her shift and she came to Ryerson with us. She lived in a small house that she rented, about four blocks west of Ryerson. We talked about what we had done, and where we had been. Even though she had come back to Medford, she had been overseas, spent time in Europe, been in love, had her heart broken, and then ended up back here.

"What about you David? Is there someone in your life?" she asked, kicking the dust with her sneaker reminding me of the sixteen-year-old girl I fell in love with in another lifetime.

I paused thinking and looking into the twilight sky. The stars were coming out and shining down on us. "Yes, well, sort of. We're separated. I'm married."

"Really? What happened..." she asked, leaning towards me. She then paused and her eyes turned away from me. "Or I guess it's none of my business."

"It's okay, really. We just sort of got so busy that we forgot what we meant to each other. One minute we're in love and the next minute my day doesn't even involve calling her from work. I never knew that a relationship like that would take so much work. My mom and dad made it look easy."

"Well I happen to think it shouldn't be work," Kathy replied, pushing herself on the swing with her feet.

I stood up and went behind her and pushed her gently. A breeze blew through the park from the Bay, and Kathy closed her eyes and let it wash over her. Her hair blew back in the wind. "Do you remember the first time you and I had a fight?" she asked looking over her shoulder at me.

"Yeah, yeah I do. It was at the Spring Dance, you asked Mike Hollins to dance."

"Oh no, he asked me to dance, I just accepted."

"Well either way, he was your ex-boyfriend, and I walk in to the school dance to find my girlfriend dancing with Hollins. I did not like that guy," I replied laughing, mostly to myself.

"Especially after that night. Neither one of you spoke to each other all through High School."

"I met him years later in an elevator at a Hotel in Toronto," I said.

"Really?"

"Yeah we spoke, laughed about old times, had a drink and haven't seen the guy since," I said.

"Did he look rich? Because if he looks rich, I should probably find him," Kathy replied. I poked her playfully in the back and she laughed. "I'm kidding. Do you know that the fight we had over him ended up being the first time I realized I loved you," Kathy said.

"Really? How did that happen, I threw him into a punch bowl," I said curiously.

"Yeah and he put you right through the locker room doors in the gymnasium," she said, still sounding disgusted over our behaviour.

"I had a doorknob imprinted on my backside for months," I chuckled.

"No it wasn't at the dance. I couldn't have been more disgusted about that, it was after I left, and you tried to follow me and I told you I never wanted to see you again. Do you remember you came to my house, you and Michael? You threw little pebbles at my window and then you stood outside and sang to me. Michael climbed the side of my house to give me a rose...," Kathy said, remembering fondly.

"...because I was too scared to go up the trellis," I said finishing her story.

"Do you remember what you sang to me?" she asked, twisting the swing around to face me.

I cleared my throat leaned in close to her and began to hum the song.

MAY 1965

I stood outside Kathy's window, guitar in hand, only really knowing one song. She had come to the window and was looking down at me when I started to belt out the song. It was barely in tune but it worked.

Kathy leaned out her window. "David, go home. It's late, my father is going to come out there," she begged. I ignored her pleas and continued to belt out the song. Michael was standing behind the large oak tree in Kathy's front yard. I looked over at him and he nodded and proceeded to expertly scale the side of Kathy's house on her trellis with a rose clenched in his teeth. I was not good with heights. He got up to the window and handed her the rose. Kathy looked at Michael startled. "This is for you, from that moron down there who is completely mad about you. He's singing, outside, in the dark, in a shirt and tie, you know he loves you. Cheers." Michael winked at her and slid back down the trellis. Kathy clutched the rose and her frown began to disappear.

She looked out her window at me standing there on the lawn, my arms raised towards the sky, my eyes closed tight. And then my worst nightmare came true, and the front door of her house flew open and Kathy's father appeared. He stepped out onto the porch and looked at me standing on the lawn. His head turned and he looked up at Kathy's window and his lips curled into a snarl. I was afraid he would show up before I got a chance to fix everything with her.

I looked at her father and over at Michael who was standing on the sidewalk ready to run. He nodded at me and whispered, "go for it, mate," but I could tell he was ready to bolt from Kathy's father. There was no reason to stop now, if I was going to die, I might as well die trying. I took a deep breath, and my voice rang out. I belted out the best rendition of Frankie Valli I could, as loudly as I could. As my song came to a close I dramatically dropped to my knee in front of her window. Her father stood there staring at me, a blank expression on his face. He was going to kill me...he was going to go inside and get a very big gun.

Suddenly his lips curled the other way and he smiled...as much as he could smile. The most he probably had smiled in a long time. I know that I had never seen Ron Carmichael smile in the entire two months that I had known their family. He shook his head and waved his hand in my direction. "Kathy, your boyfriend's at the door and he just wants you to love him," he hollered up the stairs, and then he retreated back into the house laughing out loud.

Kathy closed her blinds and a few minutes later came flying out her front door and threw her arms around my neck. I put my arms around her and we spun in circles in her front yard. I looked into her eyes and I whispered, "I'm sorry." Without warning she held my cheeks in her hands and pressed her lips against mine for the first time. The world fell around us and it was just Kathy and I floating a million miles above the earth. Her lips tasted like the very best strawberries...that you pick yourself. "Go Davey," Michael whispered, walking away from us standing in her front yard kissing. My first real kiss, with my first love. I would never forget that song, or that night.

Chapter 17

As we both sat on the swing set, reminiscing about our time together so many years ago, we began to lean in close, our lips just moments away from that first kiss all over again. It was something that just seemed to be out of our control, as we talked about our first fight, which, of course led to our first kiss. A moment that I had never forgotten and had always fondly remembered back on. Sitting here together after so many years apart, all those things came flooding back. Both Kathy and I had spent the last few months alone, without anyone to lean on or be with and there we were on our old swing set, in our old neighbourhood, together. Suddenly reality settled in and I put my hands on her shoulders keeping us just inches apart. I didn't even open my eyes. "I can't, I can't do this, I'm sorry."

"No you're right, I'm sorry too. I don't mean to make anything harder for you," Kathy said, sitting back, away from me.

"You didn't. It was me. You know, being back here in this town and seeing you again, and Michael and Brian...everything just feels like it used to. And you...you're beautiful...as beautiful as the day I met you," I said touching her face gently. We paused as I said that and stared into each other's eyes.

"Okay," she said, standing up and turning away from me. "Not helping with the not kissing."

"Sorry," I said. There was another several minutes of silence.

"I think I better go home," she said, looking at her watch. I nodded, understanding that she was uncomfortable with me.

"Alright, I guess I'll see you around town," I said. She stood just feet away from me before turning away. I knew that one of us should have said something more. Now she was walking away, across the park, her back to me.

She was almost to the other side of the park before I stood up and jogged after her.

"Kathy...," I called. She turned and looked at me in the darkness of the park. "I'll call you tomorrow, maybe we can do something."

"That'd be nice," she said smiling at me, seeming a little more cheerful.

I nodded and winked at her and then we turned away from each other again, on better terms this time. I walked towards my house slowly looking up into the sky. When I reached my front doorstep, I couldn't bring my self to go inside. My mind was racing with thoughts of Kathy and everything we had been through together in our younger years. Perhaps coming back to Medford was only confusing things but it wasn't making me unhappy. In fact, I hadn't felt this comfortable in a long time. Everything seemed to be falling into place. It was like this is where I belonged.

I stood in front of my house and looked around where I had spent so much of my life. I walked around to our back yard and smiled at the rusted out swing set leaned to one side against the fence. My mom had begged my Dad to get rid of that thing, but my Dad had refused. It was part of him and I, it was part of us. I used to go out to that swing set and sit on it until Dad came home, and then he'd push me and we'd talk about our day. My eyes began to tear as I pictured us there. I turned towards my Dad's garage. We had spent so much time going through all his things that I hadn't stopped to remember how much all this meant to him. I walked through the wooden door to the garage and turned on the overhead light. The small bare bulb, hanging from the ceiling, illuminated the room. There wasn't much left anymore, a few of Dad's things and a lot of boxes. I walked through the stacks of boxes opening a few to see what was left.

It was all the really important things that neither my Mom nor I could part with. It was all the things that Dad could never have parted with. There was a single small box sitting on Dad's workbench on the far wall. I sat on the bench and opened it. There wasn't much inside but sitting right on top was a white, metal license plate. *"304-HEW"* the plate read. They were mine, my Dad had kept them even after he had gotten rid of the car. It was the plates off my car...my very first car. I set the plate down and sifted through the remainder of the box. There were old pictures, photos of Brian, and Michael. I picked up one picture and smiled through tears. It was a photo of Kathy and I sitting on the hood of my second love. That car not only meant so much to me, it held a lot of memories for all of us too.

May 1967

It was the best spring in the world, a spring I would never forget. I was in love. Kathy and I were the happiest couple in the world. Everything could not have been better. The big news around town, for everyone else, was the car dealership opening up on the edge of town. This was big news for Medford because it meant jobs and it meant people would be coming from out of town to our little city, boosting our lacklustre economy.

For me and the guys it didn't mean much. None of us owned a car and it didn't really bother us. We didn't need a car to get around Medford. If we did, we borrowed our parent's car. They were usually pretty good about handing over the keys with the exception of the first degree we had to go through. It was always the same....where are you going, how long will you be, who is going, when will you be back? So we avoided all the questions and we usually walked wherever we needed to go. Or there were always our bikes. Although cruising was still a popular thing to do for the older kids, we didn't feel the need to do it. And unlike most boys my age, I hadn't fallen in love with a car yet. I had my girl and my friends, who needed anything more? I suppose this had to change eventually.

It was one especially hot spring afternoon. The three of us were heading up to the dump to get some pieces for my Dad's car he was rebuilding. It would mean another car for us to borrow when we wanted to. We took Michael's Dad's car and we had to drive past the new lot. We could see the flags from a distance and the huge signs advertising their new spot.

Michael thought it would be cool to pull in and take a look at the new Ford's coming out this year. None of us would ever be able to afford anything near as nice as those cars, so it was good that we had no interest....yet. As he wheeled around the lot, we checked out the newer cars. He rounded the corner and headed towards the back of the dealership where the used cars sat. My eyes scanned the scrap heap that they had behind the building. Nothing but junk, you couldn't even scrape pieces off the metal they had behind the building.
Suddenly...my eyes locked...everything faded away...nothing else

existed and I fell in love for the second time in my entire life.

She was a gorgeous aqua blue...except for the rust spots on her that were completely trashed. "Stop the car!" I belted out. Michael screeched to a halt and I jumped out and ran over to my baby. She was perfect, every inch of her. She was also a colossal piece of junk but if anyone had said that right then I would have killed them.

Michael and Brian got out of the car and walked over beside me. "What is it?" Michael asked sarcastically.

"It's the most beautiful car I have ever seen," I said, in a trance.

"That beauty is 1957 Ford Thunderbird, son. A hot car for a young man." A man dressed in a tweed suit, and a hairpiece was walking towards us. He wasn't a face I recognized so I assumed he came from out of town to work here. "Automatic Transmission, power steering, power seat, power brakes...there's more power in this thing than a tank," the man joked.

He took out a hanky and spit shined a corner of the hood. This was pointless unless he intended on spit shining the entire car. "How much?" I asked.

"David, are you nuts, your father will kill you," Brian blurted out.

I held up my hand to keep him quiet. "How much?" I asked again.

"You know, there was a man here not even ten minutes ago looking at this car...he called her Bethy...and I told him that I wanted one thousand dollars for her. He said to me that he would only give me five hundred dollars for Bethy, five hundred, a steal of course. But reluctantly I agreed. Just between you and me," he put his arm around me and looked around him like he was being watched by the FBI, "I'd let you drive out of here in Bethy for four hundred and fifty dollars."

I turned around and looked at Bethy...I mean...the car. "Well, that's a lot of money," I said.

"That's four hundred and fifty more than you have to be throwing into this junker," Michael whispered.

"We could fix it up, the three of us with my Dad, you know we could do it. I'm gonna do it," I whispered to Michael.

"You're not even going to think about this, ask your parents?" Brian asked.

"I'm almost eighteen years old, it's time I made some

decisions. Besides can you imagine what Kathy will say when I drive up to her house and pick her up in my own car?" I asked.

"Not sure, but I think it'll be something like...what did you hit and is it still alive?" Michael replied. I glared at him and turned back to the salesman.

"I'll take it...four hundred and fifty...," I said, extending my hand.

"Will it drive?" Michael asked, rolling his eyes.

"Gentlemen, I guarantee you will have no problem driving off this lot," the schmuck said, smiling. It took me a half an hour that day to pay for my car. The biggest purchase I ever made. That was four hundred and fifty dollars less in my college account, which didn't leave me with much. But I felt no regret as I went to the bank and made that withdrawl. It was for Bethy and that's all that mattered. Michael got in his car and I slowly opened the door to my new car. It took some convincing but I finally got Brian to ride with me. We were going to go back to my place and "surprise" my Dad. I sat in the driver's seat and Brian got in beside me. The interior was beautiful and actually in very good shape. "See, never judge a book by its cover," I said to Brian proudly.

I stuck the key in the ignition and without another thought the car turned over. I smiled again and Brian reached for the radio. He turned it on and sparks bit out at his hand and he jumped back and looked at me stunned. I shrugged. "I said it needed work."

I put it into drive and slowly took her out of the lot, following Michael. The engine sounded rough but as far as I was concerned it purred like a kitten. I kept looking over at Brian and smiling a stupid looking toothy grin. He gripped the dashboard like the car was going to blow. It rocked and bumped and sputtered up the road.

We drove several blocks from the car lot, following Michael in his Dad's car, and I slowly applied pressure to the brakes as we approached a stoplight. There were three distinct sounds when I stopped at that light....a snap, a bang, and a hiss. The car sputtered twice, coughed once and stopped dead at the red light. Thick, white smoke hissed out of the front of the hood.

My eyes widened and Brian held back his laughter. Suddenly the reality of what I had just purchased all came flooding to me at once and I felt a lump in my throat. We got out and Michael stopped his car and joined us in the middle of the road. He popped the hood and it flew open gladly in order to let out more smoke. "Looks like you dropped your donk," Michael said shaking his head.

"Excuse me?" I said.

"The Engine, the motor stopped."

"Oh Bethy," I moaned, banging my head on the roof of the car.

"What are we going to do with her?" Michael asked, looking at me.

"We have to get her home. We have to get her back to my house. If I have to call my Dad before he sees her, I'll be dead meat," I said.

"Well in case you hadn't noticed already Davey, she's not exactly moving anywhere, how are we going to get her home?" Brian asked. I thought about this carefully.

"We'll push her, I'll put her in neutral and we'll push her to my house," I said.

"Push her? Are you out of your mind bloke?" Michael said laughing. "You want to push this baby eight blocks around four different corners and through three traffic lights?"

"We'll take her through the side streets, and maybe I can get some speed on her, a few miles an hour or something just to make it easier," I said, begging my friends to help me. "If my Dad has to come down here and see what I did, I'll never be let out of my room before I'm thirty." Michael and Brian looked at each other and then at me with my pleading eyes.

Michael nodded and stripped off his shirt, tying it around his waist, "Let's do this mates," he said and positioned himself behind the old Ford. Brian rolled his eyes, like he was prone to doing, and sat in the driver's seat. I positioned myself at the side of the car and together we started pushing. Brian gripped the steering wheel and carefully turned us in the direction we needed to go. We got around the corner and made our way up the side streets, getting maybe five kilometres an hour out of the old girl. It never made another sound as the three of us pushed her up the streets.

Brian laughed at us and Michael groaned as our muscles began cramping. People came out on their front porch to see what we were doing. Old men looked up from their newspapers to look at the "crazy kids." "What are you looking at?" Michael yelled at one old man, who quickly returned his stare down to his newspaper. I looked over at Michael and we both laughed.

It took us over an hour to push that car to Ryerson. We rounded the last corner and Brian got out too and pushed with all his strength leaving one hand on the steering wheel. My Dad was out on the front lawn watering the grass and I could feel my stomach sink.

"He's going to kill me," I whispered.

"No he's not, don't worry," Brian said. I looked at Brian.

"Are you kidding me, the first thing he's going to say is 'what did you do now, boy' and then he's going to come over and put his hands on the hood of the car and say, 'I think we need to talk David'," I quoted. I knew my Dad. Michael laughed. We finally pushed the car out side my house and my Dad looked up. No reaction yet. The three of us collapsed beside the car panting. Sweat poured from our forehead.

My father walked towards us. "Oh David," he said. He looked at the car, checking out every inch of it. The three of us stood up and stepped back from the car.

"Do you like her Dad?" I said. "She....uh...she needs some work," I stuttered.

He glared at me and I cringed. "What did you do now boy?" he said, as previously forecasted by me. He put his hands on the hood of the car and shook his head. "David...," he began.

"I know, we need to talk," I said. My Dad walked towards the house and I thanked Brian and Michael for their help. Michael told me to call him when it was all over and I nodded. I had lived with my father for eighteen years and I knew him inside out and backwards.

"Sit down, David," he said as I walked into the house.

"Yes sir." I sat down on the couch as he paced the living room.

"How much did it cost David?" he asked me.

I cleared my throat and thought about lying...that would be impossible. "Four hundred and fifty dollars."

My father groaned loudly.

"And I assume you didn't just have that money on you so where did you get that kind of money?"

"I took it from my savings account," I replied looking at the carpet.

"I can't believe you would do something so foolish David. I am truly surprised that you would do this. That money is for your future and you went and did something like this. Did it ever cross your mind to see me about this first? I could have gone up there with you, and we could have discussed the idea of you getting a car. You're not a child anymore David, you should start acting like an adult."

So far, so good…I could handle a stern lecture. "Did I not tell you that the money in your account was to be saved for College? I even said to you more than once, when you decide to buy a car, we'll discuss it and get the one that's best. But you didn't even think about that did you?"

"No sir," I replied quickly.

"No I guess you just didn't think. Well maybe it's time you learned to do some thinking. That car won't be set foot in or even touched for two months, including repairs," my Dad said, sitting in his chair.

I sat up quickly. "Dad no," I said.

"You're right, lets make it three months. You will put every dime of your pay cheques and allowances and any money you make back into your savings account until every penny of that four hundred and fifty dollars is back in there, is that understood?" he said staring at me. His eyes dared me to argue.

I broke eye contact. He had won. "Yes sir," I replied. I waited several minutes for anything else but that was it. Without another word I ran up to my bedroom and called Michael and Brian. Michael was still downtown getting his Dad's car from where we left it. I told Brian all about it, and he even seemed disappointed. I think we all wanted to believe in the dream of Bethy, our own car to love and cruise till death do us part.

Later that night, my father knocked on my bedroom door. I was sitting in bed staring out my window. I hadn't left my room since the lecture. He came in and smiled at me. I half-heartedly smiled back at him. "Son…," he said sitting on the end of my bed. "It's been a long time since I was eighteen. I do remember my Dad lecturing me too and I used to think he was being unfair. Do you honestly think that I tell you things just because I'm your father and fathers should make their sons lives harder by forbidding things?"

I shrugged. As stupid as it sounded coming from his mouth, that was pretty much what I assumed.

"You think that I became a parent just so I could stop someone from doing things?" he asked. Again, I responded with a shrug but more or less agreed with that statement. "I tell you things and lecture you about things that I know about. I've been there, and I know a little more than you do about life believe it or not. I wouldn't tell you not to do something if I didn't know how hard it would be later on to accept the consequences. I knew that money in your account would be important for your future and I know how hard it was for me when I lost all my savings when I was younger than you were...I was sixteen."

"Where did you lose it?"

"A card game, with two guys I didn't even know."

My eyes widened. "Grandpa must have whipped you," I replied.

"No, he didn't whip me, but he gave me an earful for two solid hours about responsibility." My Dad chuckled at the memory. Then he turned around to look at me. "And because of that I did learn responsibility and I learned it even harder because when it came time to go out on my own, I had no money. I learned the hard way and because of that I think that I can help you go the easy way. I don't lecture you because it's fun or because it's my job, I lecture you because I want to help you avoid the hard way. I'm just trying to be a good Dad," he said.

I looked up at him. I loved my Dad. "You are the best Dad," I said.

He smiled back at me and patted me on the legs. He stood up and walked towards my bedroom door. "You better get some rest, you have a lot of work to do in order to fill that account back up," he replied.

"Yes sir," I said but this time I didn't resent his punishment I considered it a lesson in responsibility.

Chapter 18

July 1967

Well my father always was a better man than he had to be. I woke up on my eighteenth birthday to find my beautiful baby blue 1957 Ford Thunderbird actually purring like a kitten out in the driveway. My mom told me later that my Dad had towed it to the garage over on Main Street and worked on it there with Brad, the mechanic.

He had painted the body, fixed the rips on the interior and when I got inside the radio hummed out tunes like a perfect jukebox. She was a beauty. Dad leaned in the window as I sat there listening to the Beach Boys with my eyes closed.

"Do you know how much you should have paid for this car?" my Dad asked.

"Please," I said holding up my hand, "just let me pretend that I didn't spend so much on her."

My Dad smiled and squeezed my shoulder. "Why don't you go pick up that beautiful girl of yours," my Dad said. I will never forget backing out of the driveway on my birthday, my parents standing in the front yard with their arms around each other waving to me. I waved back and pressed my horn at them. I guess the horn was over looked because it sounded like a Tuba with a beach ball stuck in it.

I pulled into Kathy's driveway and she rushed out to take a look at my prize. "So are we gonna cruise or what?" I asked her. She jumped into the passenger side and that day we drove all over Medford. The radio blasting, holding hands, joking around with each other, whizzing by all our friends who had to walk.

That night we went to the drive-in for the first time in my very own car. The movie was something about a kid being seduced by an older woman...to this day I never bothered to see it again. Something about seeing that movie would bring back the memory of that night. Five minutes into the movie Kathy was leaned over the seat, in my lap and our heads were locked together by the lips.

If I ever manufactured a car for teenagers it would have anti-steam windows. It was like a sign to all people at the drive-in when you saw steamed up windows, there was no lying your way out of what was going on inside. Honestly, Kathy and I never really spent too much time alone in a car or anywhere. At times our hormones got the better of us and we had to step back and remember to take things slowly. We were responsible and well raised. Things were different then, over active hormones didn't mean a trip to the drug store for a box of condoms like it does now.

Our heads parted and we both looked at the windows. We couldn't see a thing out of them. We had done a good job this time at steaming them up. Kathy reached over behind me and traced a heart in the centre of the steamy window. She then traced K+D in the window. I smiled at her and ran my hand down her smooth cheek. "I love you Kathy," I whispered.

"I love you too," she said.

We leaned in close and started our marathon kissing again. Kissing Kathy was not something I could put into words. Every kiss was like a kiss for the first time. My body shivered, my heart pounded to the point I thought it would jump out of my throat. Her lips were so soft, her eyes closed so tightly as she put everything into her kiss.

At some point during "Mrs. Robinson's seduction," Kathy was in my lap. Our arms were wrapped around each other, our lips never parted, we hit the horn several times and the steering wheel was becoming more of an obstacle.

Any time we did part to take a breath it was only to tell each other something sweet, and loving. If we had been smart, we would have stopped there and watched the movie. My hands, in grand tradition of all teenage boys, began to roam ever so carefully. It became a little mind game to see how much exploring you could do before she would react either with words or by actions. My hands roamed down her back and across her stomach. Her loose fitting T-shirt made slipping underneath to her skin a little easier. She jumped when my hands touched her stomach.

My hands shot out...that was a sign....stop there. But as I discovered it was less of a sign then just shock on her part. She took my hands, never once parting from my lips and led them back to her bare skin. Touching Kathy was like touching Heaven.

I couldn't breath as our kissing got heavier, but it was the best kind of not being able to breathe. If I could have chose to die from suffocation kissing Kathy Carmichael I would chose to do so right there that night. Kathy's hands started to find their way to my body and I jumped when she touched me. We parted again and looked into each other's eyes. There was love there...underneath our raging hormones, we did love each other.

We started kissing again, and my mind was racing as expected from a teenage perspective. It had nothing to do with my feelings for Kathy per se, it was all about the male conquest and I don't mean sex. At that time sex was not necessarily the ultimate goal, in fact, it was a rare thing to hear a guy discussing how he "went all the way." It was the creation of "the bases." You know...first base was the infamous French kissing, which Kathy and I were in the process of actively practicing. Second base was sort of the goal for most teenage boys...in my circle anyway. This was the accomplishment of actually getting your hands on the mysterious female breasts.

More than once in the locker room after a football game I had been informed by Bobby and his gang of thugs that my girlfriend had the greatest 'rack' in the whole school. I couldn't honestly say I disagreed but until this very night I hadn't thought much about it. And now there they were...inches from me. And suddenly I lost all reason and sanity and second base was my goal. You could say quite honestly that I was a breast man, and if I wasn't before, I became one that night at the drive-in.

My hands roamed her stomach and over her bare back. She shivered and I felt proud of myself that I could have that affect....ah the male ego. My hands passed over the gateway to greatness...her bra strap. Her shoulders felt so smooth and warm. When I passed my hands back down she seemed to lean in closer, and closer to me. Was that a sign? Did she want me to go further? My circles started to get smaller and I made my way more subtly towards her straps.

Finally my hands were tracing the strap and toying with the idea of going for it. She made no effort to stop me, it wasn't as though anyone could see us, and the windows were white with steam. My hands went for it and I took the small metal clasps in my hands. I had always just naturally assumed that they would be no more difficult to operate than a button. How wrong I was...and how much you learn from your first bra experience.

I wondered to myself, at that very moment, who exactly had come up with the bra clasp? It had to have been a very concerned mother who also invented the chastity belt. I pictured a mother sifting through leftover war shrapnel looking for the material to make a bra clasp...something from a world war two tank perhaps. Something that would be undoable, unstoppable, un-passable. My hands fiddled with it hopelessly.

It was becoming increasingly difficult to kiss her and attempt the world's hardest puzzle at the same time. Finally we stopped kissing and she smiled at my frustration. I was ready to give up and pack it all in. I did give up on the clasp for the time being and kissed her neck, resuming my circles on her back with my hands. She seemed frustrated that I gave up so easily. "Are you alright?" I asked her, looking into those dark brown eyes.

"You can do it, if you want to," she whispered. "It's just hard...when you stop like that, it's frustrating," she said. Frustrating? Frustrating? She had no idea of the frustration I was feeling. We resumed kissing and I delicately took the clasp in my hands and pushed and tugged with all my might. It snapped in my hands, the clasps coming free and I felt like jumping out of the car and yelling..."I did it! I undid her bra!" but that would not have been a good idea. We both seemed to relax more, which was strange considering the connotations of having her bra undone.

Now it only remained to go for the gold. My seat was starting to recline under the pressure of both of us sitting in it. I reached down and pulled the lever on the side and the seat went back. Everything else around us didn't matter as my hands reach for Kathy's perfect body. Suddenly she froze and sat up pulling away from me...I was so close.

"What is it?" I asked.

Both of us were breathing like we had ran ten miles. "We can't do this David, I can't do this," she said. She rolled off my lap and sat in the seat beside me pulling her shirt around her tightly. I sat there in astonishment. What happened?

"What do you mean we can't do this, we can do this, trust me," I said.

Kathy looked at me and reached over and took my hand. "I just think that we're not ready to, you know,...do that...," she said.

"Well we don't have to do *that*, you know, we can just do stuff," I said. I knew at this point that I was sounding like I was begging but I didn't care. "I never thought we were going to do *that*."

"Still I just think we should slow down, I mean, I don't want to ruin anything between us, and I love you so much." Kathy said.

Aw geez, see that wasn't fair, she was using my feelings for her against me. We sat there in silence for several minutes. We couldn't see the movie, the windows were still steamed. We could hear the movie in the speaker hooked to the side of the car. Even Kathy's heart that she had traced on the window had been steamed over. I looked over at her. She still looked beautiful.

Ben Braddock was professing his love for his beautiful young girlfriend and I looked over at Kathy. She looked sad. I leaned over and kissed her cheek. "What's wrong?" I asked.

"You're angry with me," she said lowering her head. I slid over closer to her and put my arm around her.

"Kathy, I could never be angry with you. How can I be angry with you for saying what I knew too. We're not ready to do anything stupid, it's just hard...but you know what...I'll get over it. I love you Kathy Carmichael, and I don't care what we do as long as we are always together," I said.

Kathy looked into my eyes, and we just stared at each other. "Oh man," she said regretfully. "You aren't making this any easier," she replied. I smiled at her. "Can you turn your head while I...you know...," she asked me.

"Oh yeah okay," I said, turning my head towards the window while she did her bra back up. After all that hard work and I was back at square one. Deep inside, although I would never admit it, I was relieved one of us stopped when we did. If we had done something stupid that night, it could have changed our lives forever.

There were always a few girls our age every year that ended up "getting in trouble," and soon after the news spread they would mysteriously go to "stay with an aunt." And when they came back most of them were married to the boys who got them in trouble. You could tell them from a mile away. They were the guys with a look of terror on their faces for weeks.

The movie ended and I drove Kathy home. She sat beside me with my arm around her as we drove through the streets with the top still down. I pulled over in front of her house and stopped. "I hope you still had a good birthday," she said.

"I had a perfect birthday because I was with you," I said.

We leaned over and kissed for several minutes before she pulled away. She reached into her coat pocket and pulled out a small gift wrapped box. She handed it over to me. "Happy Birthday," she said.

I smiled and took it from her, unwrapping it carefully. I opened the box and inside was a small gold key on a chain. I took it out and put it around my neck. "It's the key to my heart," Kathy said smiling. She pulled a chain around her neck and she was wearing a small heart with a lock in it. The key matched the lock perfectly. "Now you'll always have it," she said.

No one had ever given me anything like that before. She leaned across and hugged me and I could smell her hair, and feel the softness in her touch and I forgot all about not scoring and just remembered how much I loved her. She kissed me on the cheek and got out of the car. "Happy Birthday my love," she said and then went into the house. I don't know how long I sat there outside her house after she left me. I just kept turning her gift over in my hands and thinking about the whole night.

"My love" ...I was her love. Nothing beats the feeling of loving someone who feels the same way about you. I sat there outside her house still feeling the spot where she had kissed me on the cheek. Finally I threw the car into drive, which accidentally turned out to be reverse...once I got myself straightened out I steered ol' Bethy towards home. I tuned in the radio and cranked it right to the max and I drove through the streets towards home that night on my birthday singing at the top of my lungs.

I got home and spent the better part of an hour sitting under the coldest shower you could possibly imagine. Parts of me were blue when I got out of that shower but it worked and I felt better. I came out of the washroom ready for bed just as Dad was coming upstairs.

"Did you have a good date son?" he asked and I nodded.

He took me by the shoulders and whispered in my ear, "reading a good book keeps your mind busy, which helps too." Then he disappeared into his bedroom. I couldn't put anything past my Dad and what I learned was that he wasn't only my Dad, but he was a person first and foremost, and a male person, and he knew more about life and love than I would ever know.

So that night I sat down with war and peace and shivered myself to sleep, it was one of the best birthdays I ever had.

Chapter 19

Present September 1990

I smiled and set the picture of us in front of my car back into the box. I leaned against the shelf and sighed deeply. Maybe this was too much all at once. I mean, staying here seemed like a good idea, after all my Mom needed me here. But was being here, with everything, and everyone, healthy? In some ways it was like everything fit into place when I was in Medford and yet in another way it made me feel sad and lonely. I taped up the box and placed it underneath the shelf. I walked to the garage door and turned out the light. I guess whether or not being here was good for me or not, I was here now and I was going to make the most of it. Maybe I'd learn something about myself.

June 1965

Two years before my birthday, and before my first car, Kathy and I had made it through our first two months as a couple. School finally was let out for the summer and we had every day to spend together. The very first day of summer vacation, I hopped on my bike and rode over to her house and picked her up. I even remember that she was wearing a pink T-Shirt and jean shorts with a red ribbon tied through her hair. She got on her bike and we rode off together.

I rode all the way to the lake behind her watching that red ribbon flip in the air. We rode down to the river, and through the dirt paths until we got to the little spot on the lake where Brian and I often went fishing. We spent the last mile racing each other through the paths. Kathy tossed her bike aside, letting it roll to the ground and then fell onto her back beside the water. I did the same and sat down beside her.

"I beat you," she said, teasingly.

"I let you win," I replied.

We sat there together, Kathy staring into the clouds and me watching the fish jump in the lake. I lay back beside her and looked up at the biggest, fluffiest summer clouds I had ever seen or have ever seen since. "There's a bottle of coke," Kathy said, pointing at one cloud that looked more like a rocket ship to me but I nodded in agreement. "And there's a house, with a dog outside."

Her imagination was too much for me, what I saw was a boat in the water...and even that was stretching my imaginative qualities. The breeze was so warm that day and when I stand outside years later in the summer time and I feel a certain wind...I think back to that day.

"Do you watch *Peyton Place*?" Kathy suddenly asked, propping herself up on one elbow.

I looked over at those big brown eyes and shook my head. "It's my favourite show. I think Rodney should definitely pick Allison...she's so much better than that silly Betty Anderson is. And I just know that Allison's mother is hiding something from her."

I don't know why but I started laughing. Kathy looked over at me and laughed too and slapped me playfully. "What is so funny?" she asked.

"You're so serious about it, its just a show. My Mom says that its about the worse thing to ever happen to television," I replied.

"Well I have to sneak the television into our pantry to watch it so my Dad doesn't catch me," Kathy laughed.

Kathy jumped to her feet and pulled off her sneakers and her socks and waded quickly into the lake. I sat up and watched her curiously. I couldn't help but stare at every move she made. She splashed around and kicked water in my direction. "Come on, let's walk out a little ways," she said. She turned and ran through the water causing little waves on the sand. She was so full of life. I pulled my shoes and socks off and ran after her. I remember that day so well now, even more than twenty years later. It probably seems so insignificant and yet just us being there at the lake, or two years later in my car at the drive in and all the times we spent together in between. It was the best times of my life.

Present Day 1990

After sitting in the garage reminiscing, I didn't really want to be alone anymore so I went inside the house. Brian was sitting on the couch leafing through a magazine. He looked at me and I noticed he had tears in his eyes. I looked up the stairs and I could hear my mother crying. "Has she been like this long?" I asked.

Brian shrugged and tossed the magazine aside. "A half hour or so, I knocked on the door and tried to talk to her but she said she just wanted to be alone."

I nodded and went upstairs. I gently knocked on the door and opened it. My mom was sprawled across her bed, her head in her hands, crying. She had a box of tissue on the bed with her. "Mom, can I come in?" I asked. Despite her response I was going to come in no matter what. She said nothing, just continued her gentle sobbing.

I sat on the bed beside her and rested my hand on her back. She sat up slowly, her eyes were puffy and red and she looked so sad. Tears began to well in my eyes as I looked into hers. "Oh honey," she whispered and fell into my arms. I held her close and leaned my head down against hers. "I miss him so much."

"I know...I miss him too..." I replied. "You know he wouldn't want us like this, he hated people being upset, especially over him."

My Mom's sobs subsided slightly and she looked at me and I actually saw a smile on the corner of her lips. "I always knew how to win an argument, all I had to do was cry. He hated to see me cry," she whispered. I smiled back and nodded. She sat up and we embraced each other tightly. "I don't think in all the years I knew your Dad, I ever saw him cry. He was the most sensitive, caring man but he never shed a tear."

I thought about that and then shook my head. "He cried, I remember," I said.

"Really when?" she asked.

Chapter 20

I came home from school and tossed my knapsack on the floor beside the front door. School was out early that day because of teachers' meetings. We had the whole afternoon off. I was so excited that Dad had said, when I came home tonight, we'd work on his car together. Dad bought the '57 Chevy from a guy in Colpoy, but it needed a lot of work and he had spent long evenings in his garage working on it piece by piece.

I thought it was a beautiful car but Dad said it wouldn't even make it to the end of the driveway in the condition it was in. Tonight, Dad had said he would let me work on it with him. There were some conditions to working on this car, some chores I had to finish, but by the time I got home from school I forgot about the conditions. I headed back towards the garage and my mom and Dad were standing in the kitchen. My Dad had his arms crossed and the look on his face was not a good one.

"Would you like to explain this?" he asked me, his face drawn and stern.

My mother looked upset but she usually let my father deal with things like this. My mind raced as it always did when I knew I was in serious trouble but didn't know what for. There was always a list of things that I thought I got away with when in fact they probably knew most of them and were saving them up for a rainy day punishment.

"Did I forget to do the trash?" I said, walking over to the trashcan and looking inside. The trash was empty. There was a clink on the table behind me and I slowly turned around. My father had set a very large and very empty bottle of Hiram-Walker's Whiskey on the table.

I licked my lips and planned my speech. "Do you know where I found this David?" he asked. I shook my head. "I am willing to bet you do know where I found this," he replied, moving his crossed arms to his hips.

"Yes sir," I said, correcting myself.

"Where?"

"In my clubhouse out back," I said. Several years ago Brian and I had built a little clubhouse from old wood planks and some other things. It was a pretty decent job actually and was good enough to keep the weather out.

"And how do you suppose a bottle of my whiskey and a pack of cigarettes with four cigarettes still in it, ended up in a fourteen year old boy's club house?"

My mind raced, my stomach had that knotty feeling in it, and I was caught bad. "Well Michael...he took the cigarettes from...," I began.

"Yeah I know where the cigarettes came from; I spoke to Michael's Dad already. But Michael did not take this from my locked liquor cabinet, and I suggest you start with the truth. Michael is already grounded for the better part of his natural life...and you are definitely next." My mother still said nothing.

I opened my mouth to come out with a story that might not be so damning but nothing would come out. I might as well come clean. "I took the bottle last weekend. We wanted to drink, and we were playing cards out in the clubhouse and we wanted smokes...I mean cigarettes...and something to drink. So I got your key from the desk drawer and took the bottle." I looked up at my father and his eyes flared. "I...I...took the bottle with the least in it," I stuttered, trying to justify my decision.

My father took the bottle and slammed it into the trashcan making us all jump. "I can't believe you'd do this. You went into my personal things and you stole...you actually stole something that belonged to me and not only that but you stole and drank something that is meant for someone twice your age. And by drinking that bottle, all three of you put the others in danger. Do you have any idea what happens when you're drunk?" My father stared at me. "You drink too much of this crap and your mind loses all control. You could have all gotten yourselves killed or hurt. You...David..., by giving this to your two best friends, you are responsible for putting Brian and Michael in danger."

"I never meant to...I mean...we just wanted to...," I pleaded, tears coming to my eyes.

"I have never been as disappointed in you as I am right now," he replied to my tears.

My mother reached out and held my father's arm. "Enough," she mouthed to him.

He nodded and sat down at the kitchen table beside my mother. "You're grounded, three weeks, no spending money, no working on the car, and your baseball mitt goes into storage, end of story."

My mouth dropped and through my sadness and tears boiled an insatiable teenage anger that was uncontrollable. "You can't do that!" I screamed at the top of my lungs. Both of my parents were taken aback by my tone of voice. "That's not fair," I screamed.

"What you did was foolish and inappropriate and I won't have my son drinking booze at fourteen years old or influencing anyone else to do the same. I also know that this is not the first time the three of you have been drinking or smoking, so this punishment will stick."

"How could you do this to me...it's your fault...for leaving the key in the stupid drawer, I hate you, I hate you, I never want to see you again," I screamed and I turned towards the front door and ran for it. My mind was going a million miles and my heart pounded.

My father stood up and chased after me towards the front door but I was out the door and across the field before he could catch me. I don't know if he called after me...I didn't hear anything if he did, but I know that I will never forget that day. It was really the first time I ever got in any serious trouble. It certainly wasn't the last. I remember it though, more importantly, because it was the first day I ever saw my father cry. Believe it or not, it wasn't what I said to him, although I'm sure that hurt too, but it was something else that happened on that day.

After I stormed out of the house I went down to the malt shop to drown my sorrows in a soda and watch the young waitresses flirt with the older boys. The waitresses at this time did not include Kathy Carmichael.

My father retreated into his study to read his newspaper and think about everything. I can only imagine what he must have been thinking about. He and I had never argued that way before or since. We had disagreed about a lot of things, and we had some definite arguments but after that day I never spoke to him in that tone again. My father sat in his chair staring out the window. It was starting to snow, and the sky was grey and cold. My mother was sitting in the living room with our television on. Every afternoon my mother took time out to sit down and watch her drama...as she called it. She referred to it as her one guilty pleasure, my father thought it was ridiculous. It was *As The World Turns*," and several times when I had been home sick from school I had snuck downstairs and watched it from the hallway. My mother was relaxing and watching as one of the characters explained to her Grandfather about her marital problems with her ex-husband. The screen flashed and went black before "Bulletin" appeared several times across the screen. My father sat up in his study when he heard my mother cry out "no, Oh God..." She repeated it several times before my father stood up from his chair. "Diane? What's wrong?" he called.

"Gary...Gary come here quickly," she said. Her voice was quivering and tears were starting to form. My father ran to the living room. My mother was standing in the centre of the room watching the television with her hands over her mouth.

"Honey, what is it, what's wrong?" he asked frantically.

On the television set, people were scampering around and screaming. Some of them were crying. *"Here's another late development, and this news keeps coming in...as...we're talking here. President Kennedy according to the Associated Press.. and Texas Governor John Connally were shot from ambush today in Dallas Texas."*

"Oh Jesus no," my father whispered collapsing into an armchair near the television. The newscaster cleared his throat and continued on. My mother's hand covered her mouth as tears streamed down her cheeks.

"...and it is not known whether either Mr. Kennedy or Governor Connally were killed." The voice of the newscaster reporting from the scene trailed off and the anchor from the station flicked back on the screen. My father leaned forward and held his head in his hands. My mother sat down on our living room carpet in front of the television and began to cry.

"We're cancelling all regular format during this emergency. All regular formats cancelled...we will continue to bring you news and bulletins, no commercial formats." My mother looked over at my

father and tears began to fall down my father's face.

"They killed him...they actually killed him," my father whispered. "What is happening?"

My mother stood up and walked over to my father and they held each other. Eventually I had decided that I couldn't hide in the malt shop all day. I reached home and slowly and quietly entered the house. I didn't hear anything except quiet sobs and the drone of the television. It sounded as though my mother was crying. My stomach fell...what if she thought I had ran away? I had only been gone less than half an hour but maybe she thought I left for good.

I walked into the living room and found my parents both sitting in the big armchair, their arms wrapped around each other. I looked at my mother and then to my father and my father had tears in his eyes. I immediately began to cry. My father...had never cried...I had never seen him shed a tear. I had made my father so upset that he cried.

"I'm so sorry Dad," I said kneeling beside them in the chair. My Dad looked at me and lowered his head. He still had tears in the corners of his eyes as he tousled my hair with his hand and then wrapped his arm around me squeezing me tightly.

That was the day that I discovered my father was human. I think so many of us young men see our fathers as the invincible super hero that will live forever, and keep us safe from everything. They are everything we want to be, and we try to make them proud and do what they want us to. And then one day in each boy's life something happens that makes us realize our Dad is as human as we are. I knelt there on the floor looking into my Dad's eyes...and I realized that Dad was just like everyone else. This isn't a bad point in a boy's life, in fact, it's a turning point that pushes him towards adulthood.

"President Kennedy...was shot today," my father whispered to me.

"Shot...by who?" I asked. My eyes were wide as I looked at the TV Screen. "Who would want to shoot President Kennedy, he's very nice," I said.

My Dad smiled and my mother began to cry again. *"Here's other information just in, from the Correspondence traveling with the Presidential Party. It says, President Kennedy apparently was shot in the head. President Kennedy was given blood transfusions just a few moments ago at Parkland Hospital in an effort to save his life."*

The three of us sat there on that cold Friday afternoon glued to the Television. There were no phone calls, or people at the door, it was almost as if the entire world stopped for that hour as we waited. I don't remember feeling restless or wishing I could be outside or anywhere else than watching television with my parents. I only remember waiting to hear what was going to happen to that nice man.

The clock had just passed "1:30." My mother had made us sandwiches but neither my father or I had taken barely more than a bite. The TV flickered and Walter Cronkite flashed across the screen. He was shuffling papers in front of him and everything in the house went quiet, my father in his arm chair, my mother standing in the doorway to the kitchen, myself at my father's feet. The man cleared his throat.

"From Dallas Texas, the flash apparently official....President Kennedy died at 1:00 PM Central Standard Time, Two o clock Eastern Standard Time, some thirty-eight minutes ago."

My mother began to sob and my father covered his face with his hands. I didn't cry, I could only look at the television screen as the man who never had a crack in his voice, also began to waiver and the sound of tears in his voice made me afraid. There was a long pause, as Walter Cronkite tried to regain his composure. He glanced at the clock and when he began to talk again...his voice was choked.

"Vice President Lyndon Johnson has left the hospital...." his voice trailed off as my father stood up and gave my mother a hug.

"I don't understand.." I whispered.

"There is no way to understand David," my father said to me, as he knelt down beside me. "People do things to other people because they think their way is the only way, and if someone thinks differently than they do, they do stupid horrible things to them."

"So someone killed President Kennedy just because he thought differently than they did," I asked.

"Probably yes. He believed in some things that a lot of Americans don't. But let me tell you something son...don't ever let anyone tell you how to think, or what to believe. You go out there and you decide for yourself what is truth and don't let anyone take that away from you, no matter what."

What perhaps I didn't realize, that day the President was shot, was the difference it would make in the world. It was like in a single moment the entire world became a different place. I remember that day now...years later...as a turning point, not maybe so much for me, but for the entire world.

Suddenly things changed in the world, people stopped taking things sitting down. We watched from the comfort of our homes on television as "coloured people" were beaten for simply trying to have lunch, or sit on a bus. I never really understood, when we watched these things, why my Dad and Mom let me sit there and see these horrible things happen. But I know now, that they were trying to un-shield me from the world. Being fourteen and living in Medford, Ontario did not give me the grand picture.

For the most part Medford was free from injustice, prejudice, racial tension, or any of the things that the people out there had to deal with. Sitting there experiencing it through television made me who I would become. It made me see the world the way my parents wanted me to see it....truthful, open book, and just the way it was.

Everything I saw going on in the states, from the "hippie movement" to the freedom riders, shaped the way I thought about everyday things, even here in Medford. I don't mean to imply that Medford was such a utopia, and better than the rest of the world, but the fact is our morals were never really tested the way they were down south. People all over North America were fighting for their beliefs and their rights during that time. The new American President sent people of all races off to die in a foreign country, for a cause that was not our own, unprepared and completely untrained. Meanwhile their own country fought an internal battle. I felt ashamed, not as a Canadian, but as a human being watching those men and women shed blood just to earn the right to live amongst their own people.

My biggest regret was that I could not have been with those people on that bus that was burned, or the lunch counters they were beaten against. Although none of that should have happened, some of us should have been there to help them with their cause.

I felt in my heart, long before the idea of a conspiracy arose, that perhaps Mr. John Kennedy was killed simply because he felt that equality was necessary. Segregation was not American in his ethics and I think ultimately perhaps that is what ended his life. How can someone be so closed minded that they would actually want to take another man's life just to stop him from expressing his beliefs? I asked myself that question so many times during the 60's as I watched four great men fall to an assassin's bullet.

Chapter 21

APRIL 1965

"Ladies and Gentlemen...I'm only going to talk to you for a minute or so this evening...because I....uh...have some very sad news for all of you and I think....uh...sad news for all our fellow citizens, and people who love peace all over the world and that is...uh...Martin Luther King was shot and was killed tonight in Memphis Tennessee."
I was at Brian's the night Bobby Kennedy stepped up to the podium to announce the death of Martin Luther King. Brian, Michael and I sat on the floor dead silent as everyone in the crowd screamed and cried out in pain and anguish.

I didn't understand Mr. King's death anymore than I had understood President Kennedy's death two years earlier. Being sixteen as opposed to fourteen didn't effect my understanding as to why this was happening all around us. And to think, if I knew sitting there watching the faces of the people, that it wasn't even over yet. In fact, it would end with the assassination of the very man who led the country through the death of his brother, Martin Luther King and Malcolm X. I don't think any of us could have been prepared.

Bobby Kennedy to me was a man like no other. I felt so personally affected by everything going on down in the states, and he was their rock, like a big brother who was there to hold us when all this was going on around us, no matter where we were in the world.

After Martin Luther King was killed in Memphis, I think everyone in the entire world had enough death. Those of us who lived through that decade now know that the expression, "bad things happen in threes" know that just isn't true. However, after Malcolm X's death none of us actually expected anything else to happen. We had lived through watching a fallen President and our neighbouring nation mourning for their leader.

In 1968 I was almost nineteen years old. I was working at a garage in Medford, saving my last pennies to go to College the following year. It was quite a cool day for June and I was feeling pretty good. Michael, Brian and I had planned to go camping for the weekend, just the three of us out in the bush, fishing, and bonding, all that kind of guy stuff. But even that wasn't the highlight of my day. I was more looking forward to going home that night after work and listening to Bobby Kennedy vie for the Presidential nomination on the radio with my Dad.

That probably sounds ridiculous...a Canadian kid, nineteen years old, who was more excited about listening to an American radio broadcast than going camping with his best friends but politics was something my Dad and I shared an adult interest in. I thank God to this day that we found that adult connection. Sometimes when a son gets older, the father becomes less of an important figure in the man's life. He no longer needs a hero, and the father has hopefully taught the son everything that he could without experiencing it for himself. So when that happens it's important to find something you both love as adults that you can share...for my Dad and I, that was politics...and baseball to a lesser extent.

I finished cleaning the garage and ran out of there towards home. I can remember the smell of the summer air as I ran through downtown in the twilight. I never stopped running and, to this day, I don't really know why I ran home. I wasn't late, but something that night just compelled me to run home. I rushed in the house and together, my Mom, my Dad and myself sat in our living room over our dinner and listened on the radio to the man who should be President.

Bobby was well spoken and he made us all remember his equally charismatic brother that, even as Canadians, we loved and appreciated. My Dad and I both cheered together when the Democratic Party announced that Bobby Kennedy was their choice for presidential candidate. It might have been close but nonetheless he was on his way to the Whitehouse. We were done our dinner by the time Bobby was leaving the Convention. Dad and I huddled around the radio anxiously listening. The reporters threw questions at him, but it did not phase his cool demeanour. He seemed ecstatic, and ready to take on the campaign.

"My thanks to all of you, and now it's on to Chicago and let's

win there," Bobby said to the crowd, brushing his hair from his handsome face, and the crowd responded with cheers and shouts.

Andrew West, a reporter we were familiar with, followed Bobby from the podium after his speech. The crowd chanted *"we want Bobby, we want Bobby!"* as the Senator moved through the crowd. *"Senator how are you going to counter Mr. Humphries and his background as far as the delegate votes go?"* West asked Bobby.

The crowd continued to chant and my mother looked up at the radio from her knitting in time to hear a crack from the crowd. It sounded more like a whip snapping, but in actuality it was something we should have all been familiar with...a gunshot.

My father froze and I dropped my fork down onto my tray. "Was that..." I began but stopped.

"Senator Kennedy has been sh...Senator Kennedy has been shot, is that possible? Is that possible?" the reporter cried out. The crowd was screaming and scampering and it sounded as though a brawl was happening in the background. Men were shouting and there was a definite struggle going on. My father put out his cigar and leaned forward. I set my tray aside and got up on my knees.

"It could...is it possible ladies and gentlemen? It is possible...he has been...not only Senator Kennedy...oh my God, Senator Kennedy has been shot...and another man, a Kennedy Campaign manager...and possibly shot in the head." The reporter's voice began to crack and women in the crowd were still screaming.

"What happened? What's going on?" I asked, turning to my Dad.

My Dad shook his head and sighed. "I think they shot Bobby," he said.

"No," I whispered, turning back to the radio.

"I am right here, Roosevelt Grier has a hold of a man who apparently has fired the shot. He has fired the shot...he still has the gun...the gun is pointed at me right at this moment." The struggle seemed to get louder as the reporter yelled at the men. *"Take a hold of his thumb and break it if you have to, get his thumb,"* he screamed.

My father stood up and walked in front of me and suddenly turned the radio off. "Dad, no, wait," I begged.

He looked at me and his face was solemn and very stern. He shook his head. "We don't need to go through this again. We've had enough. We'll turn it on later and see if there is any more news."

It was several hours before my father turned on our television set. We stayed away from the radio and after my Dad shut it off I went straight upstairs to call Michael and Brian. Both of them had heard the news as it happened and they kept me posted. I was getting ready for bed when I heard the television downstairs interrupt for a news flash. I rushed downstairs. My mother was already gone to bed, but my father was sitting in his chair drinking coffee. He looked at me as I came into the room. We both waited for the news. *"This is NBC News with a special report from Los Angeles, a statement is now being made at the hospital in Los Angeles. Here is Ray James for NBC News at Good Samaritan Hospital."*

"The Press Secretary, the Press Aide for Senator Robert Kennedy has just arrived here. Let's go to the podium and pick up his statement," the reporter said.

"Robert Kennedy died at 1:40 AM this June 6th 1968. With Senator Kennedy, at the time of his death, were his wife Ethel, Brother-in-law Steven Smith, and sister-in-law Mrs. John F Kennedy. He was 42 years old."

"That's it ladies and gentlemen, very quick, short announcement, on the fact that at 1:40 this morning Robert Kennedy died here at the hospital. This is Ray James, NBC News, Los Angeles."

My father stood up, turned the television off and then reached down and turned off the lamp. He patted my shoulders gently and gave them a squeeze before heading upstairs to bed. I will never forget...I sat down on our couch in the dark living room and I cried, I actually cried. I would never admit until this day that I ever shed tears over a man I didn't know.

After all, I was not even an American and I had never met the man. Yet still his death effected me the way that President Kennedy's death had effected everyone years earlier. I don't think I understood how anyone felt that day when President Kennedy was shot. Maybe I was too young to realize the full impact, but years later sitting there on the couch shedding tears for a man who had no pull or power over me I realized what it was like.

Bobby Kennedy's death opened up a rebirth, a violent revolution of sorts. Riots in the streets, angry police, everyone angry about the death of another great leader and they took it out on anti-war protesters. They beat them with clubs and all the things that both Kennedy men stood for went up in a cloud of tear gas. Television became more important to everyone as the camera's caught every minute of kids my age being beaten for chanting what they believe.

So on top of what you might consider typical pubescent changes, I had all these other things going on in the world effecting my transition to adulthood. Each death, each assassination, each uprising changed me and the way that I thought about the world for the rest of my life. Years later, a Canadian singer released a song called "*The Summer of '69*." That song, every time I hear it, has a lot of meaning for me. It was actually the summer of 1968 that I felt like was my transition from just a kid who didn't understand why people do the things they do, to being just an adult who didn't understand why people do the things they do.

Chapter 22

July 1968

I was working long, hot shifts at the garage and then doubling over to Sam's Place to put in hours there. I was doing whatever it took to put some money in my pocket. High School was over...officially. We had survived, my friends and I. In between my jobs, Brian, Michael, Kathy and I spent as much time together as we possibly could. Although none of us ever said it, we knew in our hearts that this would be our last summer together.

It was the day after I turned nineteen when Ray came to town. When my Dad told me about Ray Herst I was immediately fascinated. All I knew about him was that he was an amazing ball player and I was anxious to meet an actual baseball player from the States. Just to give you an idea of my small town ignorance, I thought the best part was when my Dad told me that Ray was black. After sitting at home and watching the injustice of racial differences in the states, I had always wanted to have a friend who was black. It was as though I thought befriending someone of a different race would make me a better person. Technically Michael was of a different race but he looked the same as we did more or less so in my mind that didn't count. I wanted to show my acceptance, and help where I could help. I thought I would be doing the world a favour by taking on a black person as my friend. I understand now that I was looking at Ray as a skin color and that I was upholding a certain type of racial prejudice myself without meaning to.

Ray was from Detroit, Michigan. He grew up in a 'bad' neighbourhood with his mother and his two sisters. His father, he told me, had run off years ago and he hadn't heard from him since. I had never met anyone like him before. He hadn't grown up with the same privileges that I had and I didn't consider myself all that privileged. But I realized just how fortunate I was when Ray told me his stories.

Ray was 26, from Michigan and he could hit a homerun further than any other player in the History of the Colpoy Vikings. The coach from Colpoy had seen Ray play in Windsor, down south.

He had offered Ray a two year stay in Ontario if he played for the Vikings. Ray reluctantly agreed. He didn't want to leave his home and his family for two years, but playing minor-league baseball for Colpoy would mean getting twice as much pay than he would get playing for the minors in Michigan. We took our baseball seriously. Ray was an incredible player; he could hammer that ball right out of Ryerson and way past the first row of houses. I knew he'd make it big some day.

Dad read about Ray Herst in the local newspaper and talked with Mom about him staying with us. We certainly had plenty of room and the Vikings were always looking for "home away from homes" for the ball players. He called up the Colpoy Vikings' head coach and offered Ray a place to stay. I was thrilled. I welcomed him with knowledge of his baseball stats and we played ball every single night that first week he was in town. My mother insisted to me that I let Ray alone and give him some space but Ray said he didn't mind, it was good practice.

He was tall, 6'2, dark hair, and dark skin. He told me how he went to Alabama once with his friend and almost got killed when they were in the wrong place at the wrong time, and police officers actually chased them with clubs for standing somewhere looking at a map. His stories were so different than what I saw on the news. Up until that point, everything I heard about the civil rights movement came from TV. Now I had this man, who played the greatest game on earth, and also had the greatest stories.

Ray was the first person in my life that was like a big brother to me. He was everything that I could possibly want to be, and at his young age, he was like a mentor to me. After the first few days his color was completely forgotten, he was just Ray. It seemed like no one in Medford cared what color he was and Ray liked it that way. At first, the whisper was, "Who was the new black guy? Where was he from? Why was he here?" But after a couple of weeks, everyone knew Ray and he was just Ray. At least I thought that's the way it was.

After a ball practice in Colpoy I asked Ray if he wanted to go down to the Malt Shop. Ray thought that was a great idea and together we walked downtown to my hang out. The Shop was not very busy.

There were the Thompsons, a young couple eating at the far booth, and there were a few kids hanging out around the Jukebox but not playing any music. Ray and I sat down on the swivel chairs at the lunch counter. Ray had been in town the better part of three weeks but his training schedule and his out of town games had kept him completely exhausted so we hadn't had a chance to visit all my hang outs yet. This was the first time I had been able to bring him to the Malt Shop.

Ray and I talked about his next game, and what he thought of the other teams. We talked baseball a lot. Sometimes, I really wish that I had talked about more important things with him, but he never seemed to mind what we talked about. Jack Simons, the owner of the Malt Shop since...forever...(we called him JL) was talking to a man at the end of the counter who was sipping coffee. Both of them looked down at us sitting at the lunch counter. The man said something to JL and JL nodded and they whispered back and forth. I didn't pay much attention to either of them.

It was several minutes before JL finally made his way down the counter to us. "Hey JL how are you?" I asked. I ignored the fact that he didn't greet me back. "We'll have two cheeseburgers, extra fries, and two cokes please," I said passing him the menu back.

JL stood there wiping the counter with his cloth. He leaned in close to me and whispered across the counter. "Davey, do you think...maybe...you could sit in a booth?" he asked.

I looked at him puzzled. "What?" I asked.

"Maybe over in one of the booths, like by the window where you and Kathy sit," he explained.

Ray said nothing, he glanced at the man at the end of the counter.

I laughed at JL, not understanding at all. "Why?" I asked. I thought he was messing with me.

"Well...I just think it might be better if you save these seats for the regular customers," he replied.

"Regular customers...JL...I am...," I began.

Ray finally interrupted. "He means me, let's go sit over here," Ray said, standing up off the stool and moving towards a booth.

"You're kidding me...JL...come on, Ray has been in town for three weeks."

"The gentlemen at the end of the counter...well...he's not really comfortable with your friend sitting here."

"He's got a cup of coffee," I exclaimed.

Ray pulled at my jacket. "Come on, David, let's just sit over here."

I pulled away from Ray. "No. JL, I have been coming here my entire life and you're gonna tell me that I can't sit at the counter with my friend? I can't believe you'd do this."

"Davey, it's not like that. I have to keep my customers happy."

"He's not even a regular," I argued.

"David, please, let's go sit right here." Ray sat down at a booth near the front door. I turned and looked at Ray who motioned me pleadingly to come sit at the booth. Finally I shook my head and went and sat across from Ray.

"I'll get you boys your burgers," JL replied.

"Ray...how can you just let them do that?" Ray stared at the counter where we had been sitting and he shook his head.

"How can I let them do that? Well...mostly because where I come from if sat at a counter where white people were, I'd be beaten, smacked around, and dragged out of the restaurant before being tossed into a gutter in the street. Then if I'm lucky they'd leave me there rather than hurting me worse. So when I come here and I'm asked to sit somewhere else in the same restaurant and still get served, it seems like heaven to me."

I was speechless. I realize now that JL was torn. I know that asking us to move probably wasn't what he wanted. He was doing what he felt was best for the business. Knowing that Ray held nothing against him for doing so, but sadly, appreciated the fact that he was even allowed to stay and get served made me realize just how important small things were in such turbulent times.

When I got home that night, I told my Dad what had happened. He was quite surprised by the whole ordeal. I explained to him how angry it made me, and how badly I wanted to fight. He understood but before going to bed he assured me that the time would come when I would need to stand up for what I believed in and say my piece. At the time, it kind of seemed like my Dad short changed me on the advice and that everyone was just letting such a big thing go un-noticed, but I understand now that there really is a time for everything...including fighting, and also sitting down and taking it.

Ray never said much of what was going on down South when

he was in Medford and Colpoy playing ball. The United States was still in turmoil, and the entire country was watching their young population die in a war that no one understood. Some nights I would come home from Brian's and Ray would be sitting on the front porch with a cigarette staring up into the sky. I'd sit with him but I sensed that he wanted quiet so I never said much.

I never knew on those nights what exactly made him so quiet and withdrawn but one night he told me he was just thinking about home and how he might never return to the home he remembers. One night, I came home to find him sitting on the porch, his head in his hands, and his baseball mitt in front of him. "Hey Ray, what's up?" I asked, sitting beside him. He didn't say anything. "Maybe I'll just leave you alone, give you some space," I said, standing up to go inside. He reached up and grabbed my arm and pulled me back down beside him.

"I'm way past due Davey, I can't get away from it much longer," he said.

"What are you talking about?" I asked curiously.

He had tears in his eyes.

"I've been able to avoid it this long but I can't afford to go to school, and I've gotten away this long but my time is coming. My birthday is September 21st," Ray replied. The more he spoke, the less it made sense to me. I didn't understand. I looked at Ray questioningly. "Never mind, no tears my mother used to say. Strong men, strong hearts." Ray stood up and stretched. "I'm going to go for a walk," he replied.

"I'll come with you," I said, standing also.

"No David, I want to take this walk alone," Ray replied, and he set out towards the park. He left his ball glove sitting on the ground. I picked it up and turned it in my hands. It was worn and used and broken and torn but it had so much power in it, so many memories, so much strength.

I went to bed thinking of what Ray had said, but they still made no sense. He seemed like he felt so hopeless and yet I couldn't think of why. He had a great career ahead of him and he had just got wind of a rumour that the Yankees wanted him for first draft next year. Unfortunately, they weren't the only ones who wanted him for draft apparently.

I got up the next morning and I thought I heard my mother

crying. I crept to the top of the stairs and looked down into the hallway below. My father appeared from the living room with suitcases in his hands and Ray followed close with the rest of his things. My eyes widened and I bolted down the stairs.

"What's going on? Ray where are you going, the season isn't over?" I asked.

Ray looked at me and smiled his big toothy grin that I loved so much. "I gotta go David, they called my birthday this morning," he said.

"What are you talking about, would someone please speak English?" I demanded.

Ray set his bags down and looked at me. "They drafted me into the army. They're sending me to Vietnam next week. See they put guys like us into a bucket and draw out our birthdays. I was getting pretty lucky being put off this long. My time's up David, you take care now," he said, and picked his bags back up.

"No, you're not leaving, they can't make you go over there. You can't go, you'll get killed," I begged.

"David Emerson," my mother scolded.

"You have to play ball, they'll understand that," I replied, ignoring my mother's comments.

"Son, they don't excuse ball players especially ones playing ball in Canada," my father replied.

"I don't understand this?" I said watching Ray and my Dad walk out the front door.

The television in the living room was on and as I walked towards the front door, feeling nothing but dread for Ray, I heard the announcer solemnly say...July 14th....that was my birthday. If I were in Ray's position right now, they would be sending me off to some foreign country to fight people I had nothing against. I would never forget that as I watched Ray leave that my birthday had been called. It echoed in my head and made me shiver. I watched Ray and my father get into the car to leave for the train Station in Colpoy.

I stood in the front yard watching them back out of the laneway. I didn't understand why he would do this, why he would leave. He was safe here, there was no draft in Medford, he didn't have to go anywhere, but it was like he chose to do so even though in my heart I knew that wasn't true. After everything that I had seen people do to Americans like him, he was going to go fight for his country.

The car stopped at the end of the laneway and Ray stuck his head out the window. "David, take care of my mitt for me, I'll come get it when I get home," he yelled, smiling and tossing me his pride and joy. I caught it and held it to me tightly. I would never let it go. I lifted my arm and waved as my friend drove away...it was the last time I would ever see Ray Herst. Ray arrived in Vietnam and was given orders to take a chopper to a base in the Viet Cong...his chopper was shot down over a river and everyone on board was killed. He never even saw the war.

Chapter 23

Present Day, September 1990

Brian continued to go to Colpoy a few times a week for his work outs. He enjoyed the bigger city, and had a great time there. He spent a lot of time in Colpoy as a teenager, as his mother worked there, so part of visiting his old home was visiting Colpoy. This is why by 9:00 PM, Friday night I was not surprised that Brian was not home yet.

Usually, he was home by dinnertime but it was no reason to be alarmed. He had stayed home several times in the last week to be with Mom while I was out, and he needed his time by himself. I hadn't done much that day. I helped Mom with the yard work and then spent the night relaxing, reading, and catching up on some work that the office had faxed me. They had told me for ten years that I deserved a vacation and here they were faxing me work.

Michael and I had planned on going for coffee that night but he hadn't called me yet. Michael was sitting in his hotel room watching a movie and having a drink when his phone rang shortly after ten. Michael picked up the phone. "Ello," he said.

"Mike?" said the timid, broken voice.

"Hey Brian, what's up?"

"I...I need some help," he replied, almost in a whisper.

"Brian?" Michael sat up on his bed and muted his television. "What's going on, where are you, is everything okay?"

"I need you to come and pick me up," Brian said. Brian need only ask once. Michael, without even an explanation, was in his car and heading for Colpoy. Brian's instructions had been simple. "Don't call David, I need a ride, I'm at the hospital."

As Michael sped towards Colpoy his mind raced. It's funny, in times of possible crisis, the things that can go through your mind.

But usually none of them are ever right. Michael got to the Colpoy General and Marine Hospital just after eleven. He went into the front foyer and asked the woman at the desk where she could find Brian Parker.

The woman typed the name into her computer and then gave Michael directions to the trauma ward. There were several nurses and a doctor around the desk. "Excuse me, Doctor, my name is Michael Finn, I'm looking for Mr. Brian Parker."

The elderly doctor looked down his nose through his glasses. He did not smile, or greet Michael, or even show any interest in his being there. Finally, after examining Michael, the doctor nodded. "Are you a relative Mr. Finn, or are you Mr. Parker's...umm...uh...his...," the Doctor stuttered.

"His partner?" Michael said, finishing the sentence. "No, but I am his best friend and I want to know where he is, he called me and asked me to pick him up."

"Mr. Finn, could I speak to you...over here...privately," the doctor replied. Michael nodded, glancing at the nurses who were ignoring them both.

"Mr. Finn, your friend Mr. Parker was in a fight."

"Brian? Brian was in a fight. Brian has never lifted his fists to anyone," Michael replied.

"Well...it wasn't so much a fight as he was...beaten up. Mr. Parker was attacked downtown by several men."

"Beaten? What? You're kidding, how did that happen?"

"Well from what we can make out, he had just come from a restaurant downtown, and the restaurant is usually...well...it specifically caters to...," the doctor stammered.

"Gay men, I get it," Michael said, filling in the blanks.

"Yes, now you're welcome to go and see him. He wants to go home and we are trying to convince him to stay overnight just for observation. He has a head injury that could be dangerous. But before you go in there...I should warn you, he was beaten pretty badly. When he came in here a few hours ago, he wasn't even conscious."

Michael sighed and pressed his head against the wall. "Alright, thank you Doctor. Where is he?"

The Doctor motioned down the hall to the right. Michael walked down the corridor and stopped outside the door. There was a glass window to the right and the blinds were open. Brian was sitting in a chair facing the far side of the room, looking out the window. The window was open. Michael opened the door slowly and knocked on the inside. Brian didn't turn around or say anything.

"Brian, are you alright?" Michael asked.

Brian looked down. "Give me a minute to get ready, and I'll meet you outside," he whispered. His voice was hoarse and barely audible. He sounded like he was parched.

"Can I help with anything, I mean, I can just get your stuff together while you...," Michael began, picking Brian's bag up from the foot of the bed.

"I can do it myself, just get out!" Brian yelled, banging his fists on the armrests of the chair.

Michael dropped the bag on the floor and turned for the door. "Fine, I'll be outside." Michael reached for the doorknob and stopped. "You know Brian, we've always been there for each other, all three of us, and if you want to shut me out then fine. But just remember mate, you called me here, I didn't ask to be brought in on this. But I'm here nonetheless, and I want to help." Michael stepped forward to leave.

"Wait, Michael...I'm sorry...I'm just hurt, in a few ways more than one," Brian said.

He stood up and looked at Michael. Brian had a patch on one eye but it barely covered the damage. The entire left side of Brian's face was a bruise...a dark shade of purple. A large and dark bump protruded from his forehead and his mouth was cut in four different places. Stitches ran the length of his right cheek. There were several cuts across his forehead and on his neck. The wounds were very fresh.

Michael tried to stop his instant reaction, which for Michael, should have been easier than any other person, but Brian had never looked like this. No person, any one of us had ever had contact with, had looked like this. Michael was speechless.

"Please, don't tell me how sorry you are, even though I haven't heard it yet. I don't want any pity about this; I brought this on myself," said Brian, grabbing his bag from where Michael had dropped it.

"Excuse me?" Michael said, sitting on the foot of the bed. "You think this is your fault?"

Brian looked at Michael from his one good eye. "It is no one's but mine."

"Bull shit Brian! We're not leaving here until you understand something...you did nothing...nothing wrong, do you understand me?"

Brian nodded just to be non-argumentative. Michael stood up and grabbed Brian's shoulder. "Stop, and listen." He looked into Brian's face without flinching. "No one, should ever hate you for who you are. Of all the people in the world who didn't understand who you were, I was the worst. I didn't want you to be any different than I was. And it took me less than a week to realize you aren't different than anyone else. It means nothing to me now because you've been like a brother to me. You are who you are and I love you for it. This is not your fault...what these people did to you is their sin not yours."

Brian dropped what he had in his hands and began to sob. Tears fell down his swollen face. Michael wrapped his arms around his friend and held him close patting his back. "Why did this happen?"

"They're afraid. They are cowards," Michael replied. The two friends stood in the hospital room. Brian cried his pain out and Michael stood there with him.

It wasn't until the next morning at eight-o clock that Brian came through the front door of my house. I was making coffee in the kitchen for Mom and I. Brian stood in the front hall with Michael behind him. I looked at him and dropped my coffee into the sink.

"Oh my...oh God, what happened?"

"Don't be upset David. I just didn't want you to over-react. I'm fine...I will be fine."

I looked at Michael looking for some sort of an explanation or confirmation that he was actually okay. He looked terrible. Michael nodded. "She'll be apples mate." Michael cleared his throat and sat down in one of our kitchen chairs. "He was beat up coming out of a restaurant in Colpoy,"

"What? You're kidding me...well did they rob you? What did they take?" I asked, still in complete shock. Michael shook his head at me warningly. "I don't understand...why would they...," I started to say but then, just like that, I understood. "Oh I get it. Who did this, were they kids?"

Brian shook his head. "Why don't we go outside," Michael suggested. The three of us went onto the back porch and sat down. The sun was high and the morning was already unusually warm for September. No one said anything for quite some time and then Brian spoke.

"I stopped by the Restaurant to get some lunch and see an old friend that works there. I hardly ever go to that restaurant, I don't even like the food there. I just wanted to see my friend. We had lunch and talked and then before I knew it, it was like after eight o clock. So I got up and left and walked about a block, and these guys came out of a bar on the corner. They were...middle aged...our age...and they were dressed in suits and ties and I didn't think much of it but I remember they had been right behind me two hours earlier when I had went into the restaurant. So I kept walking, not thinking anything about them. I mean, they were business men and I never would have thought to pick up my pace or take a different route.....," Brian's voice cracked and trailed off. It took him a couple of minutes to regain his voice. When he spoke again, there was the sound of tears in his voice. "After another block or so they started calling to me...'hey man, slow down, let's chat.' They were kind of laughing and smirking so I figured they were being typical drunks. I ignored them and kept walking, and then one of the guys yelled out...'If it walks like a fag, and drinks like a fag then you know what it must be eh guys.' Then I picked up my pace but by this time they had decided that I would be their nightly amusement and they caught up to me. I asked them to leave me alone, and even gave them a few choice manly words to try and get them to back off, but it was too late for that."

"Hey fag, out for your nightly street walk?"

"Do you think you can pick up some tight end out here, eh fairy?"

"Maybe you think one of us is cute eh?"

"I completely ignored them for several minutes, I didn't let it get to me. I've done it before, I know how to ignore people like that. Then the guy in front stuck his foot out, and I was so intent on ignoring them that it caught me off guard and I fell on the sidewalk. I have no idea what happened after that...all I know is, all of a sudden, their words turned to fists and I think some sort of stick from somewhere. They...they kept hitting me, and kicking me, and punching my face and after the first few hits I couldn't feel anything...all...all I could think about was that I was going to die here in the street and no one would ever know why. I don't even know when they stopped. At some point I came around and they had left. I managed to get to my feet and stumble out to the road. Three cars passed...and I begged them to let me in, take me to a hospital or even just call the police but they all drove away. Finally a lady stopped, and I think she said she was a nurse. Then I passed out for good and I woke up in the hospital. Three cars passed me by...they didn't even know I was gay...they had no reason to hate me...they just wouldn't stop because I had been beaten. What the hell kind of world do we live in?" We thought maybe it was a rhetorical question, as Michael and I both listened to Brian's story, but Brian was looking at us waiting for an answer of some sort.

"Do you know who these men were, I mean, did the police come?" I asked. Michael nodded.

"Brian spent the last three hours at the police station. The police were friendly enough and tried to be helpful but they didn't seem all that anxious to catch anyone for this," Michael explained.

"I know who it was, at least I know who tripped me first and who hit me several times. I know one of them just as well as I know half the people in this town. Greg Harrison is his name, and I saw him earlier at his store," Brian explained.

"Greg Harrison?" I said, in disbelief.

"Yeah, as in Harrison's Department Stores...all over Ontario, started in Colpoy," Brian replied.

"Oh I know who he is. Our firm in Toronto does the Harrison account. We've been doing advertising for them for years. Are you sure it was him?" I asked.

"Positive, I know him well."

"Brian you need to get a lawyer, you need to press charges, and sooner rather than later. Don't let them get away with this," Michael said. I nodded my head.

"Michael's right, the sooner you press charges, the sooner things can get resolved. We can't just let them walk away from this," I said.

"I don't know," Brian said shrugging.

"Brian, have you seen your face...have you actually seen what they've done to you," Michael demanded. Brian shrugged again. "Brian, if you don't stop this then it might be someone else next time and they might not get away with a pummelled face but rather inside a pine box."

"Look, I'll think about it. Right now, I just really need to rest and not see anyone for awhile," he replied, standing up and walking into the house. Michael and I stayed on the back porch for some time. We said nothing, not a single word. We only looked over the back yard at the birds, and the fall leaves hitting the ground. Our coffee was cold and we had nothing to say, but our minds were racing. We said nothing to each other and yet we were both feeling the same...relieved Our best friend was brutalized and yet we felt relief because right now Brian could be gone. We could have lost him because a group of middle aged men felt they could take away someone else's dignity.

Finally Michael stood up. It was already almost noon. "Well I'm gonna get some sleep too mate. Its been a long night. I'll call you when I get up, maybe we can get a drink tonight or something." I nodded and lifted my coffee mug towards him. He left me to my thoughts. Mom would have a fit when she saw Brian's face; it was going to take some explaining that was certain.

I heard Brian moving around in his room several hours later. I knocked on his door with a light lunch for him. He didn't reply. "Brian, I brought you some lunch. I'd really like to talk," I said to the door.

He unlatched the door and stepped aside. He was changing his clothes and buttoning up a stylish dress shirt. His face looked possibly even worse now that the blood was starting to flow back to it. The patch helped cover some of the damage. Brian stepped back and looked into the mirror on the wall. I had wondered if Brian had seen himself. "Well aren't I the prettiest flamer in town," he said, barely in a whisper.

"It will heal Brian."

"Want to bet on that, it might heal here...but not here...," he said punching his chest gently. "You know, since I was as young as I can remember, I used to get picked on. I was either too skinny, or too weak, or too quiet...but there was always something "wrong" with me according to everyone else. And then when I finally realized that I was gay I actually prepared myself for the worst of it but you know...until this...I never had that many problems."

"This will pass too. You'll forget all about this, and it won't happen again," I said.

"Now you're doing what you've done since we were kids David, you're trying to protect me. You can't tell me this won't happen again. As long as I'm leading a life that is unacceptable to society, I'm endangering myself and everyone else with me. What if you or Michael had been there with me? They would have done the same thing to you for nothing more than being there with me."

I didn't respond to that. He was right, I couldn't argue with the truth. "I'll help you deal with this anyway I can," I said.

"My whole life someone has been there to protect me, either you or Michael or my mom or your parents. Someone always shielded me and for the first time in thirty-nine years I found myself on that street completely alone. You don't have any idea what it was like to look in the eyes of the people in those cars and see the fear...they had no desire to help me and they had no idea. I don't need anymore help, I need to help myself."

I watched as Brian took his coat from the closet and put it on. "Where are you going?" I asked.

"Just out, I need to be alone...actually alone…and deal with this," he said, and closed the bedroom door behind him. I walked to the window and watched from above as Brian walked down the front lane and towards the park. I wondered where he was going, but I understand that wherever it was, he needed to go there alone.

Chapter 24

July 1st 1963

It was the biggest celebration of the year in our little town. All of the families in the Ryerson neighbourhood would get together for a huge barbeque in the middle of Ryerson Park to celebrate Canada's day. Eventually families from outside of the Ryerson neighbourhood started coming. We'd play baseball, eat ourselves silly, and wait for the fireworks to start in Medford Harbour. It was something everyone looked forward to all year.

Michael's Dad, my Dad, and two other of the neighbourhood Dad's would fire up the barbeques and the Moms would sit around the picnic table gossiping and swapping recipes. The other Dad's would stand around and drink their beers and smoke their cigars discussing Trudeau and his latest policy or outburst.

The three of us, myself, Michael and Brian, took this opportunity to milk the younger kids in the neighbourhood for everything they had. We'd make bets with them about how far we could hit the ball, or make trades with marbles and comic books, and since most of them were two or three years younger than us, they had no idea how much they were losing out on.

Now up to this point you would likely assume that life for the three of us was pretty good, not much to be afraid of in Medford. However, the three of us and many other children in Medford had one big fear. It was something that would literally haunt us for the rest of our lives, I know it did for me.

Through our backyards and up a small embankment there was a fork in the road that branched off in three paths. If you went down the right path it would go to our school, Medford Community School. If you went straight through the fork, onto a dirt path, it would take you to the river and eventually the lake. If you turned left on the road it would take you up to a much older part of Medford. The houses were older, and the people in them were older too. They had been there a thousand years, or so we thought, and they had let their houses run down and were too old to worry about fixing them.

The houses lined both sides of the street making for some dark and very spooky looking homes. At the end of the street was a dead end going straight up an embankment. The embankment was at least a hundred and fifty feet high and was too steep to climb. On top of this cliff was the east side of town where there was a general store, some more homes, and the local arena. So in order for the old people in those old houses to save time, and avoid going all the way around the cliff, the long way, the city had built a flight of old wooden stairs with metal railings on either side. There was 68 Stairs, with a landing on each level after ten stairs, six landings in total. There was only one lamp that hung down over these stairs, about half way up, and it did not look overly secure. At night it only lit less than half of that stairway.

It was certainly the fastest way to get to the arena, or anything in Medford that was on top of the cliffs. The other alternative was to turn right at the fork and go all the way up Maple Road, around our school, up three more blocks and then to the left. It took three quarters of an hour to walk, when it would take ten minutes by the stairs.

But for us, and for any other children in Medford, that was not an option. The stairs were never an option. Years and years later, in 1978 it would occur to me sitting in a dark movie theatre how much those stairs in Medford reminded me of that fateful flight of stairs in "The Exorcist." And whatever sent Father Damien to his death down those stairs is exactly what we were afraid of way back then.

That July afternoon, with the sun high and everyone anxiously awaiting the fireworks, Brian, Michael and I sat on the grass reading a Turok comic book. Brian had gotten it from Colpoy when his mother had been working and we were dying to read it.

We all drooled over the cover that featured Turok and Andar with flaming weapons taking on evil bad guys. "A hidden cave leads Turok and Andar underground into a nightmare world of deadly Albino men?" Michael read the cover curiously. "What kind of story twist is that?"

"Hey this is a collector's issue, and it cost me 12 cents. Mom will never just give me that much again for a comic book," Brian replied.

"What's the deal, you were dying to read the new Turok last week?" I asked Michael.

"Yeah well that was before I heard about the new issue of Justice League," Michael replied matter-of-factly.

"What new one?" Brian said, tossing the Turok aside. I scowled at Brian and picked up the comic. "I didn't see any new Justice League, you know I would have gotten that one instead."

"Number 19 Justice League American...The super heroes are banished into outer space and become the Exiles of Earth," Michael quoted, from what he had read somewhere.

"Well we have to get it now," Brian exclaimed.

"Yeah okay, like you said none of our parents are just going to give us 12 cents for a comic book," I replied.

"Well Frankie Wilmott has it and he said he'd trade me if I got something good," Michael replied.

"Are you kidding, Turok, brand new, who wouldn't trade for that, I don't even care if we read it," Brian said. Justice League was everything to us! We'd do anything to read an issue that we didn't already have. Our lives were so simple to be excited by something so...wonderful.

The sun was starting to sink fast in the sky, another hour or so, and it would be dark and everyone in Ryerson would be heading to the docks for the fireworks, including Frankie Wilmott and his family. "We'd have to go right now," I said. "He'll be leaving for the fireworks soon." Together Michael and I ran over to my Dad, while Brian grabbed his comic and prepared it to trade for Justice League.

"Dad, can Michael, Brian and I go over to Parker Street to see Frankie Wilmott? We wanna trade a comic book with him," I begged. I tried not to sound needy but it didn't work.

"Well son, we'll be leaving for the fireworks soon," he said.

"We'll be back in time! We'll hurry, and we'll meet you guys down at the harbour, maybe Frankie's parents will give us a ride," I pleaded.

"Frankie's parents don't have a car," Brian interrupted, not helping my case. I glared at him and shoved him with my elbow. He got the drift to not help with any new and unimportant information.

"Alright, the three of you can go, but you be down at the harbour by dark or you'll never see that comic," my Dad instructed, pointing his burger flipper at us. We both smiled and thanked my Dad profusely. As we left the park, my mother stopped us.

"Where are you boys going?" she asked.

"Dad said we could go to Frankie Wilmott's before the fireworks but we'll be back before they start," I explained, as quickly as possible. We were still walking backwards towards the street as I talked to my mother.

"Well if you're going past the store then you can pick me up a gallon of milk and a loaf of bread," she insisted. She already was reaching for her small change purse.

"Mom, no, we don't have time," I whined. She looked up at me and her eyes widened threateningly.

"Yes, Ma'am," I said, lowering my head.

"Now here's a dollar ten for the milk, and the bread should be about a quarter, you can keep whatever is left over but don't gorge yourself on candy."

"Thanks Mrs. Emerson," Michael replied, and we bolted for the road, leaving the mothers laughing at us. The truth was we'd really have to move if we wanted to make it to Frankie's and back by our "curfew."

We made it to the fork in the road and the final rays of sun were creeping up the side streets making way for the evening. People were coming out of their houses with blankets and sparklers getting ready for the festivities down at the Harbour front.

The three of us stopped at the fork to catch our breath. We were all panting like out of shape old men. We had really ran hard to get this far and now we were all pooped out. "We're never going to make it," Michael said, doubling over from a stitch in his side. He looked at his wristwatch. "It's quarter past eight, it'll be dark by the time we hit the hillside."

Brian nodded in agreement. "Frankie will be gone by the time we get there and we won't make it back by dark so we'll have no comic book and be grounded. This idea is not sounding so hot."

"Well...we could take the stairs and be back before our parents even leave for the harbour," I suggested. Brian looked at me wide eyed and glanced up the street in the other direction towards the stairs.

"You're crazy, it's almost dark. We don't even take those stairs in the daylight, there is no way I'm going up those in the dark."

Michael looked at me curiously. He didn't quite show his fear the way Brian did but I knew he wasn't crazy about it anymore than

Brian was. "Take the stairs? David, you got a few Kangaroo's loose in the top paddock?" It was getting quite dark now as the last rays of sun disappeared in the distance. Michael appeared thoughtful for a moment. "He's right though Bri, it's the only way we'll make it," Michael said, shrugging.

"You guys have both lost your minds; every time we try to take those stairs we get two steps up and end up screaming for home. There is something up there, we heard it," Brian pleaded. The escarpments, or cliffs as we called them, were fielded with heavy forest on either side. No one ever bothered to remove the trees because they couldn't build on the steep cliff side anyway.

The stairs were lined with trees, and in the dark you couldn't see a foot on either side of the railings. We had tried to get up them before, many times, after dark, when my Mom had sent us to get bread or milk but we always gave up and went the long way. Michael had actually made it to the fourth step before we heard loud rustling heading right for us. Michael said he saw eyes coming through the bushes and that was enough for us and we went home screaming.

That was the last attempt at the staircase. "We have to try it Brian, Justice League remember, once in a lifetime chance to read it," I said, trying to persuade him.

He gave in. "Alright, we'll try it. But if any sort of monster comes at us, I'm throwing you guys at him to save myself."

"Deal, let's go mates," Michael said, smiling. He looked excited to be trying this again. By the time we walked up the block the roadway was dark. Twilight had more than arrived. The three of us stood at the base of the stairs looking up. The single lamp, halfway up, swung in the wind and creaked threateningly. The shadows bounced up and down the stairs as we looked up at them.

At the very top of the stairs, very faintly, we could see the street lamps from the neighbourhood above. Hard to believe it was that close...but so far away. "So who's going first this time?" I asked, swallowing the lump in my throat.

"Not me, I did it last time, and I am not looking at that monster again," Michael said.

"Well someone has to go," Brian replied, looking at us.

"Please don't let us stop you," I said, jokingly to Brian. I knew he wasn't going to be the one to go first.

He looked up the stairway, tilting his head slightly. Branches and leaves fell from above making crunching noises as they hit the wood. "Alright," he said suddenly.

"What?!" Michael and I both said at once.

"I'll do it. I'll go first and when I get to the first platform, you guys start up after me," he said, still focusing his attention on the stairs ahead of him.

"Brian, I was just kidding, you can't go first," I said, grabbing his shoulder.

"Well you're not gonna do it, and Michael said he's not, so that leaves me."

"True enough, let him go David," Michael said, stepping back.

That night, at the bottom of the haunted stairway, I looked into Brian's eyes and I saw something I had never seen before in him....true determination, a look of courage and unrelenting bravery. I let go of his shoulders and very, very slowly Brian set his foot on the first stair. More leaves fell through the trees across the wooden stairs. Michael and I grabbed onto the railing at the bottom. We held our breath as Brian took the second step. We could actually see the first platform in the dark, just six short steps away.

"Go Brian, you can do it," I said, as he took another stair, keeping his eyes ahead of him. If we had been thinking logically, which is impossible at fourteen, we would have realized that taking these stairs so slowly would take ten times longer than the actual long way around. We didn't care, it was about excitement and cold-blooded fear.

"Woooooo," Michael whispered, doing his best ghost imitation and then laughing.

"Knock it off, Finn," Brian said, still not turning around.

Brian took another step and suddenly another after that. Before we could blink he was whispering down the stairs..."I made it, I'm here, the first platform."

"Are you serious?" I whispered back.

"Alright, we're coming up Bri," Michael said.

I went first, one foot in front of the other, trying not to look out in the forest around us. My heart was pounding in my chest. Michael had his hand on my back to guide him up the stairs. It took us a few moments before, finally, we both stepped onto the same platform that Brian had made it to. Brian was already standing on the next stair up facing us. He had such a smile on his face, I had never seen him look so proud. For the first time, he had done something that both of us envied him for. He had done what neither of us had been brave enough to do.

"Way to go Brian," we both said praising him, and giving him slaps on the back. He smiled at us triumphantly. Then he turned around and we all looked up the stairs. "Now we just have to get through five more platforms," I said.

In one moment, it was all like a flash, the bushes ahead of us and to the side moved, rustled and we heard a high pitch whistling noise, almost like a scream but it was close, very close. Something swung down from above and caught Brian on his left cheek scratching his face. Brian hollered out and stepped back into us. We all froze. Whatever had swung down to attack us was coming back again. The whistling stopped and then started again and we all began to tremble. We looked up the stairs and saw a large black thing coming towards us. It was the size of a large dog and shaped more like a bear.

Michael saw it first and pointed and then the three of us screamed until we went blue. Together we all turned and bolted down the stairs jumping the last three. We ran down the block, still screaming, not once stopping to look back. We ran all the way back to my house and straight up to my room. The three of us crashed on my bed and waited a half-hour till we caught our breath. We never said a word after that. We went downstairs and went with our families to the fireworks. We were quiet the entire night, each one of us thinking about the thing that had almost gotten us. Brian perhaps had more on his mind. He was saddled with extreme disappointment. His fleeting moment as a hero had came and went in the blink of an eye, and in the end he had ran like the rest of us.

Certainly, neither Michael or I ever felt anything against Brian for not making it up the stairs. He had in fact made it further than any of the rest of us ever would. From that day forward we never ever attempted those stairs again during the day or night. We had seen enough to convince ourselves it was not just childhood imagination playing tricks on us.

It was a night none of us would ever forget but we'd never talk about either.

Chapter 25

Last week of September 1990

Brian left my house that evening and walked around the park. He went downtown and sat under the huge oak tree outside city hall. There weren't many people out at that hour but he just sat there and smelled the clean, crisp air and watched the fall mist rolling in over the streets, and off the water.

He walked down to the harbour and sat on the rocks watching the waves roll over the shore. And then he walked back towards my house, past our old High School. By the time he reached that old fork in the road, it was dark. In fact, it was past eight-o clock. His eye patch was making his face itch, and scratching his face made it ache and bleed, so it was a no win situation. He looked up the road and without much thought began to walk towards the old stairs.

Before he knew it, he found himself standing before that same stairway. The railing had been stabilized somewhere along the years but ultimately it hadn't changed, with the same old lamp swinging from overhead power lines.

He felt no thumping in his chest, or really any fear at all, as he looked up into the darkness. He raised his foot and stepped on the first stair, and then took his foot back. A bird cawed in the distance and flew up from a bush. Brian swallowed the lump forming in his throat.

"This is ridiculous, you're thirty-nine years old," he said, out-loud.

He took three deep breaths and then suddenly bolted for the stairs. His feet pounded on the old wood as he flew across the first platform. He headed up the second set and flew across the next platform. His eyes focused ahead and his heart was pounding, his only thought was to get to the top.

Suddenly he heard it, the whistle, that same whistle that had come before our attack decades ago, and it instantly stopped his heart and sent him back to that night in '63. Brian stopped and froze halfway between the second platform and the third. How could he stop now? He had to keep going but he knew what he had heard.

The whistle wasn't as loud as he had remembered it being. Brian turned slowly around and didn't see anything. The lamp overhead was swinging in the breeze. Suddenly the trees rustled and Brian stepped back and looked out into the forest around him.

He looked carefully, searching for any sign of life. There was no life. Above him there were old power cords hanging down menacingly, and creaking slightly when the wind blew. Brian chuckled and turned back to face the stairs. He shook his head, in order to clear the whistling noises, and then continued much slower up the stairs. The wind still howled through the dead trees, but Brian didn't let it bother him. He had realized his childhood demons were nothing more than some noises in the bush, not much was going to phase him now.

He slowly made his way past the sixth platform and could see the sidewalk at the top of the stairs. Brian took one last step and his foot hit the pavement. He held the railing and slowly turned around. He looked down at the dark corridor of stairs that he had just conquered.

He smiled and lowered his head, closing his eyes tightly and feeling the wind brush over his face. "I did it," he whispered. He stood at the top of those stairs for several minutes, just repeating to himself that he had done it. He had walked up those stairs, the stairs that to this day none of us had ever braved. "Now I just have to go back home," he said, suddenly realizing that it was getting late.

He looked down the dark stairs that had taken him twenty-seven years to conquer and realized that to get back home quickly would require going back down those stairs....well maybe in another 27 years. With that thought and a deep sigh Brian put his hands in his pockets and turned around to take the long way home.

There was a delivery for me that arrived just before Brian got home. The man had me sign for it and I knew what it was. It had the seal of my Ad office on the front. They wanted me back in Toronto the following week, for what was described as an urgent business meeting. I couldn't argue with this, I had to be there. That night Michael and I decided to get together at the old bar downtown and have some drinks.

Brian came back from his walk in much better spirits. He didn't say much. I asked him how his walk went and he smiled and nodded. His mood had lifted and it almost made his bruises seem less noticeable, as though the emotional scars were directly linked to the actual ones. He didn't tell me about his stair-climb until much later.

After my mother had gone to bed, and we had cleaned up the dinner plates, Brian and I walked down to the bar around eleven. For a small town, the bar was a hot spot but that was because it was basically the only thing open past six. It was very busy in the little sports bar. There was a baseball game on television, and men and women were all huddled around the big screen TV.

There were younger couples at the tables, and older men around the pool table. I recognized about half of the people in there. Michael was sitting at a booth in the corner where we had been getting together the last few weeks. We walked over to the table and Brian and I sat down across from Michael. His eyes were glazed and he lifted his glass half-heartedly.

"You're here early," Brian commented. Michael looked over at Brian and Brian caught a smell of his breath, and saw the absolutely glazed look in Michael's eyes. "Whoa...okay...maybe we're just really late."

I laughed. "Starting before us eh Mike?" I said. Michael nodded.

"I had a few," he said.

His glass was empty again. He stood up in his seat and lifted the glass over his head. "Hey Dougie, some grog for me and two for my mates here," he called out. Doug nodded and waved his hand. Michael sat back down.

"What time did you get here?" I asked Michael, curiously.

He shrugged, "I don't know, six maybe, just before dinner."

"You've been here for almost six hours?" Brian asked.

Michael looked at both of us and his brow wrinkled. "Is that alright with you Mommy? You have a problem with me having a good time?" Michael demanded.

Brian was taken aback by the callous response. "I was just curious," he said.

"Yeah well it sounded like an accusation to me. I'm a big boy now, I'm not 18 anymore and I don't need you or Pope Emerson here telling me when to start drinking."

Doug came over to the table and set down the beers in front of us. "Hey Mike, that's it for you. I can't serve you anymore after that one," Doug said.

Michael had already started to guzzle the glass that he had just put in front of him. "What?" Michael said. "Oh quit messing with me Dougie, I haven't even started yet."

"Well you won't be finishing here, I can't serve you anymore," Doug repeated. He turned and walked away from the table. Michael jumped to his feet swaying slightly and grabbed Doug's shoulder.

"Screw you mate, I'm a paying customer, I'll drink however much I want to."

Brian and I jumped up and grabbed Michael off of Doug. He struggled in our arms as we held him back. He reeked of more than beer, he smelled like tequila and vodka, on top of everything else.

"Hey!" Doug yelled. "Smarten up or get the hell out of my bar, Michael Finn. This isn't the big city, I don't have to put up with your crap. Now keep him calm, both of you."

We nodded and apologized to Doug profusely. We let Michael go and we were about to sit down when Michael bolted again towards Doug, this time spinning him around, and laying his fist into Doug's chin. Doug went down on the floor on his hands and knees and Michael stood over him staggering slightly. "You don't mess with Michael Finn, Dougie," Michael said, sarcastically.

Both of us ran over to Doug and tried to help him to his feet. He pushed us off. "Get the hell out my bar now, I'm calling the police."

"We're really sorry, we'll leave Doug, I'm really sorry," I said.

"Just get out!"

Michael was already stumbling towards the front door. He turned towards the bar and threw his hand up towards Doug. "I hope your chooks turn into emu's, and kick your dunny down." Brian threw a twenty on the bar to cover the drinks we hadn't even drank, and we followed Michael out. Michael was already on the sidewalk bent over retching onto the ground. Eventually his liquid dinner came up and we were graced with the vision of his vomit on the sidewalk. He stood up and wiped his mouth with his sleeve.

"Sorry about that, alright I'm good to go," he said.

"I think we better just go home tonight," I replied, and Brian nodded walking away from Michael.

"Are you guys kidding me? It's not even midnight, I'm good for more. I was just getting warmed up when that scag got in my way. Come on, let's go back to my place. I've got some vodka there and a few other bottles," Michael said.

I stopped and turned to face Michael. "Maybe that's your problem, you've got too many bottles in your life."

"What's the supposed to mean David?" he demanded.

"Exactly what I said Michael. Every time we're with you you've got a flask of something in your hand, or you're adding something to your coffee, or you're piss drunk at ten in the morning right through till ten at night. You do a pretty damn good job of making everyone around you think you're the life of the party, and the fact is most of your life is going right down those bottles."

Michael looked straight into my face. "You think I have a drinking problem, oh that's classic, that's really something. You think I'm a fucking alcoholic. You're something else, you're just so great aren't you David. No one is good enough for you are they?" Michael raved, waving his hands around.

"Come on guys, let's not do this tonight. Mike, you're drunk and you don't want to say something you're gonna regret," Brian said, stepping between us.

"Well David isn't drunk and he seems to have no problem shooting his mouth off, maybe that's why your bitch left you huh Davey?" Michael blurted.

My eyes flared and I swung out instinctively, punching Michael in the face. Michael fell backwards on the sidewalk. "Come on guys, don't do this," Brian begged. I stood over Michael looking down at him. Michael was smiling and holding his jaw. Blood trickled from his nose.

"How could you say something like that?" I demanded.

"Oh it's the booze talking mate. It's not me, you know I'm a raging alcoholic," Michael yelled, sarcastically. He awkwardly pulled himself to his feet and brushed his clothes off.

"Screw you Michael Finn, get out of my life. If you want to kill yourself with that stuff, and all the while deny you have a problem, then go for it. I don't care anymore, you're nothing but a worthless drunk," I said. With that out of my system, I turned and walked away from Brian and Michael.

"Worthless drunk? Well at least I still have a good time, and I'm not a bitter old man. It took you forty-one years to realize how pathetic your life is David. I've known you for a long time and your life is boring. One day you'll look back and wish you could have been that much more like me," Michael yelled after me. Brian looked at Michael bent over on the sidewalk, and blood running from his nose. He looked at me, walking away from Michael, and he began to come after me. I didn't say anything to him as we walked together away from our best friend. Michael swore and attempted to kick the parking meter but instead stumbled onto the ground. He reached into his jacket pocket and pulled out his flask, uncorked it, and downed the contents.

Brian and I said nothing as we walked back towards my house. I knew that he wanted to talk about what had happened, but I just didn't know what to say. I had no idea this night would have ended the way it did. As we approached Ryerson Park and could see my house in the distance Brian finally spoke. "Sara left you?" he asked.

"What do you mean?" I responded.

"Sara...your wife. Are you guys split?"

"Brian, I'm sorry I didn't tell you."

"So you forgot to tell your best friend that you were having marriage problems?" Brian asked. He said it calmly without resentment although I knew he was hurt by it. I didn't respond. "I see," Brian replied, looking at the ground as we approached my house.

"We are separated right now, trying to work out our differences, and I just didn't think it was important to bring up," I explained.

Brian laughed at that sarcastically and shook his head. "You know, you've got your nerve assuming that as your best friend, whether we don't speak for months on end, or whether we do, that I wouldn't want to know everything that has gone on in your life. I understand that we didn't keep in touch after college, I even understand that maybe you might not tell me over the phone when we spoke, but we've been back home for three weeks and you never thought once to mention this to me."

"I didn't want you to be disappointed in me," I replied. We reached my front door step and sat down.

"Disappointed? You disappoint me?"

"Well you know, not being able to keep my marriage together, it's not something that I advertise to the world that I screwed up."

"You think I've never screwed up? Do you think you having marriage problems is the worse mistake any of us will ever make? You said yourself you're working things out, so this might all seem like nothing a year from now."

"I'm sorry I didn't tell you Brian, I owed it to you to be honest and I should have been."

"David, you of all people taught me that when it comes to friendship there is no such thing as disappointment, only acceptance, and I offer that to you one hundred per cent."

I nodded and we gave each other a hug and went inside for the night. I could barely sleep. The words of my fight with Michael echoed in my head. I know Brian must have been wondering what would happen from now on. Would Michael and I speak after this? The same questions echoed in my head. It was not the only fight that I had had with Michael, but it had been years, since we were kids. Any time that something happened between Michael and I, or Brian and I when we were kids, I always went to the same person for advice.

So when I got out of bed early the next morning I walked over to Kathy's house. I hadn't spoken to anyone that day, not even Brian. My mind was still on the fact that it felt as though I had just lost one of my best friends for good. Brian had been right, the three of us hardly kept in contact over the last twenty years. But that didn't matter because there was always the feeling that Michael, Brian and I could still count on each other, always. Now, it seemed after last night that my relationship with him was in real jeopardy. We both said things in anger, but they were also rooted in truth. I didn't want to see him drink like that, and I had known for several weeks that there was something more to his drinking than just the casual beer.

Kathy answered the door, still in her bathrobe, looking just as radiant as she ever did. She held the robe tight against her as she looked through the screen door. "David, are you alright, you look upset?" she asked.

She opened the screen door and I came inside. "Michael and I had a fight last night...I hit him," I explained. We sat down in her kitchen and she made coffee and we talked for some time about Michael and how much I feared for him and his problem. Kathy agreed that she hadn't seen Michael without some sort of a drink in his hands since he had been back in town.

"You can't make him see his problem David, he has to see it for himself. He has to hit bottom and I hate to say it but I think he's a long way from that."

"But what if he doesn't hit bottom before he does something stupid and ends up hurting himself or someone else."

"I think he has already done a little of both especially since it seems as though he's alienated his best friend."

I sighed deeply and sipped my coffee. "Oh...Kathy, when did life become so complicated? Where did all of our lives go? You know, one minute I'm twenty years old thinking about how I have another sixty years ahead of me to do so many things, and then in the blink of an eye I'm forty-one and I feel like life has just slipped right by."

"Life is what make you make of it. It doesn't have to be ending, and forty-one can be a whole new starting point. Fresh start, new beginnings, a whole new beginning," Kathy said. I looked into those beautiful mysterious brown eyes and I couldn't help but let my mind wander to how much I missed her soft lips. She had the softest lips and suddenly I ached to feel them again. I wanted to feel that piece of my life that I hadn't felt in so long. I had never tried for anything so hard in my life as I had tried to get Kathy to kiss me. Long before our first kiss on her front lawn that night after the school dance, I had done everything in my power to get those lips against mine.

Chapter 26

The school had suddenly become infested with rats. To us, that meant an early march break which was just fine, no one was going to argue with that. Spring was early that year and everything was in full bloom. Kathy and I had been dating for two weeks. I had taken her to so many movies I couldn't even count. We sat in the malt shop for hours and she even went fishing with Brian and I twice.

She seemed to take quite a liking to Brian. They got along amazingly but for some reason it didn't bother me. Not that Brian couldn't have attracted someone like Kathy, he was probably better looking than I was, but still it didn't bother me.

Although the two weeks had been going just perfect, something was still out of my reach, we hadn't kissed. It was not uncommon for a young couple, such as us, not to kiss. Kissing was left to the more experienced kids who parked their Dad's Chevy's at the drive-in for an hour longer than the movie lasted.

It had taken me several days to get up the courage to hold her hand. Actually, it was Michael who finally stopped in the hallway at school and said, "Oh you two make me sick, hold her hand already," and he had thrown our hands together. Her hands were tiny and warm, and felt so good. But finally holding her hand meant that the first goal of a young teenage relationship was complete and it meant I had to start planning on how I would kiss her. And I didn't want Michael to be there to put our lips together.

My plan began to fall into place. Her birthday was at the end of April and everything had to be perfect. This was going to be my hook, line, and sinker into making her believe I was the man of her dreams. I planned for days and did so many chores, my hands felt numb, just to get money for the big day.

Dad knew my plans and he exploited me for all it was worth. He waved money in front of me while I mowed the lawn and, when I moaned about weeding the garden, he made a point of reminding me how much flowers and dinner, and gifts cost.

I must have pushed that little mower around that yard for twelve hours while he sat on the porch smiling and waving at me. Michael and Brian would come by the house with their ball gloves and ask me to play and I'd look over at my Dad and he'd smile and shrug, and put the money back in his wallet. I'd moan, and sigh, and send my friends away. He enjoyed that week a lot.

Finally her birthday arrived and my plans were in effect. Mom helped me make a meal that would melt any girl's heart. I pulled out recipes for fettuccini alfredo and slaved over the stove. I made dessert...the best Cherry Cheesecake you can imagine...and I made it twice, since the first one exploded all over the kitchen. Dad took me downtown so I could get balloons and flowers, and anything else I could think of. Dad sat in the barbershop, reading his newspaper, and getting his hair trimmed while I scrambled to get everything organized. Every time I flew by the barbershop window my Dad and Jimmy, the barber, would point and laugh. I'm glad they thought it was amusing.

Everything was finally perfect and I had everything I thought I needed. I made my way back towards the barbershop with flowers in one hand and balloons in the other when I walked past the Discount Store. In the window was the biggest softest teddy bear I had ever seen. He was absolutely perfect and I could just hear him through that glass (in a voice that sounded strangely like Jimmy Stuart) saying... *"I belong to Kathy, take me home, take me home David!"*

I rushed into the store and asked the clerk how much for the bear. I could feel the pain flood over me when he said ten dollars. Ten dollars...that was exactly what it had taken me two weeks to earn and I had just spent it on flowers, balloons, food...I would never see ten dollars again.

"Do you want me to box him up for you?" the clerk asked. I shook my head.

"Sorry I'll have to pass," I replied and turned towards the front door, disappointed. The bell over the front door tinkled and a man's voice called out to the clerk.

"Get that bear ready for my boy, he belongs to a special girl."

I looked up and my Dad was standing there in front of me. I smiled at him and he put his arm around me like he used to when I was a kid. I was the happiest sixteen year old male with a teddy bear in the world. Kathy was never going to forget this birthday.

She came by my house just as I was lighting the candles in my living room. Mom and Dad went upstairs to give me my space. Of course, not before Mom gave me the lengthy speech about watching the candles, and making sure they didn't tip over, and not to burn anything, and make sure the dishes were stacked neatly beside the sink, and not to let things get out of hand with Kathy and I. "Oh Mom, come on," I said, my face going red. Finally they retreated upstairs and Kathy arrived. I slicked back my hair one more time before going to the front door.

I opened the door and Kathy looked beautiful. Her hair was pulled back and she was wearing the most beautiful red and white dress. My mouth went dry and I lost all motor function as usual.

"You are...you...I...you...wow!," I stuttered, like the village idiot.

Kathy smiled. "Are you going to invite me in David?" she asked.

I nodded and stepped aside.

I brought her in and we sat down at the table. I served my perfect meal which actually did turn out to be perfect...ha you thought I'd screw up the meal didn't you?...it was wonderful. When she was almost done her dinner, I moved smoothly over to the radio and turned it on. I thought I had it perfectly set for the station I wanted and the music that was going to be unbelievably romantic. Instead, *The Stones* started blaring that they couldn't get no satisfaction, making us both jump at the loud music.

I quickly grabbed the radio and hit the right dial and this time I got *The Righteous Brothers*. That was just slightly more romantic. Kathy smiled and we both sat down on the couch. We didn't say much, every once in awhile we'd look up at each other and smile. Everything was perfect. We just sat there looking at each other.

"I have something for you," I said.

"You've done enough already," she replied. I shook my head and stood up. I backed out of the room and grabbed the flowers and the balloons and walked back into the room. She giggled and covered her mouth with her hands.

"These are for the most beautiful girl in the world," I said dropping to one knee and handing her the flowers. She took the tulips and smelled them.

"Thank you so much," she said. She set the flowers gently down beside her and leaned towards me. My heart jumped into my throat. Was this it? Was she going to kiss me? My lips were dry, I just ate noodles, and maybe my breath was not good, what if I'm bad at it, what if I don't know how to kiss, it looks easy enough...for Cary Grant anyway. But there was no kiss, she wrapped her arms around me and hugged me tight which was equally...interesting...but not the objective.

"There's more, I have something else for you," I said.

"More?" she replied.

I nodded and reached behind the couch. After several grabs with my hand, I found the stuffed bear's big paw. I pulled him out and dropped him into Kathy's lap. He looked up at her with a stupid string-grin on his face. She squealed in delight and threw her arms around the bear and gave him a big kiss on the snout. I rolled my eyes...that was easier for the bear.

We talked for an hour laughing and joking and holding hands. It was the most perfect night, everything went exactly as I had planned. All that was left was the kiss. Just after eight, she stood up and said she had to go.

"Already?" I said.

"It's late, my Dad will want me home soon. This was the perfect night David, thank you so much."

"Okay well I will call you tomorrow," I said. It wasn't going to happen, I missed my chance somewhere along the way. I walked Kathy to the front door and then walked out to the front step with her.

"Have a good night," she said, looking at me with her head tilted slightly. Was she waiting for it? Did she want me to kiss her? Was this a hint? By the time I had weighed out the options she was turning to walk down the steps.

"Kathy," I blurted.

"Yes?" she asked, turning to face me again.

"Happy Birthday," I said, wrapping my arms around her. We hugged and I took a deep breath, when we parted this hug I would do it, I would kiss her. I held her close and then slowly we started to part.

There they were, her lips, her perfect lips.

I leaned in slowly, too slowly, but I leaned in nonetheless. I could hear the bells and whistles already. I was getting closer, unfortunately I was taking too long. Kathy was already turning around to walk home. My lips pressed against the side of her head and my mouth was filled with hair. It's a strange thing that you can miss lips by such a wide margin but here I was making out with the side of her head.

I jumped back when I felt her hair and Kathy and I looked at each other nervously. To this very day I don't know if she knew what I had tried. I suspect that she did but we were both too embarrassed to ever mention it. For two teenagers, it's much easier to pretend it didn't happen. She blushed and walked down my front pathway.

"Kathy?" I called again. She turned around at the end of my walkway.

"I really want you to be my girl. I would like us to be...you know...steady...," I said.

"I am your girl David Emerson," she said smiling, and then walked towards her house with a bounce in her step. I stood on the porch with a stupid grin on my face. She was my girl, she was my girl, MY girl. I ran out into my front yard.

"Woohoo," I yelled into the night sky. "She's my girl!" I yelled out. Dogs started to bark in the neighbourhood. "She's my Girl!" I sat on my front porch unable to stop smiling. I must have looked like such a cracker jack sitting out there with such a grin on my face. It was a feeling I would never forget. It was the feeling of love.

Chapter 27

September 1990

I was sitting in the restaurant that used to be our old malt shop so many years ago. Although you'd never know it was the same place. Nothing remained from our old haunt except one squared off piece of wallpaper that Nick, the new owner, kept up for a little memorial to the days of old. I was babying a very cold coffee and had been for over an hour. The lunch counter that once belonged to the malt shop had been moved to the opposite side of the restaurant and I sat there staring off into space.

My mind was racing, thinking of everything going on in my life. I thought of my Dad, and how things had not been the same since he died over a month ago. I thought of Kathy, and how the feelings for her seemed to be coming back full force. I thought of Michael and how much I just didn't want to lose him to something that I felt like he could have control over. And Brian, how much he was the least person to deserve what had happened to him. And I thought of Sara...my wife...and my daughter Sam. It had been so long since I spoke to either of them, almost two months in fact. Sara made it very clear that she wanted a lot of space. Things had been bad towards the end, everything seemed to set us off, and we'd throw out harsh words, no matter how badly it hurt the other person. I finally drove the knife into our marriage when I told her I never loved her. I don't have any idea what made me say that. It wasn't true, I loved Sara, I loved her more than any woman in my life...even Kathy. When Kathy and I broke up I honestly believed I would be alone for the rest of my life. I never thought I'd find another person and if I did...they wouldn't be Kathy. But then there was Sara...she was smart, and funny, she could make me laugh like no other person, beautiful and my perfect match.

I looked over at the front of the restaurant. There was a pay phone on the right side of the front door. I tossed a bill on the counter to pay for my coffee and walked over to the phone. I picked up the receiver and hit "0." After several rings the impatient voice of a woman on the other end answered. "Operator?"

"I need to make a collect call to Toronto..."

July 1976

I was 27 years old that day. My birthday had been one of the best. Although I dreaded the thought of nearing thirty, with my youth in the rear view mirror. My roommate, just months after I moved to Toronto, was a black guy named Eric. He was a guy I always thought of as someone who loved life. He was 29, full of vigour and optimism. I could not understand where his ambition came from. He was working his way through College to become an actor.

He came into my room at nine o clock that morning with two of our other friends, Julie and Steve, and poked me gently. When I opened my eyes I was met with several very large water balloons dropping down on me and into my bed. They splattered across my half-asleep body. I dove out of bed screaming as they all stood around me and laughed. Then, as I regained my composure, they broke into a round of "Happy Birthday," with Eric leading them.

That started the most amazing birthday I had ever had. The three of them took me to the stores downtown, and bought me lunch at my favourite corner deli. We spent the day just enjoying Toronto, dancing down the streets making fools of ourselves. We had our pictures taken by the guy on Young and King and had so many hot dogs I thought I was going to explode. No hot dogs were ever like Young Street Hot Dogs.

Toronto in the seventies was a world that had to be experienced. The hippies were still in full swing trying to keep their movement alive, the culture and the people, everyone had something to say. It was just the place to be. I had only left home a year ago and honestly until the day of my twenty-seventh birthday I had hated being away from Medford and my folks. I loved Eric and all my new friends but they didn't make up for missing Michael, who had went to the states for a job offer, and Brian who went out west to work for awhile. We hardly spoke anymore and it hurt.

Eric, Julie, Steve and I walked down to the harbour front, with our cokes, and sat under a bridge. Eric lit a joint and took the first long toke before passing it to Julie. He held it in for awhile and then exhaled it out. "So this is your night, where do you wanna go dude?" Eric asked me. Julie passed the joint to Steve, who passed on it altogether. I didn't hesitate to take a deep drag of the sweet smelling weed. I had literally gone twenty-five years before I even saw weed. I wasn't a habitual user by any means but it was just what we did, it was literally a hobby. I use to hate it when   Michael smoked weed and yet now it was just something I did once in awhile. My eyes bulged and I could feel my thoughts clouding as the smoke sifted through my brain. I passed the joint back to Eric who gladly took it. "I don't know, maybe we should just go home and order in."

"Forget that man," Steve said laughing. "Let's hit the clubs, we never do that anymore."

"We went out last weekend," Julie replied.

"Last weekend, that was like a week ago," Steve replied, smiling.

"Alright let's do it," I said, jumping to my feet. "Let's go change into something ridiculously stupid and go dance until the sun comes up."

Together we all retreated back to our pad and changed into, what I've decided after dressing myself through four decades, was the worst looking clothes ever created by man. I mean, these weren't clothes, it was more like a contest among people under 30 to see who could look most like Bo-Bo the clown. And the best part was we thought we looked good! I remember that night as we made our way through the streets with our shoes that had souls five inches thick, and Eric's hair that was streaked with blue and just shy of being a 70's Don King. But he thought he looked hot, and we thought we all looked pretty good.

We bounced down the street winking at the girls, yelling "hey dude" to people we didn't even know and laughing, just having a good time. The disco that we loved to go to was only several blocks from our apartment. It was the place to be, and we loved it. We had our own little table in the corner although we didn't do a lot of sitting.

Believe it or not, I could disco like you've never seen. I was good.

We got to the disco, got our drinks and sat at the table laughing at all the people who thought they had moves. Eric and I waited until we heard the song we wanted. Finally it started to blare over all the speakers, and it was time for us to start our jive. We jumped up and hit the floor, hands in the air, shoes clicking on the smooth wooden dance floor. The floor was packed and it didn't matter because everyone just wanted to dance. The music was what we were here for. No one cared what anyone else was doing around them.

I think back now and I remember walking through the front door of that club every weekend and past people who were doing some sort of illicit drug right off the tables. It's really amazing to me that it didn't even phase me. I grew up in small-town Canada and yet none of this stuff seemed to amaze me or bother me. Which is good because if you took any certain interest in the guys or girls that were snorting, shooting or smoking, you found yourself either joining them or out in the street bleeding.

I can remember looking around the dance floor at the faces of everyone around me. Some of them were smiling and having a great time, and others looked like they were just trying to forget everything in their life. I could see up into the balcony where a guy in a sequined jacket was helping a girl push a needle into her arm. The 70's for people like my friends and me were just about growing up, moving from being a child to being an adult. It was like the after party for the revolution that was the 60's.

Fortunately, even though none of the things going on around me bothered me, I also never felt the need to try any of it. I was happy with a drink, a cigarette and the occasional puff on some good weed. The song ended and Eric and I went back to the table and Julie passed us a joint. We both had a few drags and I leaned over to Eric. "Thirsty...I'm gonna go get another drink and some chips or something," I said.

Eric nodded still grooving to the music that was blaring. My mother would have called it "Noise Pollution" as she always did about Rock and Roll. I made my way through the crowd towards the bar. I finally made it to the bar and held up two fingers to the bartender. "Double on the rocks," I yelled and the bartender gave me a thumbs up.

I looked back over my shoulder into the crowd. More and more people packed in but there were never any fights or shouting matches like the bars nowadays. People were just happy to be together, they were like family. The crowd parted slightly and I could see the tables on the other side of the dance floor. I scanned the area casually and then back again. My eyes focused in on someone and I stared. I think my mouth probably opened slightly.

She was so stunning. She must have felt the stare from my eyes because she looked up and our eyes locked. No kidding! Our eyes met across a crowded room, how great is that? We kept our stare for what felt like ten minutes. The whole world stopped, and I fell in love at first sight. This was completely different than Kathy, so I would tell myself, I could see my whole life with this woman and I had never met or even spoke to her before. The bartender set my drink down and I paid him. I grabbed the glass without taking my eyes off of her. She stood up as I made my way through the crowd towards her. Within moments, I was standing in front of her, looking into her eyes. She was much shorter than I was, and she had long dark hair, and the most beautiful blue eyes I had ever seen. They were like eyes of glass that could see right into someone. "Drink?" I said, offering my glass.

"Alright," she said, and took the drink. Two words...two words and we were both in love.

Gordon Lightfoot began singing about reading his mind.

We stood together in the middle of that dance floor. My arms wrapped around her, everyone else non-existent. "Sara," she said.

"Huh?" I said, snapping back to reality.

"My name is Sara," she replied smiling.

"David," I said. "Do you wanna marry me Sara?" I asked, yelling over the crowd. Sara laughed and put her hands around my waist.

"How about we go out for dinner first?"

"Dinner...huh...well it's kind of sudden," I said, smiling. That night we spent...well that night we spent the next two days together. I think Eric thought we were never going to part enough for him to speak to me. We did everything together, and I learned more about Sara in two days than I even knew about some of my closest friends. We played the truth game for about 12 hours straight, and by the time that game was over, we had told each other our deepest darkest secrets and still we didn't scare the other one away.

It was the most unforgettable two days of my life. And those two days turned into us dating, spending the coming weeks together.

We saw the city, visited the zoo and the museums and did everything that a couple romancing each other should do. But after that first night it was easy to romance each other.

I was working at en entry-level office job when I met Sara. I was just making enough money to cover my expenses and have a few dollars left over to take her out. I tried to save what I could but it was hard when we were young and wanted to have fun.

On our one-month anniversary we decided to go to the carnival. We ate corn dogs, and threw balls at cups to try and win tiny stuffed animals. My baseball arm gave me an advantage when it came to carnival games and after two hours at the fair Sara had her hands full. In the middle of the carnival was a city park with a small bridge across a stream. Multi-coloured spotlights underneath the stream shot a beautiful rainbow of colors onto the bridge. Sara and I got pizza from the vendor on the corner and walked into the park. We stopped in the centre of the bridge and Sara dropped her stuffed prizes beside her and began to eat her pizza.

I just stared into the water. "You're quiet tonight?" Sara said, poking her head around mine to give me a kiss. Pizza sauce, from her mouth, ended up on the tip of my nose. She laughed at me and reached up to wipe it off. I turned towards her and wrapped my arms around her waist.

"I love you Sara," I said, suddenly. Throughout every day we had spent together, it was an unspoken understanding that we were falling in love...but unspoken was the key word. Neither of us had stopped to discuss our future or how we felt, or our relationship. I think deep inside neither one of us ever expected that a one-night stand was turning into much more.

There was a long pause and my stomach started to sink. Maybe I had made a mistake. "Look Sara, a long time ago I let someone walk out of my life that I loved more than life itself. She was my everything. I promised after I lost her that I would never let anyone go out of my life again without telling them how I felt. So I want you to know right here and now that I love you with all my heart."

Sara said nothing. She leaned back on the bridge and closed her eyes. "Oh," she finally said.

Not the exact response that I had hoped for. She opened her eyes. "Oh," she said again. "Oh boy."

"I don't expect anything from you, I just had to tell you how I felt," I said, putting my arms on her shoulders.

"David, no one has ever told me they loved me before. I have never had anyone buy me flowers, or hold me the way you do, or love me the way you do. I didn't know love was like this," she said, looking at me.

"That's good," I said, nodding "I'm glad things are good."

"No, no they aren't good. I mean, neither one of us knows how we're gonna pay our rent from month to month, or how we're going to eat for the next week or whether we'll be able to keep our jobs. How can we support each other when we're barely supporting ourselves?"

"Because we have each other. We'll get through things together. If we can't afford rent...we'll move in together, cut our rent in half, food...well...there's always fifty cent hot dogs on Young Street, and our lives will work themselves out. But I can't see anything working out, I can't see wanting anything to work out, if I don't have you with me."

"I love you too," she said, very quickly, without another thought.

I smiled and threw my arms around her and spun her around. "Will you move in with me?" I asked her.

"I don't know...I mean my parents would flip, and right now they're my only hope for supporting myself. There is no way they're going to help me out if I'm living with someone I'm not married to. To be honest, I don't think I want to live with someone that I'm not married too."

Sara walked over to the edge of the bridge and looked down into the water. I stood behind her and thought carefully. "So then let's do it," I said, softly.

"Do what?" she asked.

"Let's get married, today, tomorrow, a month from now, whatever, but let's get married," I replied.

Sara snorted and threw her head back. "David, you've lost your mind. We just met, and you want to marry me."

"Sara, do you remember what I said to you when we met?" I asked.

Sara nodded and smiled. Tears began to fill her eyes. "You asked me if I wanted to marry you."

"And you know, I meant it. I would have married you right

then and there because I just knew you were it for me. I know that I want to spend the rest of my life with you Sara. I don't make decisions like this without thinking, but this decision doesn't need to be thought about. I know I love you and I want to spend the rest of my life showing you what you mean to me." I cleared my throat and slowly got down on my left knee. I took her right hand in mine, and I looked up at her. Sara covered her mouth and began to cry.

"Do you wanna marry me, Sara?"

"Yes, I want to marry you David Emerson," she said.

It was less than two weeks before Sara and I walked into city hall and got married. It was pretty informal but we hardly noticed. We spent the whole time looking into each other's eyes and making silent promises to one another that this would not be a mistake. Finding your soul mate, I believe, is something you have no control over. Whether you find your soul mate in a spouse, or a friend, or even someone you pass on the street, you sense it deep inside.

Chapter 28

SEPTEMBER 1990

The phone rang several times. I sat there leaning against the wall listening to it ring. Finally, someone picked up. "Hello," she said. Her voice sounded so strong and full of life, but it also held a certain amount of sadness, and my heart sunk thinking of the pain I had caused her.

"Sara?" I whispered, hoarsely.

There was a long silence. She said nothing, and I couldn't hear her breathing and I thought for a moment she had hung up. I took my ear away and almost hung up myself.

"David?"

I held the phone close again. "I'm sorry to call like this but...I miss you," I said. It wasn't my intention to say anything like that but it was out of my control. She didn't say anything.

"How is Sam?" I asked. Still she said nothing. She must have been covering the phone and her hand slipped because I caught the sound her crying.

"Sara, I'm sorry, maybe I shouldn't have called," I said. There was a long pause before she took a deep breath and spoke.

"No it's alright. I was wondering why you hadn't called."

"You told me not to," I said.

"Since when do you listen to me," Sara said, almost jokingly. I smiled despite myself. Another long pause.

"I was just thinking about...us. I was thinking about when we met. Sara, what happened to us? What happened to the way we were?"

"I guess when we promised to love each other forever, we forgot we might not always like each other," Sara replied. Yet again, more silence. "Sam misses you a lot."

"I miss her too, and you, I miss you both." Sara didn't reply to that. "Sara, are we going to make it through this?" I asked.

This time she replied right away which made my stomach tighten. "I don't know."

"What can I do?" I asked, plainly.

"David, it's not about you making it up to me. Why can't you see that? All I ever wanted was you. I don't care about anything else but when your husband loses all interest in you," she said, and her tears started again.

"I never lost interest in you."

"You could have fooled me. You may never have been unfaithful to me with another woman, but you haven't been with me emotionally for over a year. When did I lose you David...when?"

"I thought I was giving you and Sam what you deserved," I replied quietly, as though I were being scolded.

"All we ever asked for was you, so don't bring this down on us."

"I have to come to the city for business next week. Can I come see you? Please."

"When?"

"Wednesday, at noon, I have some business to take care of but it shouldn't take longer than an hour."

"Alright, we'll meet you in the park. You know the one."

"Okay thank you. I love you Sara, and I'll prove it to you."

We hung up and I left the restaurant. I walked back home and Brian was there talking to my Mom and helping her fold laundry. They both looked at me as I came in the door and I smiled at them both. I went into the living room, sat on the couch and sighed deeply. My Mom came into the room and sat beside me. She had been so distraught the last month that I hadn't considered ever talking to her about everything going on in my life. She looked at me and put her arm around me. I laid my head on her shoulder as though I were ten again. Diane Emerson, my Mom, how little anyone truly appreciates their mothers. "How are you?" she asked.

"I went to see Kathy this morning, and then I called Sara," I said.

"Do you still love her?"

"Of course I do, she's my wife," I replied.

"I didn't mean Sara," she replied, bluntly. "You never forget your first love."

She didn't say anything else. She stood up and walked back towards the kitchen running the dishtowel through her fingers, and instantly she was transformed to that young, vibrant woman I remember. "Do you remember your first love?" I asked, as she was leaving the room.

She turned to look at me and for the first time since the funeral she smiled, a real, happy smile. "Of course...I married mine." She winked at me and left. I sat for a few minutes thinking about what she had asked me. Did I still love Kathy? Brian poked his head in and I nodded at him.

"Am I interrupting your thoughts?" he asked.

"No, of course not, come on in," I replied.

He sat beside me and lowered his voice so my mom wouldn't hear, "Sergeant James called from the police department. This morning, they found Michael downtown slumped up against a building. He had a bottle of something in his hand, and he was covered in filth, most of it his own. He was still pretty drunk and they picked him up and took him back to the motel room. They said if he paid a fine they wouldn't charge him the host of things that they could charge him with, and the Sergeant thought we should know about it."

"He must have found some more booze after we left last night," I replied, and Brian nodded.

"You were right David, he's got a problem, and I'm sorry I didn't take more notice when you first mentioned it."

"Don't worry about it Bri, I think this has been going on long before either of us could have cut in." I paused, and leaned my head back against the wall. "Maybe...maybe it's not too late. Maybe we can still help him. Let's go over there and try to get him to listen to us."

Brian thought about it and then nodded. "Alright, let's go." We grabbed our jackets and headed out the front door. "Should we wear helmets?" Brian joked, as we left.

We walked to Michael's motel room. It was almost dinnertime and I figured Michael would be up by now and hopefully sober. We knocked on the door and heard nothing. We knocked again and finally Michael opened the door and looked out at us. He stepped aside leaving the door open and returned to what he was doing, packing his bag.

He balled up his socks and tossed them into the suitcase. "What are you doing?" I asked.

"Baking a cake," he replied, dryly.

"Michael, don't do this. Where are you going? I thought you were going to stick around with us," Brian asked him.

"Well I stuck around, it's been a month, and I have work to do. Besides I think my welcome in this town is long worn out."

"Michael just stop and listen to me," I begged, grabbing his arm. He pulled away from me violently.

"Get your hands off me. Look it, you made it damn clear what you think of me," he replied zipping up his carryall. He glanced at Brian. "Both of you."

"I never said anything about how I felt about you. I told you how I felt about your drinking. Maybe you think that's one and the same but it's not. If you want me to tell you what I think of you...I'll tell you," I replied.

Michael rolled his eyes and shoved by us towards the door. I turned to face his back. "I'd tell you that you're the best friend I ever had. I'd tell you that when I was stuck in life, or wondering what to do, I'd stop and ask myself...what would Michael do? I'd say that whenever I was in trouble or just needed someone to talk to, that I wished Michael was there. And you know something else I'm not the only person who feels that way...because I know Brian thinks the same about you." Michael stopped at the door but did not turn around. "All I ask is that you stop defending yourself, stop getting angry, and listen to what we have to say. We've been your best friends for 30 years; I think you can give us five minutes."

"I'm listening," he replied, still not turning around.

"Mike, we're worried about this. Maybe you're not worried about it, you might think it's not a problem, or maybe you don't care, but we do. And since we are your best friends and you supposedly care about us, then you should care that we are worried," Brian said.

Michael lowered his head. "I do care, I just think you're wrong and you don't understand."

"What is there to not understand? Last night you were saying things just to hurt us. That's not you. You're a completely different person. You're not even relying on yourself to do anything, you drink to get you through...everything."

Michael finally spun around and I knew by the look in his eyes that he was defensive again. "You don't know shit about me. It's been 20 Years since you've even seen me and you think you know what gets me through a day."

"Stop!" I yelled back at him. "You promised you'd listen to us."

"Well I listened, I've had enough," he said, and turned back towards the door. Brian blocked his way closing the door and standing in front of it. "Move Brian," he said firmly.

"No."

"Parker move!"

"No." Brian folded his arms across his chest. "If you want me to move, you'll have to move me. And I know you won't hit me...not well you're sober anyway," Brian replied, looking Michael in the eyes.

I walked closer to him and cleared my throat. "Think about it Michael, I want you to think back to what you told me. You told me you lost so many jobs, and you've had two ended marriages, and all this other bad luck that has come your way. Just humour your best friends and think back to those things and look me in the eyes and tell me that you can remember not being drunk during any one of those bad things that happened," I demanded. Michael still faced Brian.

He seemed to look off into space, hopefully recollecting what I had asked him to. He turned to face me. I looked at him and shrugged. "Tell me your wives didn't have a problem with your drinking, tell me you didn't lose your jobs because you were drunk more than sober."

Brian spoke up. "Tell us that right now if we searched you we wouldn't find at least three different bottles of alcohol on you. Do you think that's normal?"

"Oh what the hell do you know about being normal, look at you, you're busted up like a heavyweight boxer," Michael shot back.

Brian frowned. The comment hurt him, cut him deeper than Harrison had done by beating him. "I won't let that get to me, Michael, because I know you're just trying to drive us away."

"Yeah take the hint, let me out," Michael replied, putting his face inches from Brian's. Brian could smell a faint odour of booze on his breath. He had probably been drinking again this morning.

"Michael you woke up in the street for God's sake, what does it take for you to hit bottom?" I asked him. I reached out and put my hand on his shoulder. He whirled around, shouting something as he did it, and next thing I knew he was landing a punch into my face. I fell back on the floor with blood pouring from my lip.

Brian's eyes widened. "Michael what the hell....?" he yelled, rushing to my side.

Michael looked down at us, and I noticed something I had never seen in Michael's eyes, fear. When Michael finally spoke he stammered nervously, he had lost his edge. "Now we're even," he whispered. But now I could tell he had just seen a glimpse of what we saw. He turned and rushed out the door. Brian looked at me and I waved my hand towards the door.

"Let him go, I give up," I said holding my face. His punch hadn't hurt as bad as the thought that our best friend was killing himself.

Chapter 29

Both Brian and I left the motel feeling hurt by everything
Michael had said and done. We knew where it was coming from but it
didn't change how much it hurt us both. We didn't discuss it and we
didn't try to find out where Michael was going, maybe we both felt that
it was over. Our childhood trio, and our reunion to that effect, seemed
to have ended with Michael punching me...or maybe it ended the day
before when I called him a worthless drunk, either way, we all felt like
it was over.

I lay in bed that night thinking about how much Michael had
done for me. He had given me strength and taught me how to be
assertive. He helped me with Kathy, and he told me not to let her go,
the one thing I didn't listen to him about. Before Brian and I met
Michael we were scared of life, of growing up, of experiencing things,
and Michael showed us how to stop worrying and start enjoying.

That night I laid in bed staring at my old ceiling as I had done
so many times in my life. I sighed and sat up in bed knowing that sleep
was just not an option. There was too much going on. I walked over to
my closet where my Mom kept all my things that I never bothered to
take with me. I turned on the bedroom light and pulled out a box of
junk. It had everything in it from old letters that friends had written
me, to yearbooks, to a football jersey, still carrying dirt stains that
would never come out.

I pulled out the jersey and smiled. My eyes became teary as I
also pulled out one of my Yearbooks. It said "Reach For The Stars---
1964" I flipped through the pages and stopped on a group picture of our
football team. None of us liked Football, not even Michael, but it was

something we could all do and as Michael put it, it was a good way to meet girls. I scoffed at that when he first said it...but that is when I saw Kathy for the first time.

September 1964

It was the beginning of grade ten. We had survived our first year in High School, and it was actually kind of uneventful, not much had happened. We kept our friends close, and we figured out the flow of the world that was high school. We knew who to stay away from, we knew which kids sold cigarettes and which kids were popularity death if you were seen speaking to them.

Michael was determined that we had to find our outlet that would rocket us to the top of the social ladder. He spent the first week of grade ten flying around the halls trying to find something that would be our special niche in the big ocean of secondary school.

Brian and I were sitting in the cafeteria at lunch, in the second week of school, when Michael came flying into the huge eating area. "Guys!" he yelled from across the room. Everyone in the cafeteria looked up at Michael and he waved them off casually and ran over to our table.

"What's up?" Brian asked.

Michael slapped a flyer down on the table. It was yellow with bold black lettering that said "FOOTBALL" "COME JOIN OUR TEAM" "Yeah so what?" I said.

"So what? This is it, this is what we have to do," Michael replied, sitting down beside Brian. Brian glanced at Michael and then at me. We both burst out laughing. Michael scowled. He was serious. "What's so funny? This is our key to popularity, this is our key to meeting beautiful women, cheerleading types," Michael said winking at us.

I laughed again and shook my head, returning to my pudding. "Brian, you can throw a football, I've seen you do it," Michael said, pointing at him.

"Yeah well that's just in the park, not in a game. There is no way we'll make it onto the school team. And imagine the humiliation if we don't make it. That'll drive us further back down this popularity ladder. Besides I like the level I'm at now, I don't get beat up, and I don't have to go to every party everyone has...I'm socially ignored...it's a good place to be," Brian joked, and I laughed at him and gave him a "high-five."

"Guys be serious, I really want to do this. I think if we work together we can get on that team."

I looked at Michael. His eyes were determined. This was very important to him. "Okay so what do you say Brian? Do we amuse our friend and give it a try, what have we got to lose?"

Brian thought about it for several minutes. "I suppose that's true, maybe it'll be fun," he replied. Michael smiled, he was pleased.

We hustled out to that field the following Tuesday and we threw balls until our arms ached, and caught catches from sixty yards from the Coach. We were tackled, jostled, bumped, thumped and shoved. By the time we left that field, the three of us, and about five other sophomore suckers, were limping away. The junior football players were laughing at our expense as we hobbled to the bleachers on the sidelines. I sat down slowly and moaned aloud. Seven other guys did the same. "Is this really worth it?" one of the guys asked in the back.

"Yes," Michael replied, glaring up at him. "It won't always be this bad," he added.

A freshman got smashed into the ground as they practiced right in front of us, his face going into the mud and all our eyes widened. The Coach was jogging towards us. "Oh please don't take us on this team," I begged, quietly.

"Alright boys, as you know we can only take four of you seven. You all played pretty good and anyone who survives the first practice has to be commended but I have to choose four. So I'd like to see the following boys at tomorrow night's team practice right here on this field. Finn, Emerson, Ritchie, and Parker. Night fellas." The coach turned and walked away. None of us moved. The three boys who didn't make it were whispering..."Thank God."

"We did it," Michael said, suddenly getting a burst of energy and jumping out in front of us. "We did it guys, we're on the team."

"Yeah, we so are," Brian moaned.

The next day we hurried out of class and headed towards the field. Although neither Brian or I would admit it, when the coach said our names, we were excited. As we hurried towards the field, we felt proud and anxious to be part of the team.

The four of us new recruits stood at the edge of the field, our assigned gear in our hands. The Coach and the Captain of the team, Bobby Gallagher, came over to us. "Alright boys, put on your gear and hit the field, we're running patterns, and practicing for the game on Saturday. Bobby here will run down the patterns with you, and I want to see you do them right the first time."

Bobby then belted out a bunch of complicated plays and runs and other things that none of us had any idea about. When he was done we hit the field and played our very best, which usually meant running really long and standing there while the play was being completed...thank goodness.

Finally the coach blew his whistle and we headed back towards the locker room to shower and change. The coach stopped us as we were heading into the locker room. "Ritchie, you need to keep your eyes on the plays even while you're running downfield. Finn, you looked good out there, Emerson, throw long and deep, not high and wide, and Parker, you run like a girl."

He then walked towards his office leaving us with those pearls of wisdom. "I run like a girl?" Brian asked us. Michael laughed.

"Yes, yes you do," I replied, slapping him on the back. We went into the locker room and did our regular locker room things. We listened to the juniors talk about the girls they parked with and the television they watch and we mentally kept notes so we could keep up with the conversation at a future date.

As we were leaving Bobby Gallagher and two of his stooges caught us at the door. "Now hold on there boys, you didn't think practice was over did ya?" Bobby asked us. The three of us looked at him curiously. Greg Ritchie had already escaped the locker room. "See, you guys are new recruits to the team, and you can't really be a part of the team until you've done your entry test."

"Entry test?" I asked.

"Yep that's right Davey-boy." The other two guys laughed. "Now what would be an appropriate test for three buddies such as you."

I clenched my eyes shut when I realized what they meant. It was an initiation. "I think you need to do something outrageous, something embarrassing, and something that all of us that have to work with you on the team can laugh at for years to come."

"What about Ritchie, he's a new recruit?" Brian said.

"Oh we already spoke to Ritchie, he's gonna stand outside the school in his underpants. I figure that'll do it for him." Our eyes widened. Suddenly our stomachs turned. This could be devastating. "We thought something different was in order for you guys. In fact, we thought you guys are so close, you'd want to do something together. But you know what I'm a fair guy, I'm gonna let you guys pick what you want to do. I think something in front of the whole school would be good...and since the coach thinks Brian runs like a girl, maybe you guys should all do that, dress like one, walk like one...the whole get up, get my drift," Bobby said winking at us. They all laughed and walked out of the locker room.

Michael and I looked at each other and swallowed the lumps in our throat. Brian looked at us and shrugged. "I don't get it," he said. We both looked at Brian and flashed him dirty looks. "What?" he asked innocently.

"Nothing at all Brianna...," I said, sarcastically.

We all sat in my living room the next morning before school. Laid out in front of us were three of our mother's dresses, hair ties, shoes, stockings, and most importantly make-up. "So who's making the change first?" Michael asked.

"Who will be the easiest to make into a girl?" I asked. Michael and I both looked at Brian.

"Oh come on," he said, throwing his hands in the air. We both smiled and threw him down in the chair. I grabbed the lipstick and smeared it on roughly. "You're not doing it right, you're not putting it on straight," Brian complained.

"Yeah, because that's what really matters right now," I said.

"Give me the lipstick, this is how you put it on," Brian replied, carefully and perfectly applying it to his lips and then dabbing his lips on a tissue. He smiled at us, with his perfect lipstick. We both looked at him curiously. "What...I have a lot of girl cousins," he said.

Together we made ourselves into the three best-looking girls in Tenth Grade. Okay, maybe not but we looked good...nah we looked ridiculous. My father was just coming downstairs as the three of us were heading out the front door in our wigs and dresses, our faces in make-up.

"Bye Dad," I said, as we flew past him.

"Bye Mr. Emerson," Michael and Brian said.

"Goodbye....boys?" he said, yawning and waving at us. He froze his hand in mid-air and looked closely at us and then shook his head.

There we were, the three of us walking towards our high school dressed completely as girls. Brian and I hobbled along in the girls' pumps but Michael seemed to have a knack for it. High School...the last thing you need to do is draw attention to yourself. As teenagers we certainly didn't need to do something like this to get embarrassed. We could see the school ahead of us, looming over us. As usual, this morning everyone gathered outside waiting for class to begin.

"Just act cool," Michael whispered, through clenched teeth. Every kid in our school looked over at us as we approached the crowd. Hands began to point, laughter began to erupt as we got closer to our peers.

We pushed our way through the growing crowd. Everyone was laughing now and whistling crudely. I looked over at all our classmates and Michael and I flipped our hair provocatively which was met with applause and cheering. The three of us smiled at each other and hobbled towards the front doors of the school. Michael turned to the crowd before going inside the school and flexed his arms and yelled, "Yeah!" The crowd cheered again and we disappeared into the school.

In all the excitement we had drawn the crowd away from the fact that on the front lawn of the school shivering in the cold was Greg Ritchie, standing alone, covering himself from the fact he was wearing nothing more than a pair of navy blue briefs.

Chapter 30

First Week of October 1990

We didn't hear anything from Michael after he left town. I assumed he would go back to the States but neither of us knew for sure. I had called my office earlier on in the week to let them know I would be at the meeting that they requested I attend. I begged Brian to come with me into the city but, to a certain degree, he still preferred to stay inside.

His face had healed a lot over the last week, and his eye patch was gone, but the emotional bruising wouldn't go away for a long time. The city scared him, not only Colpoy, but also just the idea of leaving Medford. Medford had become more of a hideaway for him now than a vacation. Brian had actually planned on leaving at the beginning of October but he had called his work and took a leave of absence after his attack. I promised him nothing would happen if he went with me to the city, but he opted to stay home with my mom. I couldn't have cared less for the big meeting that my boss promised would change all our careers, my mind was on seeing Sara and Sam. I checked my watch as I entered the city. It was just after nine, I was making great time. The meeting was at the office at ten and I could make it to the park by noon to meet my wife.

My wife...I had missed saying that. I remember when Sara and I first married I would go out of my way to be able to say to people....my wife...my wife is at work, my wife made me dinner last night, my wife loves me. I hadn't said it to anyone in over three months now. I hoped more than anything that we could just find some morsel of hope in our meeting for lunch today.

I got to the office and walked through the massive lobby. I didn't miss this lobby at all. It meant stress was upstairs. The walls were covered in our most recent and successful ad campaigns. Behind the desk was our biggest client to date...Step Lightly Kitty Litter....a multi-million dollar campaign done by the senior partners themselves. "*Step Lightly Mr. Whiskers, it's clean!*" the poster boasted.

The girl at the counter was someone I didn't recognize. We went through front desk clerks like coffee. The turnover was mostly due to the fact that we hired University girls who left at the first sight of a better job.

I took the elevator to the twenty-first floor and got out. The office hadn't changed. Several cubicles with familiar faces, downing coffee and punching away on computers searching for clients. Two women answered three different phones constantly, a call coming in every few seconds.

"David! David Emerson, a sight for sore eyes," a man said, from the other side of the cubicles, where there was a line of doors leading to different offices. Mine was one of them. The man was standing in the doorway of my office. It was Harvey Brooks, one of my "work" friends. I never spent any time with the guy outside of work, but somehow we managed to call each other friends.

He came over to me and hugged me, slapping my back. "You're back for the big meeting huh?" he asked.

I nodded. "Yes, Paul sent me the memo about the meeting and asked...or well...demanded I be here today, pretty important I guess. Any idea what it is?" I asked. Together we walked towards my office.

"No idea, they are pretty tight lipped but I think it has to do with Harrison's Department Store," Harvey said.

"Excuse me?" I replied, looking at Harvey.

Harvey smiled and nodded excitedly. I cursed under my breath and walked into my office. They hadn't touched anything except to clean it. It was just the way I left it. I had a great view of the CN Tower from my office window. I could see Young Street thousands of feet below me. I thought it very ironic that I spent the seventies trying to get off Young Street and now I was thousands of feet above it.

I looked out the window and put my hands in my pockets. Harvey sat down in a chair and cracked his knuckles. "Things have been crazy around here without you. Paul and Matthew had to unload your accounts on all of us, and we've been working double, triple, quadruple, hours. Are you back for good?" he asked.

"I don't know. I have an old friend in Medford who was hurt pretty badly, he was beaten up in Colpoy. I can't really come back to work until he's ready to go home."

"What happened to him?"

"Well actually...and this is just between us...he says Greg Harrison, from Harrison's Department Store....," I began my story but was interrupted by a large bodied figure in my doorway. He looked very regal and had wavy grey hair and was dressed in a dark suit.

"Mr. Emerson, welcome back. I hope you found things satisfactory," said Matthew Schwartz, our senior partner and my boss.

"Yes sir, things were just like I left them," I replied.

"I heard you mention Greg Harrison, he'll be joining us for our meeting this morning," Matthew replied. Harvey and I nodded. "Shall we adjourn to the conference room?"

We followed Matthew down the hallway into our enormous conference room. It had been weeks since I sat in this room. The walls were lined with different ad campaigns that we had come up with at this very table. The right side of the room was all glass windows. In the middle of the room was a long rectangular table. There was a handful of men including Paul McKay, the other senior Partner, sitting around the table talking and laughing and drinking coffee. We walked in and shook hands with several of the partners, and I took a seat near the end of the table beside Harvey.

The men were all ad agents for the company. I knew them all by name but had only worked directly with a few of them. Each one of us had different clients and only consulted with each other in business meetings such as this one. We waited several minutes before the conference room door opened again and Greg Harrison, with two other men, entered the room.

Mr. Schwartz stood up and greeted Harrison. Harrison was as Brian had described him, late thirties, nice looking, clean cut, and bright eyed. I could feel my anger build as I looked at him, thinking of what he had done. What made me angrier is that my hands were tied. This man was our second biggest client in the history of the firm. Although based in Colpoy, their fourteen department stores spread out over Ontario used over 1.5 million dollars in our advertising expertise.

Greg was introduced to each one of us. I was last on Mr. Schwartz's right, and therefore, last to be introduced. Greg greeted me with a smile and shook my hand. I clenched his hand and nodded, without smiling.

"Alright Gentlemen, we are all here today because Mr. Harrison has some very exciting news. I will let him explain the details," Matthew said.

Greg nodded. "Thank you Mr. Schwartz. Well, as most of you know, my father started doing business with McKay and Schwartz in the early eighties. Since then our company has grown and by 1995 we hope to have well over twenty-five stores in Ontario alone. My announcement is this...we are expanding our company to include Quebec and Nova Scotia, we are hoping to expand this year and open two stores in both provinces."

"And Harrison's expansion into other provinces means National Ad Campaigns. They want to expand all over Canada in the next ten years. This means we will be launching a campaign immediately...and this account...well Mr. Harrison?" Mr Schwartz passed the conversation back to Greg.

"This account will bring revenues to your company to the tune of 15 Million dollars," Greg replied. Conversation erupted among my colleagues; I glanced at Harvey who was wide eyed. I could see the money signs rolling in his eyes.

"Now I will need each and every one of you to take on a portion of this project. However, Paul and I have decided that we need one of you to head up the entire campaign. And we've decided that person will be...David Emerson." My friends and colleagues erupted into applause and I felt pats on my back, though I could hardly believe I heard my name. Schwartz held up his hand to quiet everyone. "I can assure you though that each and every one of us will benefit from this." Everyone in the room applauded including Greg Harrison. They were all looking at me. I didn't know if I had even heard Mr. Schwartz's speech. I don't think I knew he had appointed me to this account. My mind was spinning.

"Oh Mr. Schwartz...I don't think that I'm right for this account," I finally replied, through the applause. Harvey was patting me on the back.

"No son, your time has come, this is your big chance," he replied, whispering in my ear as everyone continued to applaud.

I shook my head looking for the words. I pushed back my chair and stood up, waving my hands for them to stop. It took several moments before everyone stopped clapping. "I am truly appreciative of this opportunity but I can't do it, I have to turn this down."

"Excuse me?" Schwartz said. Everyone was staring at me now.

"Mr. Schwartz, Mr. McKay, you know I have worked hard for this company for the past eight years. I put my sweat and blood into my clients and I love my job, but I can't do the Harrison account," I repeated, looking at Greg. He was looking at me as well, curiously.

Mr. Schwartz stood up and stuck his face in mine. "Emerson, are you out of your mind? You can't turn this down, we don't even have a scenario for you turning this down. This account will make you rich, and could turn you into a future partner." I stood back away from my boss and continued to shake my head. I didn't even know how to tell them subtly that I didn't want this account. I couldn't bring myself to do it.

"Sir," I cleared my throat and looked at everyone. "Greg Harrison beat a friend of mine to an inch of his life. I can't justify working for this man and especially working side by side with him," I replied. The other men in the room began to converse again when I made the statement.

"You're kidding me? Surely you're not taking a friend's squabbles over a commission of three million dollars. And that's just to start. Greg told me about the lawsuit your friend has against him. It's hogwash, he'll never win, and he's got no evidence. Besides Greg told me about your friend, he's a fag David, a fag, and I don't have any problem with that, but they just aren't like you and I. Don't throw everything away for a friend. Friends come and go, three million dollars will last forever. You want your daughter to go to the best school, have everything she could ever dream of."

I glared at Matthew Schwartz, a man I had actually considered my mentor. I had worked so hard for him, done everything for him, and every ounce of respect I had drained away with one tiny three letter word. I gathered the papers in front of me and without another word walked towards the door. "Emerson, take this account and sit back down with us or you're fired," Paul McKay shouted across the room. All eyes were on me as I turned to face my colleagues.

"I quit," I said, matter-of-factly. I pointed at Greg Harrison and chuckled at him. "And you Mr. Harrison are an asshole, and I hope you burn." I turned on my heels and walked out of the office. My heart was pounding and my head hurt.

I just walked away from my entire career, and walking away from McKay and Schwartz would probably mean I'd never work in the ad business ever again. I'd be blacklisted. Even without the thought of three million dollars to start, I made a very good living, and in one hour it was all gone and I joined the list of unemployed.

I felt sick but my heart...my heart didn't hurt. My heart soared because I had stood up for what I had believed in. I had defended my friend, and stood my ground. Maybe I didn't sit at any lunch counters and get beaten, or ride Freedom Buses or hear Martin Luther King's dream speech in person but, in my own way, I walked out of that office and felt like I had accomplished a revolution. I walked out of the building and into the streets. The sun was high and felt warm for Fall.

I looked at my watch. "Oh no," I said to myself. The hour-long meeting must have gone by fast because it was five past twelve already. "Sara," I whispered and tried to flag a cab. It would take at least a half-hour to get to the park. I prayed she'd wait for me as I jumped into a cab.

"McArthur Park," I said, and the cab drove away from the curb. I watched my office building disappear into the distance. Perhaps I would never set foot in that building again, unless it would be to clean out my office, but I didn't even care about anything in there. I didn't care if I left my pens and pencils behind, I was free.

I got to McArthur Park and it was almost One o'clock. I had missed it, I had screwed up. In my celebration of standing up for Brian and myself, I had forgotten the most important thing about this trip. I dug around my pockets and pulled out my cell phone. I hadn't used it, or turned it on, since my Dad died. I figured if I was going to take a break and "find myself" in Medford I'd do without the benefits of a cell phone.

I hit my directory and flipped through the numbers until I found...*Sara's Cell*...and I hit dial. Within seconds the phone was ringing. "Hello?"

"Sara, oh thank God, listen I'm in the park looking for you, where are you?"

"Hmm David let me think, am I at the park, oh no that's right I was there an hour ago. I'll tell you where we are, we're nowhere near that park or you. How do you think Sam feels? I tell her that today we are finally going to see Daddy and we wait and wait...and it was cold and finally she looks at me and says, I don't think Daddy is coming. Would you like to tell me how the hell I deal with that David Emerson?"

"Well...I...listen...I can," I stammered.

"No don't bother, that's not even the worst of it, do you know what the worst thing is David, I actually couldn't wait to see you. I actually believed today would be different, that today might be a new chance for us. I actually had hope...that's the worst part," she added, and then the phone line went dead.

Maybe her phone died, or the battery was low, or perhaps she was going into a tunnel but no matter what scenario I could come up with, there was no doubt in my subconscious she had hung up. I sat in the park, on a very large rock with my phone in my hand. In the same day, my greatest moment and my worst fears had all come true. My greatest moment is that in forty-one years I finally got to stand up for something and make a small difference, and my worst fear, I had finally driven away my family. I had lost them.

Perhaps, you may wonder why I didn't go after them that day, why I didn't fight. The truth is when it came to Sara and I, my fighting days were over. I didn't have the strength. Selfish? Yes, but I couldn't do it. I couldn't handle it.

So I walked back to my office, got in my own car and headed back towards Medford. I got back to town around dinnertime and my Mother left a note on the front door. She had gone to her bingo game with Mrs. Clarke next door, and Brian had gone down to Sam's Restaurant.

I had walked by Sam's many times since Michael, Brian and I had dropped by there. It looked so cold and empty and I tried not to think about how much I missed old Sam. He had been more of a mentor to me than anyone had...except my father. Sam gave it to me like it was, no holds barred. I walked down to the old shipyard on the Harbour front. The streetlamps were lit giving a perfect atmosphere of serenity. The air was getting a little cooler in the fall breeze and there was a heavy mist rolling in over Medford.

I stood at the waterfront and pulled my jacket around me tightly watching the fog surround everything. Boats in the docks below clinked against the metal poles. I could see Old Sam's place in the distance, with a few lights on inside.

I walked down the boardwalk and stood outside the restaurant. I never got to say goodbye to Sam, punishment for not keeping in touch with those that mean the most to you. Sam meant the world to me, he was kind of like my Grandfather, after my real Grandfather passed away. He was more than that though, he was a friend, a confidant and just someone who made life seem so much easier.

Chapter 31

August 1971

It was very cold for an August evening. I had everything packed and was almost ready to leave for Toronto the next day to start my University classes. Brian and I did one year of community College and then it was time for me to head off on my own. I was both anxious and excited all at once. I decided that since I had everything ready, I would walk down to the harbour and see old Sam before I left.

I walked down the same streets, and past the same old boats, and listened to the sound of the birds above me. I got to Sam's place just after dinner. Sam would be cleaning up inside and getting ready for any late night eaters. I opened the front door and I looked around. There were only two couples and a family left in the whole place. They were done eating and just enjoying themselves with conversation.

Sam was sitting at the bar on the far side of the Restaurant. He had a coffee in front of him and a book opened up on the counter. I walked over to him and sat down on one of the barstools. He looked up at me and smiled. "Well Davey Emerson, you're off to the big city tomorrow, huh kid?"

I nodded. I could feel tears building up behind my eyes, not just for Sam, but for leaving everything behind. A serious chapter of life ending right before my eyes and it was all catching up to me. "Thank you for everything Sam," I said.

He waved his hand at me, "Aw I never did anything special for you. You did more for me, you were a great help around here son and we'll miss you a lot."

"Thank you sir," I said.

"Here, I want you to take this with you, and hang it on your wall, so you don't forget good ol' Medford," Sam said, turning around. Above the bar he always kept a painting that his Grandfather did of the old shipyards. He painted it from the top of the break wall down on the bay and you could see the whole town from there, with each little light and horse and buggy in finite detail. It was a beautiful picture and in the front was old Sam's Restaurant, but of course at the time it was "*Richardson's Ships*" and a different color altogether, but still the same old place.

"I couldn't take this Sam. This picture...it means everything to you," I said in shock, taking the artwork from him and looking at it. I had never held it before.

"Nah, I'm everything in this old place, and when I go someday this place will probably go with me. Now, I said I want you to have that, you take it from Old Sam and don't argue," he said smiling.

"Yes sir, thank you sir," I said. I leaned over the counter and Old Sam and I hugged for the first time since we knew each other. I held him close just like I did my own Dad and he held me back. Finally we let go of each other and Sam cleared his throat.

I could tell his eyes were tearing up. "Get on out of here boy before you waste all my fluids. At my age you can't afford to be dehydrated," he said chuckling. I smiled at him again and nodded. I tucked the picture under my arm and headed towards the front door. Before I left, I turned and looked around at Sam's. Perhaps I knew it was the last time I would ever see Old Sam, or his restaurant, the way I remember it, where I had spent all my years growing up.

Maybe I knew that I would never see another dirty dish, or another smiling family sitting in the booths, or have another one of Sam's amazing burgers. Tears began to creep from the corners of my eyes and I smiled and turned to leave.

"Hey David?" he called from the bar. I looked over my shoulder at Sam. "Don't you let anyone tell you what truth is, you go out there and find your own truths."

"I will, thanks," I replied, and left.

"Goodbye son," Sam whispered, and then began to wipe down his bar.

October 1990

I tried the front door of the restaurant and it was open, as it had been the day the three of us had come down to see it. I looked around the old place, the same way I had done years earlier before I left. The tables were mostly in the same places. The same old-fashion lights hung above each booth. It seemed darker and without as much life as it once had.

I looked towards the bar and there was Brian sitting at the counter holding a drink in his hand. James, Sam's son, was behind the counter talking to Brian. I walked over to the two men and sat down. Brian looked over at me and nodded.

"David, how are you?" James asked, offering me a beer.

I shook my head at the offer of a drink. "Not bad, exhausted."

"How was the meeting?" Brian asked, looking at me closely. He could tell things were not going well. Brian always had this amazing ability to figure out what was really going on inside me.

"Well...I went to the city today, lost my job, my wife, and my kid. Not bad for one day's work."

"How did that happen?"

I looked at Brian, the faint markings of Harrison's beating still on his face. I could see the troubled expression as the memory of being beaten lied in the back of his mind at all times. It had hurt him far worse than any physical bruising. "Let's just say they weren't living up to my principles," I replied, and smiled at Brian.

"Such is life I suppose," James said. I agreed with him whole-heartedly. "I mean look at me, I'm thirty-five years old, single, no kids, never been married, a degree in Psychology, and I'm here babysitting a restaurant I can't even sell. Not exactly my dream life come true. This old place is becoming more of a burden than a memory."

Brian looked thoughtful for a moment. We had started some sort of pity party right here in the restaurant. "I'm 39, single, no kids, a dead end job that I hate, my face is covered in bruises, my ribs still hurt when I sneeze and I'm gay."

James and I both laughed at Brian's facial expression. He said his piece as though he were happy about each thing. "If I were gay, it would be my pleasure to have a guy like you," James replied, patting Brian on the back.

"If you were gay what makes you think I'd have you?" Brian retorted, and we all laughed. That night was a release of anxiety that I had been waiting for since I first came to Medford. We sat there until the small hours of the morning, eating stale pretzels, and trying to top each other with our pathetic life stories. But it wasn't just talking about everything that helped, it was just knowing that we weren't alone. We all had our faults and our problems, but we knew after that night that we weren't the only ones.

The next day Kathy woke up to a banging at her front door. She thought to herself that it was probably me. We hadn't spoken in a week since I came to her house after my fight with Michael. I missed talking to her but I thought, at the time, it would be best if we didn't see each other while I tried working things out with Sara, although now it appeared that Sara and I were done.

She wrapped her housecoat around herself and went to the door. She opened it slightly and looked out. There was no one there. She opened the screen and stepped out onto the front porch. She looked to her right and there was Michael leaning up against the front of the house.

"Michael?" Kathy said, standing in front of him. "What are you doing here, are you alright?"

Michael looked at her, his eyes trying to focus. "Your mailbox is drilling into my back," he said matter-of-factly. Kathy exhaled deeply and waved a hand in front of her face.

"Oh Michael, you smell like a brewery, where have you been?"

"I have no idea, please can I come in?"

Kathy nodded and she threw her arms around him and dragged him into her house. He dropped himself on her couch and buried his face in her pillows. Kathy sat down beside him. "Michael look at me," she said.

Michael said nothing. "Michael, look at me," she demanded again. Michael sat up slowly, moaning as he did, and looked over at Kathy. "Why are you doing this? Why are you hurting yourself and the people you care about?"

"I hit David," he said quietly.

"What?" Kathy asked.

Michael nodded. "I hit him; I actually hit my best friend." Kathy was more than surprised when suddenly Michael began to cry.

"I never meant to hurt anyone," he sobbed. Kathy moved over and wrapped her arms around Michael. He buried his head in her shoulder and sobbed like a child. "I had nowhere else to go and I couldn't go to David or Brian."

"I know, I understand. Michael, I will get you help. We all will, we just want to see you safe and happy, and not like this," Kathy replied, looking into Michael's eyes. Michael nodded. Kathy could see in his eyes that he was still pretty drunk as they spoke but even still she could also see that he understood everything going on.

"I want to stop," he said, looking at her. He wiped his eyes and looked directly into hers. "I want to stop drinking," he repeated.

That same morning, I was on my way out to the store to get some things Mom needed. I just got down the front steps when I looked up. Kathy and Michael were walking up the front path. They stopped at the bottom of the stairs.

"Hi," I said to both of them, in shock at seeing either one of them.

Kathy smiled at me. Michael stared at the ground. "Michael wants us to help him David."

"I know I don't deserve your help," he said, looking up at me for the first time. "But I'm sorry, and I just really can't do this without you or Brian."

Brian came out the front door behind me. He had been listening from inside the porch. "Of course we'll help you, that's what friends are for," Brian said. He walked down the stairs and put his arm around Michael. Michael nodded and smiled at Brian. The three of them looked up at me and I frowned.

"It's just a really good thing," I began. "That you hit like a girl, because otherwise I'd be really mad at you for punching me." Michael smiled and I nodded at him. I walked down the stairs and gave him a hug. "We'll get you any help you need. We will help you through this."

Michael and Brian went inside to get some coffee and Kathy and I sat out on our front porch. "I'm sorry David if I made things complicated for you. I had coffee with Brian yesterday and he told me about you and your wife. I just didn't know how this would go, seeing you again after all these years. I don't want to make things hard for you," she said.

"No, Kathy, you didn't complicate anything. You mean the

world to me, you've always had a place in my heart and that won't ever change," I said. "Besides...well...things didn't work out the way I had hoped when it comes to Sara and I." We were silent for several minutes, just staring across at the park and the leaves falling from the trees. "Kathy, would you like to go out with me tonight?" I asked.

"Excuse me?" she said looking over at me.

"I want to take you out, not just to catch up on old times, or remember our past, or play games with each other, I just would really like to take you out and get to know you. The you now, today, not yesterday, not tomorrow, just today. Will you go out with me?"

"A date? An actual date?"

"Yeah, I mean if you don't want to, I understand, I haven't been exactly fair to you."

"David, I've waited twenty years for you to ask me out again. Yes, I'll go out with you tonight."

Chapter 32

The next few hours, after Kathy left, were spent with clammy hands, sweating, and a whole lot of teeth grinding. Michael and Brian helped me dig through my closet to decide what to wear. I hadn't been on a date since I met Sara. Let alone the fact that this was Kathy...Kathy Carmichael.

I changed clothes three times, showered twice, tried to get my hair to do something less "middle aged." At six-o'clock that evening the doorbell rang and Michael, Brian and I made our way downstairs. My mom opened the front door and I could hear her greeting Kathy. I stood at the top of the stairs, Brian was halfway down. "How does she look?" I whispered.

Michael was sitting on the stairs behind me. "It's Kathy, she's gorgeous, how do you think she looks," Brian replied.

My mom walked into the hallway and Kathy followed her. My eyes widened and my heart just stopped beating. Kathy looked like she did that first day I had seen her on the football field. Her smile lit up the room. She was wearing a light blue skirt and a beautiful sweater to match. Her long hair was tied back into the same ponytail I used to love so much.

I sat on the stairs staring down at this beautiful girl that I had loved so much. Brian looked up at me and smiled. My expression must have looked ridiculous, but she was breath taking, literally. Finally, Michael nudged me and I walked down the stairs. She looked up at me and smiled. I was wearing my very best dress pants and shirt, and my tie that was too tight. "You are stunning," I whispered to her. She smiled and blushed.

I offered her my arm and together we waved goodbye and headed off to Colpoy. We drove and talked, and laughed, we didn't have a single moment of awkward silence. That drive went by too quickly but by the time we reached our restaurant, we both felt something...sparks. Up until then I think our attraction was based on memories of old times past but driving in the car, looking over at each other, our hands brushing up against each other, we felt something that was all new.

The restaurant was one of those places that you only go to once in a lifetime. It was the most beautiful spot in town. There was a well-dressed gentleman in the centre of the restaurant playing soft Sinatra music on a beautiful grand Piano. I escorted Kathy inside and we waited for the maitre'd to come over to us. He sat us in a corner, at a table set for two, with candles and wineglasses. I uncorked the wine and I poured us both a glass. We lifted our glasses into the air and I cleared my throat.

"I would like to make a toast," I said and Kathy smiled at me. I looked into her eyes and felt that same old feeling. I paused for several moments, both of us holding our glasses in the air. She was beautiful.

"To the most beautiful woman in this room," I said.

We clinked our glasses together and she blushed again. "Do you remember the first time we kissed?" Kathy asked.

"Yeah I do, thought about it recently, actually. You jumping into my arms and kissing me," I said, reaching across the table and taking her hand in mine.

"Well, seeing you stand on my front lawn belting out that song, you deserved something."

"True," I said, laughing.

"You treated me like no other person ever has," she said, looking at me seriously.

"Well you don't deserve to be treated any other way."
We held hands and looked at each other across the table. The piano player began to play *The Way You Look Tonight*. Several couples got up to dance beside the piano to the old ballad. "Would you like to dance with me?" I asked.

Kathy nodded and I led her up to the dance floor. I held her in my arms and looked down into those familiar, and beautiful eyes. The piano player continued to play the song as we swayed gently to the music. I began to mouth quietly the words to the song in Kathy's ear.

"I had forgotten how much I missed your voice," she whispered.

I spun Kathy around and dipped her slightly before we started dancing again. "I think I'd forgotten how much I missed everything about you," I replied. Kathy laid her head on my chest as we rocked to the music.

Kathy tilted her head as she looked at me, in that way that only she ever could. I smiled at her and continued to sing to her,. I leaned in and touched her nose with mine. The song began to come to a close. Our heads tilted ever so slightly and our lips came closer. Slowly, but without hesitation our lips came together for the first time in so many years. As I held my lips against the girl I once loved, my mind flashed through everything that had happened over the last few months. Everything going on that seemed to complicate my life seemed to fall in place as I stood there kissing Kathy.

I suddenly pulled away from her and she looked at me curiously. We stood there in the middle of the dance floor and said nothing. "I can't," I finally said. Her eyes widened, everything I had said to make her come out with me tonight, and it all seemed to just crumble away. "I'm sorry, I can't do this." I paused and then turned walking quickly out of the restaurant. A few minutes later I sat outside on the curb in my good suit but I didn't care. I could still taste Kathy's kiss on mine.

It was several minutes before I could sense her standing behind me. She tucked her skirt under her and sat down on the curb beside me. We didn't say anything, we just sat there. Finally Kathy looked over at me, I didn't look at her. "You still love her?"

"I never stopped loving her," I replied.

There was more silence before I looked over at Kathy. This whole night seemed all too familiar.

April 1969

Every spring, since 1962, the town council put on a dance at the arena and Community Centre in Medford. Most parents discouraged their children from going to any dance, let alone an chaperoned by a few senior members of town council. It cost fifty cents per person or seventy-five per couple and the money always went to some great cause in town. For high school kids, it was like our senior Prom. Our school never did a prom, not even once, they left it up to town council to organize the dance.

Everything, literally, up until this very day had been perfect. There was no reason to think that anything in my life could go wrong. It was the day of our four-year anniversary. I was excited that it fell on the same day as the Spring Dance. I hadn't really asked Kathy to go, but I assumed that it was where we would be. We had gone the last three years in a row. I picked her up for our anniversary date, with Brian and Michael in the back seat. She got into the car and looked at both my friends and then at me. She didn't say anything but she seemed a little upset. Kathy didn't say a single word the entire time we drove to the arena. She stared out the window. I didn't notice, because the three of us were looking forward to the Medford Dance. "I'm taking you to the dance tonight," I whispered to Kathy, as Brian and Michael horsed around in the back, punching each other playfully. Kathy didn't speak to me. She just stared out the window.

We usually had a great time but Kathy didn't seem interested in the dance. I opened her door when we got there and she got out, but still said nothing and wasn't looking at me. "What's wrong with Kathy?" Brian asked me. I shrugged, I had no idea.

Music was coming out the front doors of the Arena and Michael was already dancing to the music. He and Brian went ahead of us as I stopped Kathy at the doors. "Kathy, what's wrong?" I asked.

"Nothing," she replied coldly.

"Kathy what is going on, talk to me please, if you don't tell me we're never going to have a good night," I said.

"Seems like you're not having any problem having a good time," she snapped back.

"What's that supposed to mean?"

She rolled her eyes at me, something she had never done and I must admit, it hurt. "This was our night together and you're bringing me to some stupid dance, where we can't even be alone, and you're all happy and excited about it. It's like you're glad to not be alone with me. We talked about driving up to the beach, we talked about going for dinner,"

"Are you kidding me?" I said, getting annoyed. Kathy turned away from me and looked out into the parking lot. It was getting dark outside. I sighed. "Kathy, I just thought we always love to go to the dance. I just figured tonight wouldn't be any different," I replied.

"Well it is different. This is our anniversary, and you'll be leaving for college soon and I'll be leaving soon, and I just thought we'd want to spend as much time as possible together," she replied, still not turning to face me.

"Kathy, we've got a whole summer before we have to think about college, we'll work it out, we'll make it work, and it will be fine. Is that what this is all about?" There was a long pause and Kathy wouldn't look at me.

"Well maybe it won't be fine. What happens when you meet all those college girls?" Kathy said. Her voice was less defiant now and sadder.

"Kathy it's you I love," I said, touching her shoulder gently.

She pulled away. "Well you don't show it anymore," she replied.

I was confused, where was this coming from? "What...I...how...oh forget it, just forget it, you're not ruining my night here with my friends," I fired back. I turned and walked into the dance leaving her alone at the front of the arena. She turned and watched me walking into the dance and tears began to fall down her cheeks.

I knew as I made my way through the crowd that I had hurt her with what I said. Spending time with my friends was not what was important to me right now, I truly wanted this dance to be a great memory for Kathy and I. She was right, we would be leaving for college soon and I wanted tonight to be special. It was our last spring dance, probably forever. I didn't understand why Kathy wouldn't want to be here with me.

I sat on the sidelines watching Michael and Brian having a great time, laughing, dancing with friends, just being happy. I was confused and hurt and angry. I hadn't seen Kathy come in and I was too proud and too hurt right now to go out there and talk to her. I needed to cool down.

"Hi David," said a female voice from beside me. I looked up at the person speaking to me. It was not Kathy, it was Carol-Anne Morrison.

"Oh, hey Carol-Anne," I replied, returning my stare to the

ground.

"Where's Kathy?" she asked.

"Who knows," I replied bitterly. I'm sure Carol-Anne picked up on that. The music changed and they started playing our song...the song Kathy and I loved together. It only depressed me more. I slumped my shoulders and lowered my head further.

"Do you want to dance with me David?" Carol-Anne asked.

Immediately the word 'no' came to my mind but apparently my mind and my mouth are not one and the same. "...yeah sure why not," I blurted out. Next thing I knew I was on the dance floor with Carol-Anne Morrison. A girl I could barely stand to talk to, let alone dance with. A hundred couples were swaying together on the floor and my mind was barely on what I was doing as we danced to *When A Man Loves A Woman*. I was listening to the words and thinking about Kathy.

My lack of attention suddenly ended, and I was snapped back to reality, when I realized that Carol-Anne was leaning in close to me, so close she was going to kiss me. Our lips touched for less than a heart beat, and everything came down in a crash in that heart beat.

"What are you doing?" I screamed at her, shoving her away. The crowd seemed to part and I looked across the room between the couples and there was Kathy standing there looking at us. Her face was blank and her eyes were full of pain, I could see her heart breaking before me. I stared at Kathy, my mouth open to say something, but nothing would come. Kathy turned, tears in her eyes, and ran back outside.

Murmurs rippled through the crowd. I looked at Carol-Anne who seemed to have no real opinion on the situation. Then I looked at Michael and Brian who were both dancing with girls from our high school. Michael looked disappointed. He motioned for me to follow her.

"Kathy, wait," I called out. I followed her outside and across the parking lot to a large empty field across the road. Kathy kicked off her shoes and ran into the middle of the field. Finally, she slowed down and I caught up to her. If she had been wearing something other than heels, and didn't have to take them off, I never would have caught her. "Kathy please stop, just let me explain," I said.

"Explain what David? We're still in the same town and you're dancing with someone I hate, let alone when we're miles apart, what then?"

"I was upset, it was nothing, I was thinking about you, and she asked me to dance and I just wasn't thinking clearly, we just had a fight."

"So every time we fight you're going to go out and dance with some other girl, or kiss them, or do whatever else?" Kathy demanded. She was crying now and I wanted to hold her so badly. "How could you do this to us?"

"I thought we understood each other Kathy, I wanted this to be a special night for us," I said.

"So much for that I guess," she replied.

We stood in silence underneath a spring sky full of stars. A huge full moon was rising in the east casting an orange glow over us. We could hear the dull hum of the music across the way. "It's not going to work is it?" she asked, suddenly.

"What?" I asked.

"Us. Being apart, you in the city, me on the opposite side of the Province, it's not going to work."

"Are you saying you don't want to be with me anymore?" I asked. I could feel tears building in my own eyes. I couldn't cry in front of her.

"Is that what you want?" she asked me, looking into my eyes. We stood face to face looking at each other.

"I don't want anything that means I can't be with you."

"David, how can we be together, if we're never together. Maybe we just have different paths."

"So then you want to break up?" I asked. Tears squeezed out of the corners of my eyes and ran down my face. Kathy saw them and began to cry as well.

"I think its best," she cried.

We stood in that field for an hour, saying nothing,. That was the final word and we just stood there looking at each other. Neither of us wanted to move, if we could have stayed standing in that field forever we would have, if it meant being together.

"I love you," she said.

I looked into the eyes of the girl who was my everything, I could remember every smile, every laugh, everything I ever did that made her happy. I lived to make her smile. My whole life meant nothing without her voice and her touch. With all those thoughts going through my mind I turned away from her. I was the first person to walk away that night, and left her standing in that field. I don't know how long she stayed there, and I had almost forgotten my biggest regret in life but now I remember what it was...I never told her I loved her back, and I did. I loved Kathy so much. If I could have stopped the world that night just so we could be together I would have done it. But that night standing under those stars, we were over.

Chapter 33

October 1990

"If you love her than you need to be with her," Kathy replied, interrupting my memory.

"Kathy," I said, looking at her. "I don't want to hurt you again."

"David, listen, for the last twenty years I wondered every day of my life...what if you and I got a second chance. We got that chance tonight...and now I know."

"You know, twenty years ago I walked away from a girl that I loved with all my heart, and I've never forgiven myself for it," I said.

"Well, don't make the same mistake twice, go after her," Kathy said. She had tears in her eyes but she was smiling and I could tell she meant what she said. I looked at her and reached over and touched her face gently. She smiled at me through her tears and squeezed my hand. "Go get your family back," she whispered.

The night I went on my date with Kathy, Brian and Michael stayed at the house. Brian assured me that what Michael needed right now was a night home, just to talk. And they talked and talked, and talked some more. Brian helped Michael through his first night. It didn't seem like much to us but Michael told us the next day that it was the first time in twelve years that he went an entire day without a drink.

The night passed without many problems, although Michael

seemed to get very agitated before he fell asleep. Brian never left his side. They talked about anything to keep his mind off drinking. I came home from my date with Kathy and crashed on the couch beside them. They were sitting at the coffee table playing cards. Michael seemed almost hyper.

"How was your night?" Michael asked, without looking at me.

"Kathy and I decided that it won't work," I replied.

"Again," Brian said, glancing over at me. I nodded.

"So how are you feeling Michael?" I asked.

Michael shrugged and laid his cards down. "I'm alright, I'm feeling a little anxious. I just don't really know where to go from here."

"Well tomorrow we'll make some calls, and find out where the closest AA meeting is. Then you make that first step and go to a meeting. You can go from there," I said.

"You want me to go to an Alcoholics meeting?"

Brian and I looked at Michael. "Yes," we both said.

"I don't know if I can do that," he said, standing up and pacing the floor.

"Michael, you said you wanted our help, you said you wanted to stop," Brian said.

"Well I didn't really think it would involve other people, I mean, I can do this on my own, we can do this. I don't need someone quoting their beliefs at me and telling me how to quit, I can do it on my own."

"Really, cause you don't look so good at the moment and I think if we let you out of here, you'd be at the beer store before we could blink," I said.

"Not true, although just a few tinnies wouldn't be so bad," he replied. He was joking but we weren't impressed.

"Promise me that you'll go to a meeting," I said.

Michael looked from Brian to me, and then nodded half-heartedly.

We stayed up late that night and both of them listened to me talk about Kathy just like they had so many years before. The night Kathy and I broke up twenty years ago, they sat with me out back of the arena, listening to me cry. We sat there for hours, just lying in the grass looking up at the stars. Michael kept telling me that this would pass, and Kathy and I both had great things ahead of us. I didn't believe him, at the time. He was there for me that night, and he was there for me even now when I was dealing with the same thing all over again. I would be there for him during anything he needed me to be.

It was almost three-o clock in the morning before Brian decided to go up to bed. Michael and I got some coffee and sat on the back porch looking at the same stars we had lived under for the last forty years. We didn't speak for the longest time. We sat on the edge of the deck drinking our coffee and listening to the fall breeze.

I couldn't help but think about how much I loved the sky over Medford. I had walked the streets so many times looking into the twilight thinking about how beautiful the stars were over this little town. God must have liked us a little more to give us such a beautiful sky.

"Do you believe in God?" I asked, suddenly. I don't know where the question came from, and I knew the answer, I mean it was Michael Finn, God was not in his vocabulary.

"Yes," he said, without hesitation.

I looked over at him. He was looking up at the sky like I was. "You do? Really?"

"Yeah I do, I always have. I mean, if we don't believe in something bigger than us, if we don't believe there is a bigger picture than our little lives, what's the point. God is just a given in my mind...how could a life this beautiful be created by natural process. Someone had to have a hand in it."

I was a little astonished to hear Michael say that. Maybe being sober really was affecting his mind. We were quiet for several more moments before either one of us spoke again. "I used to have this bible my Nana gave me when I was twelve. It had this great hand sewn cover on it. She told me a friend had given it to her years ago when she was a little girl and now she wanted me to have it. At first I thought it was kind of stupid...but then I actually opened it one night and started reading it. We had just come over from Aussie, and I felt like I was the only kid in the world, and I would never make any friends. I opened that old bible and right in the cover someone had written...Friends Are Friends forever. I started reading it and I never stopped, read the whole thing cover to cover," Michael replied.

His eyes seemed so deep in thought as he took another sip from his coffee.

"Is that why you believe in God?"

"No, not completely. Do you know what my biggest fear was when I came to Canada from Aussie?" he asked. I shook my head. "Snow." I looked at him curiously. "I was scared to death of snowstorms, the idea of driving in them was even worse. One winter my Nana was flying in to spend Christmas with us. We had to drive to the airport in Toronto to pick her up. The snow got bad about half way there, it was just piling up and my Dad couldn't see a thing and I huddled myself in the back, and tried to hide but it was like the snow was getting us. I sat in the back seat, my arms wrapped around my knees and I was just praying for that snow to stop...I was so scared. We got to the airport and picked my Nana up, and she sat in the backseat with me and we started the drive home and you know what? The snow had stopped completely, the sky had cleared and it was like this brilliant greenish yellow color that just seemed to light up the night like I have never seen before or since. I said to my Grandmother, 'look at the sky, it's so light,' and she looked at me and smiled and said, 'yes, God is lighting our way.' I knew from that moment on that God really was lighting our way, not just hers and mine, but everyone's. And you know I can't honestly ever say I've given Him anything back, or even done anything to make Him proud. If I were Him I would have turned my back on me years ago...but somewhere inside I always felt like He never has. That's why I believe in God, just faith."

I nodded at him and we returned to looking up at our great sky. We didn't discuss anything else that night but he definitely made me think. My mother never stopped telling me how much God loved me, but I don't think it ever really sunk in. I had always depended on myself to survive and maybe that was my problem. That night, I think, deep inside my head I even talked to God. I only asked for one thing...I asked for him to take care of Michael, give him strength. My Grandfather always said the Lord works in mysterious ways. That night as Michael and I watched the night sky, for me it seemed to glow...it had a strange green glow that was almost like it was lighting a path.

The next day, when I got up, I called around and found the closest meeting, which was in Colpoy. I could tell that Michael wasn't crazy about the idea of going. But he was doing it...whether it was for him, or for us, I don't know.

After dinner Michael headed out and drove to a small church in Colpoy. It was dark by the time he got there and there were only a few lights shining from the basement of the church. The lot had several cars in it and Michael pulled into a parking spot and got out. He looked towards the back of the church. There was a back door propped open with a cement block and several guys were standing outside having a cigarette, talking and laughing.

Michael stood beside his car and took a deep breath. The guys he could see standing outside the church didn't look much like drunks to him. He took a couple of steps towards them and then stopped. They didn't see him in the parking lot, and he didn't want them too. If he walked through those doors, it would mean ultimately admitting he had a problem. It meant admitting that the last twelve years of his life were not his own but controlled by his problem, it meant admitting defeat, something Michael Finn didn't do.

He took a step back and was about to turn around and leave. It would be that easy, he would kick this thing on his own without being preached at. But then he knew that his two best friends would never forgive him if he didn't try it. He had to prove to us that he could do this.

He turned back around and walked steadily towards the back door of the church. A couple of the guys looked at him as he pushed by them but none of them said much. He walked through the back door of the church and down several stairs. He stood at the bottom of the stairs in a church basement. It was a large rec-room set up with old wooden chairs, a podium at the front of the room and a table of food and snacks on the far side. Men and women of all ages 20-80 were in the room and they spoke to each other like they were the best of friends. There seemed to be no generation gap, or any differences of opinions, they were all here for the same reason.

Michael stood at the bottom of the stairs looking at each person. They seemed so happy, and content to be with each other. Michael swallowed the lump in his throat and suddenly turned on his heels and headed up the stairs. He wasn't going to stay here another minute. "Hey!," someone called.

Michael stopped at the top of the stairs and turned around. A middle-aged man was running after Michael. "Yes," Michael asked.

"My name's Bob, how are ya?" he asked, offering Michael his hand. Michael looked at it carefully investigating for ulterior motive and, not finding any, he shook the man's hand. "I'm an alcoholic," he added.

"Excuse me?" Michael said.

"I'm an alcoholic, how about you?" he asked.

"I'm here for the meeting," Michael stuttered.

"Good, good for you, are you a member of the Colpoy West Group?"

"Oh no, I didn't realize you had to be a member, I just came for the meeting," Michael replied.

"Oh good, no membership required. You're welcome any time, we're glad to have you. How long have you been sober?" Bob asked.

"Well, including this last hour, a day...," Michael replied, trying to joke. Bob nodded approvingly.

"You know what, every day counts. One day at a time brother," he replied.

Someone at the front of the room was calling for everyone to take a seat. "Do you wanna come sit down, I'll sit with you at the front, maybe we can go out for coffee afterwards and talk about getting you a sponsor," Bob said.

"Yeah I'll think about it," Michael replied.

Bob nodded and shook his hand again and went to sit down. Michael watched from the door as everyone took their seat. *"God Grant me The Serenity to accept the things I cannot change, the courage to change the things I can...,"* the group recited. His mind was racing, did he belong here? This wasn't where he would normally belong and yet something compelled him to stay. He looked towards the front door, and then back at the meeting. The crowd stood and they all bowed their heads.

"Our Father who art in Heaven, Hallowed be thy name...," the crowd said in unison. Michael nodded and stepped into the room. He walked behind the crowd and stood beside Bob. Life for Michael had been one big party. If things got a little too serious, it meant in his opinion that he hadn't drank enough. He had done everything he could to make people believe he was someone that he wasn't. He did all he could to make people believe he was in control. Underneath all that Michael was caring, and understanding, and protective and he loved and hated just like anyone else. Brian and I understood Michael more than anyone but even that was not much. Michael Finn would always be a mystery to the world but someone...anyone would be honoured to have him as a friend.

Bob looked over at Michael and nodded. Michael nodded back and took a deep breath, maybe things weren't so bad after all.

Chapter 34

"David," my mother said, from upstairs. "Can you please make sure that trash gets out before you go to bed?"

"Okay I'll do it right now." Brian and I were sitting at the kitchen table playing a couple rounds of poker waiting for Michael to come home from his meeting. It was past eleven, and we hoped it had gone well for him.

I left the table and grabbed the heavy trash bag by the front door. It was cold outside, and the air was starting to feel more like winter. It was nearing the middle of October, almost Thanksgiving, and winter was well on its way. I hauled the big trash bag out the door.

Up the street, there was a car turning down towards my house. I thought maybe it was Michael getting back from his meeting. He had decided to stay with Brian and I, at my Mom's, until next week when Brian went back out west, and then we would take things from there. I set the garbage down to get a better grip and the car pulled up out front. It was not Michael, it was a police car.

I waited several moments before a police officer got out from the front seat of the car. His female partner got out of the other side. Their radio was yammering in the background but they seemed to not notice it. The two officers walked towards me as I stood on the front step with my garbage.

"Mr. David Emerson?" the female officer asked me, looking

down at a notepad. She could barely read it in the glow of the streetlamp in front of the house. I nodded.

"Yes, is there a problem?" I asked.

"Mr. Emerson, we understand you're a good friend of a Mr. Michael Finn, temporarily listed at the Pine Hill Hotel, room 309."

I rolled my eyes. This was typical, I knew things were too good to be true. I peered through the darkness trying to see if Michael was in the backseat. I knew he was late, he had probably lapsed into a bar and beat somebody up. The officers looked at me sternly. I couldn't read their faces. I sighed deeply.

"What has he done this time, I knew we should have gone with him, I knew this wasn't going to work. Whatever it is, we'll deal with it Officers, I'm very sorry you had to come out here...," I began, shaking my head.

The male officer held up his hand and they both took a step towards me. "No sir, Mr. Finn isn't in any trouble." He cleared his throat gruffly and his gaze turned from stern to sympathetic. I looked from one officer to the other.

"What's going on?" I asked.

The front screen door opened and Brian stepped out onto the porch behind me. "What's going on David?" Brian asked.

"I don't know, something about Michael," I answered over my shoulder.

The officers looked at each other and the man spoke again. "Mr. Emerson, Michael Finn was in a car accident tonight, he was on his way towards Medford on Highway 12, and he was hit...head on by a drunk driver in a pick-up truck."

"What?" Brian said, his voice wavering.

"Is he....alright," I asked. The big cop looked up at me and cleared his throat. His hands fell down to his sides.

"I'm sorry Mr. Emerson, both cars were totalled, he's dead."

"NO!" Brian's scream rocked the quiet neighbourhood as he dropped to his knees right there on the porch. Tears began to fall from my eyes, I sobbed and dropped beside Brian. We wrapped our arms around each other. We sat on the porch sobbing. My mother ran to the front door and instinctively dropped beside us both and held us.

The officers stood there in our front yard, keeping straight faces as we cried together. I told my mother through tears and cries of pain that Michael had been killed. "Oh god," Brian cried, hearing it again.

"Oh no, how could this happen," my mother cried.

"Michael, oh God Michael," I sobbed.

Brian fell to the cement and pounded his fists against the ground as my mother held me tightly like she hadn't done since I was ten years old. Michael was gone.

"So are you goin to stand there all day, and look at it, or are we goin to play some damn Baseball?"

"Hey, Blonde girl? My friend wants to know your name, he thinks you're just cool. There ya go, Mate"

"Doesn't recognize me from a Koala in a tree"

"Change is what you make of it Davey, I mean, no one truly changes, we just stay the same and the world around us changes. It's an illusion, kind of like a trick with mirrors you know."

"Fun? Fun? My fun involves women, now I've spent a lot of years accepting Brian's life choices but I am straight, completely straight and so are you...I think."

"It's College, never tie yourself down when you're swimming in a sea of hot, young fishes,"

"Brian...focus...and you're gay remember, start acting like it,"

"No one, should ever hate you for who you are. Of all the people in the world who didn't understand who you were, I was the worst. I didn't want you to be any different than I was. And it took me less than a week to realize you aren't different than anyone else because of your sexuality. It means nothing to me now because you've been my best friend. It never stopped you from helping me when I needed you, it never stopped you from loving your family, and it never stopped you from being someone I could always count on. This is not your fault...what these people did to you is their sin not yours."

Honestly, I don't even know where to go from here. My best friend was gone, it was like a nightmare, it was like it would all end in just a few more minutes and everything would be the same and Michael would not be...dead. Dead...what a horrible word, so short, so scary, so permanent.

I felt numb from the ankles up, like I couldn't feel anything coming at me. I didn't want to hear "I'm sorrys" all over again and put up with the sympathetic stares of Mom's neighbours who felt sorry for Brian and I because we had lost my father and now our best friend.

It didn't seem right, it didn't seem even remotely possible, that I could be putting someone else only a few months later into the ground. I would never see Michael again, never hear his ridiculous wisecracks, or see him laugh at something that no other person would ever laugh at.

I sat in my room with the door closed as though I was sixteen again and sulking about something. I left my yearbook from 1965 open in front of me. It had a picture of Michael and I in our football gear near the front. I looked down at Michael's face and tried to come to terms with the fact I would never see it again.

Maybe I should have spent that first day with Brian after we got the news. Maybe we could have used each other's support but I wanted to be selfish about my grief...again. At night, as I sat there on the floor still staring in the dark in the general direction of the yearbook. I could hear, faintly, Brian crying in his own room. I knew how much we were both hurting, but neither of us wanted to be with the other. When we were together...the two of us...it only made us realize that one of us was missing.

It seemed like only moments later that all of us were standing over an open grave with Michael's cold grey casket hanging over it. The wind was icy cold that day and blew like an angry breeze. I stood beside Brian and my mother, pulling my long coat tightly around me and staring down at the casket as the minister spoke.

I didn't give a speech like I had done at my Dad's funeral. I didn't feel like I wanted to share anything about how I felt about Michael. My Dad, was my Dad, and everyone had something different with him. Michael was different, he was my best friend. I don't know if Michael ever planned to be buried on the hilltop in Medford beside his Mom and Dad but that's where we put him. It turned out he had left his estate in the hands of his first wife Shannon, Brian and myself. His second wife, was nowhere to be seen at the funeral.

Shannon was stunning, as expected. She shook my hand and gave me a warm hug and thanked me for everything I had done over the last few days. Whatever I had done, I had done it like a zombie barely remembering ever leaving my house.

The minister announced his final wishes and said, "Ashes to ashes, dust to dust."

I noticed as the minister spread the sand across the casket in a "cross-like" pattern that despite the howling wind, the sand did not move as it fell onto the casket. I wondered if anyone else noticed but the thought passed. Everyone turned away and began to walk towards their car. We would all go back to the church and spend the most depressing two hours talking to friends and family, eating and pretending life would go on.

As the crowd walked away, Brian and I stood there by the grave, beside each other. We didn't speak or move. We folded our hands in front of us, and stared down at our old friend. So close...yet so far away.

"God is just a given in my mind...how could a life this beautiful be created by natural process, someone had to have a hand in it."

I felt a hand on my shoulder and I turned. It was Kathy. She was wearing a black dress and her eyes were streaked with tears. "I am so sorry," she said.

"Thank you," I replied. She offered a hug and I held her in my arms. I needed to feel her warmth against me again just to allow me to feel something. She smiled at me encouragingly and squeezed my hand before turning and walking towards everyone else. I turned back to Brian and put my hand on his shoulders.

He looked at me and I saw in his eyes how I felt in my heart. "What's life going to be like without Michael Finn?" I asked. We both looked down at the casket again.

Brian reached up to his lapel and unpinned the white rose they had given to his closest family and friends. Brian leaned down and touched the casket gingerly. He placed the rose gently across the top. "G'day Mate," he said, touching the casket one last time.

Together the two of us turned away from our best friend and if

I didn't know better I'd say I could feel Michael walking with us, waiting to say his piece.

It was only several days before I packed my things and got ready to leave Medford. It was just after a very quiet and uneventful thanksgiving and it was time to go back to my home in the city. Brian had decided after Michael died that he would stay in Medford for as long as he felt necessary. My mother certainly didn't want to be alone and I was relieved that Brian would be with her.

I carried my bags out to the car and Brian and my Mom stood by the car to see me off. I hugged my mother tightly, holding her close. I felt like I was leaving her for good. I felt like something was missing as I left Medford that day.

"Take care of her Brian," I said to him, and he nodded. "Thank you."

"Don't thank me, I'm happy to stay," Brian said.

"Tell Kathy I said goodbye if you see her," I asked. Brian nodded. "Take care Bri," I said, and I put my arms around him and hugged him. We slapped each other's backs and then shook hands after our hug ended.

I pulled away from that driveway and looked in my rear view mirror. I could see my best friend and my mother standing in my old front yard and I could feel that familiar lump in my throat. I didn't want to leave, the last two months had been full of heartache and adventure and awakenings. No matter what, I was going to miss what I was leaving behind. But right now I had to remember I was going back to my family, I had to show them that they were what I wanted. Maybe everything that had happened here was so that I could figure that out, and I could only hope that I didn't find it out too late.

Chapter 35

It was almost 5-o clock by the time I reached the city. Kathy's words rang in my head over and over again, like an echo..., "Go after her," she had said. I drove towards the familiar neighbourhood where Sara and I had a two-story house. I hadn't been there in over two months. Things looked good, the lawn was as green as everyone's on the block, the windows spotless, and it looked a lot like all the other houses on the street. I never realized how bland everything was.

I pulled into the driveway and sat there, not moving. It looked as though no one was inside, but Sara's car was parked in the garage on the left side as if she was waiting for my car to park beside it. I sat in there for the better part of forty minutes listening to the radio, and the weather with the possibility of the first snowfall tonight.

I lowered my head and closed my eyes, everything seemed to be such a blur right now. When would everything just stop. "So what are you waiting for? She's right through that door, everything you decided you wanted?" Michael said.

I looked over at Michael sitting beside me in the passenger seat. "What if she doesn't want me?" I replied.

"Doesn't want you? You know as well as I do that she tried harder than even you did to make this marriage work. Now you made up your mind, and left your first love to come all the way here and make that beautiful woman in there as happy as she has made you. But instead you're sitting out here in your car, talking to someone who doesn't exist," Michael said, matter-of-factly.

I nodded in agreement and looked over at the now empty seat beside me. It was time to make an effort for something that mattered to me. It was time I showed my wife and daughter how happy they make me. I got out of the car, closed the door, and made my way towards the front door. The garden on either side of the front walkway was wilted, and pretty much gone, preparing to be smothered in snow until next spring.

I got to the large oak front door and lifted my hand to knock. I had keys, I could have walked right through the front door and yelled, "honey I'm home," but I felt like I didn't quite belong to this house anymore. My hand hung in the air, not quite knocking, and then I dropped it back to my side. We had put a small garden bench on the right side of the door and I sat down on it. Sometimes I came out here after dinner on Sundays to have a cigar. I didn't do it often but sometimes, so I could hear the kids playing street hockey and my neighbour washing his car, just to watch another day turn into night. It was perhaps one of my "old man" habits I was starting to fall into. I sat on the bench and just looked out into the street.

The front door of the house opened at some point and Sara stepped out onto the porch. She was facing back into the house telling Sam to sit still, she'd be right back. She turned and faced me and jumped back in surprise. We both stared at each other without saying anything. "What are you doing here?" Sara eventually said, getting over the initial shock. I didn't say anything and she cleared her throat and tried again. "I didn't mean that the way it sounded. I just meant...why are you sitting out here," Sara corrected.

"This is where I always sit after supper," I replied.

"You drove three hours after dinner to sit outside your house," Sara replied.

My house, she had actually said my house. I took this as a very good sign and it gave me a ray of hope. I looked at my wife and I thought back to the first time I saw her across that dance floor. She was so beautiful, stunning, moved my whole world. How could I feel anything for her except love? How could I have forgotten what she meant to me?

"I have to get something from my car," she said. "I'll be right back." She took a few steps towards the garage and I stood up.

"I love you Sara," I said. She stopped, but didn't turn to face me.

"You don't love her?" she asked. There was no bitterness in her voice, she was just asking.

I walked over to her and put my hands on her shoulders. "There could never be anyone but you."

She bowed her head and I thought maybe she was crying but she wasn't. She turned around to face me and she looked at me with eyes of curiosity.

"Where is this coming from?" she asked. "Where were you months ago when you left here? Why didn't you tell me you loved me before you left the house, slamming the door behind you?"

"It took me this long to realize what I wanted and how much you and Sam meant to me. Sara, Michael Finn was killed in a car accident last week," I explained. Sara covered her mouth with her hands.

"Oh no, David, I am so sorry, I had no idea. Why didn't you call me?" she asked.

"I didn't want that to be something you felt you had to support me through. I mean...when my Dad died, I know that we decided it was just too much to pretend everything was alright and I didn't think that was any different. It was horrible, Michael passing away. But the funeral was beautiful...it suited what Michael would have wanted." I hated saying that the funeral was "good." People often used that term to describe my father's funeral but it bothered me. "Good" was not a way to describe a funeral. I leaned against the wall of our garage and closed my eyes thinking about Michael again. "It was a shock to everyone's system, and we miss him so much. But you know when Michael died, things just seemed to finally fall into place. I started to realize what was really important to me. He told me once that if I'd stop being so pigheaded, and start listening to my heart, I'd be that much further ahead and that just seemed to make even more sense after he was gone. And I realize that coming back here, and telling you that I loved you might not be enough to make you see that I know how wrong I was about everything...but Sara, if you let me I will spend the rest of our lives making that up to you. I want to be with you, and I want us to be a family again. You are my whole world, no one else but you. I actually thought for a flash that I belonged somewhere else and then it seemed like when I got to that other place, with that other person, all I could think of is why you weren't there with me."

Sara reached up and put her arms around my waist. It was the first time she had held me or touched me in so long. "Did you ever think that I wouldn't want to make things work with you? I feel the same way about you that you have always felt for me" Sara said.

I looked into those beautiful, crystal blue eyes and I fell in love with my wife just like we had so many years ago. "I will do whatever it takes, anything, to show you what you mean to me."

"All I need to do is look into your eyes, David, to see what I mean to you. I've waited so long to see you look at me like that again."

We leaned in close and I kissed her, a kiss that was deeper and meant more than any other kiss in my life because I wanted her to feel how much I had missed her, and how much I wanted to spend the rest of my life with her. No matter what had happened, for those few minutes that we stood in our driveway, that kiss absorbed all the pain. We had a lot to deal with but it all seemed that we could do it, together.

The front door opened and my little girl stepped out and saw us standing there in each other's arms. "Daddy," she squealed, and jumped into my arms. I tossed her into the air and then held her close to me rocking her gently.

"Oh Angel, I missed you so much," I cried. Tears began to come down my cheeks as I held my little girl, with my wife by my side. Sara offered me her hand and I smiled and took it. Together with Sam in my arms, and Sara on my hand, we walked into our house and closed the door.

Sara was actually overjoyed that I had walked out of my job. She had hated my job since the day I started and she hated most of the people I worked with. Harvey always hit on her at staff parties, and my boss made me miserable and I believe her words were, "oh thank you," when I told her I walked out and sort of quit and sort-of got fired. Either way I was free from employment. Certainly we both had enough money to get by without worry for awhile. My job may have been terrible, and one of the causes of our eventual separation, but a six-figure salary makes things seem worthwhile, at least for a time.

Sara wrote for a magazine out of Brampton. It was a quaint little publication that decided what was stylish for the new season and who was wearing what. Sara was the Assistant Editor and she enjoyed her job for the most part. It was a far cry from journalism, which was what she was trained to do, but she had worked her way up to that position within the magazine and she was proud of it. She worked hard. So it might have been a little harder for her to walk into her office the next Monday morning and tell them she was leaving. She handed her resignation in and then walked out.

They begged her to stay, and they offered her a raise that even made my eyes go big, but she stood her ground and left. You might wonder why she did that? The weekend I came back to be with my family was the best weekend of my life. I made love to my wife all night long, she slept in my arms, and if I was the type of guy to kiss and tell...I'd tell you it was the best sex of my life. Then we'd get Sam up and we'd make breakfast, and we laughed around the dinner table and Sara and I couldn't keep our hands off each other under the table.

We showered together, dressed each other, got our daughter ready and headed for parks, museums, carnivals, anything we could think of that would be the most fun to do. We had missed so much, and I wanted to make it up to both of them, but going to these places was not about retribution, it was about making up for lost time. It was about being together, it was about giving Sam a chance to smile again which she hadn't done a lot of since her Mom and I separated.

At the end of that weekend we even made a three-way-promise to each other as we sat at the kitchen table playing with clay, and making little clay people. We promised each other that we would never be apart again and I think we all meant it. Things were not fixed, nothing is ever immediate, it takes time, and growth and communication but Sara and I gave it a good start. We spent hours talking about everything, how we felt and what we had done without the other person.

I told her about Kathy, and everything that had happened in Medford in full detail, no omissions and she told me she was glad that I came to the conclusions I did. I think I still saw a flicker of jealousy in those shining eyes but we were being honest and that was what was important. She told me about being asked out by the mailroom guy at the magazine and I laughed at her and she slapped me with a pillow. The guy in the mailroom was nineteen!

It was Sunday night, as we were going to bed, that our lives changed forever. I lay beside her as she read a book and I just watched her as she seemed so entranced by what she was reading. She looked down at me and took off her thin rimmed glasses. "What are you staring at, Mr. Emerson?" she asked.

"A beautiful creature, Mrs. Emerson," I whispered back.

She went back to reading her book and I lay on my back looking at my old familiar ceiling. "You know, us being here together, after everything that has happened, my Dad dying, Michael getting killed, Brian getting beat up, Kathy, and my Mom, and just everything that has gone on over the last month...it makes me really, really think," I said, looking at my wife.

"What do you mean by that?" Sara asked setting her book down.

I turned over to face her and put my arms around her. "How often do people actually get the chance to realize how short life is and that every moment should be seized and appreciated."

"You are getting entirely too philosophical on me, David," she replied.

"No, but seriously, people never do what they dream of doing and if Michael was here, he'd tell me that I should learn from everything and to go for my dreams."

"Okay so what are your dreams that you're not going for...and don't say Kathy Carmichael because I'm not okay with that," Sara replied, jokingly.

"No...I mean life dreams. What is something that you have always dreamt of doing but never done it because you think life is too short, or that it will never work, or things got in your way?" I asked Sara.

She appeared thoughtful for a moment. "Write a book," she replied finally. "Write a book, stay home with Sam, and learn to do something new every week, just be my own person and not have to follow someone all the time."

"So do that," I said.

"Excuse me? You're unemployed, someone has to bring home the bread," she replied scoffing at me.

"You know what I really honestly believe that if we follow our dreams right now, today, that the bread will come to us," I replied.

"You are turning into a senile old man," she said, patting my head.

"Sara, when is there going to be a better time to do this?" I asked her, getting on my knees at the foot of the bed. "Sam is young and living in a big, cold, impersonal city, and I miss Medford. I want to be there with my mother, and Brian, and you. Just think, you could write your book, and we could buy the little house with the picket fence you always wanted and we wouldn't have to have bars on the windows."

Sara was smiling so I knew that my ideas were sinking into her head. I looked at her and leaned over and kissed her gently on the lips. "I could buy Sam's place, I could buy that beautiful old Restaurant and turn it into the place that I remember."

"Sam's place?" she asked, cynically.

"It's an old Restaurant where I used to work when I was a teenager. Sam died and James, his son, is having trouble selling the old place. He has so many dreams of his own, and he just wants to leave his Dad's pride and joy in good hands and no one loves that old place like I do."

"You want to run a restaurant?" she asked me unbelievingly. I nodded and smiled like a kid. Sara looked at me and shook her head. She stared into my eyes and she saw that everything I was saying was more than just a sudden rant of insanity, I was serious. "Let's do it," she said without any more hesitation. "Let's pack it up and see where we go."

That was the conversation that sparked Sara walking into her office the next day and resigning, much to everyone's shock. By the middle of the week, Sara was on the phone with my mother telling her that we were moving back to Medford. My mom was so happy, and Brian was just as excited.

I called several real estate agencies, one to sell our house in the city, and one to find us a house in Medford. Sara cried a little when they nailed the "For Sale" sign into the ground outside the house. We had so many memories there, and it wasn't quite as easy to leave as we thought it would be. But our future was more important. It was quite amazing how everything could change in a heartbeat. Within three days, our house was up for sale, and we had all our household possessions loaded into the back of a moving van, with the help of some very large gentlemen from the moving company, and we were off to Medford by the end of the week.

Thursday afternoon, we pulled up outside my old house, with my Mom standing on the front porch waiting for us. We got out of the car and Sam ran towards my Mom. "Grandma," she cried out, and my Mom picked her up and swung her around.

"Oh how are you my pretty little girl, I missed you," Mom

said.

"I missed you Grandma. Mommy says we're going to live right near you, so I can come see you every day now," she said, smiling.

"Well won't that be wonderful. Now if you run inside, there are some cookies for you on the counter," she said, winking at Sam. She squealed with delight and rushed inside the house. I smiled at my Mom and gave her a big hug. So much heartache in the past few months that sometimes I forgot how great she was.

"How are you doing Mom?" I asked.

She nodded and smiled at me. "Every day I miss your Dad a little more. I sometimes forget he's not here and I still set an extra plate at the table, or I almost call him to come cut the dinner meat, but having Brian here has been wonderful," she said. I smiled and nodded and I stepped aside so my Mom could see Sara. She smiled and waved lovingly. They hadn't seen each other for almost a year.

"Oh Sara, how are you?" my Mom asked, putting my arms around her.

"I'm very good Mom, thank you," she said.

"We missed you around here, but I knew my boy would come to his senses. Emerson men can be pretty pig headed," my mother whispered, and Sara laughed. Brian came to the front door and stepped outside. His bruises and scars were almost gone, barely noticeable.

"There is a cookie monster in the kitchen that is devouring everything in sight," Brian said.

"Hey Brian," I said. He smiled at me and shook my hand firmly. It had only been a week since I left but I had missed my old friend. "Sara, this is my best friend, Brian. Brian this is my wife Sara," I said, introducing them. Sara shook Brian's hand and smiled at him.

"I've heard so much about you," she said.

"I'd like to say the same but I haven't yet." Brian looked at me accusingly, and I shrugged. "I can't wait to get to know you," Brian replied. "And I would assume that little bouncy brunette in the kitchen is Sam?"

I nodded. "That's my little girl."

"Well supper is almost ready, are you guys coming in for dinner?" my mother asked. We agreed that both of us were starving, it had been a big day for moving and the furniture wouldn't be at the new house until well after seven that night. We had rented a small house only a few blocks from Ryerson, until we figured out where we wanted to live. We didn't really have the luxury of time to look at different houses yet.

We had the greatest meal, I loved my Mom's home cooking, and nothing tasted better. When our dinner was almost over and Brian was playing ball with Sam on the floor, getting to know her, I stood up as Sara and my Mom cleared the table. "Sara and I have an announcement to make," I said.

Brian looked over at me and my Mom stopped what she was doing. "You're already married, so that's not it, and you're not pregnant cause…well you're both old," Brian said jokingly.

"Watch it," Sara warned threateningly.

"No nothing like that. I spoke to James about his purchase price for Old Sam's Restaurant, and I've decided to buy it." The room went quiet, no one said anything. My mom set the plates she had in her hand down on the counter. Even Brian said nothing, the only noise was Sam making car noises on the floor.

"You're gonna buy Sam's Place?" Brian finally said.

I looked over at Sara. "Yeah absolutely, James is ecstatic about it. He wanted someone that would love the place like his father did, and let's face it, I'm the only one who could love that old place like that. I'm giving him his asking price. I would have bartered a little more but I know James wants to travel and go back to school and I want to help him do that."

"Well, I wondered what you and Sara were going to do when you came back to Medford. But…you don't know anything about running a restaurant, David," my mother replied.

"I know, you're right, but I do know this town. And I know what made Sam's Place special for everyone that lived here. I know what they remember and I know what old Sam loved, so I think that I can do it and I really want to do it. It's the most exciting thing I've had come across my mind in a long time."

"What about you Sara?" my mother said, looking for her approval.

"Well, I'm going to write my novel that I've always wanted to write, and take care of Sam, and I'll help David wherever I can in the Restaurant," she replied.

"So my question is…raise your hand if you want a job in my

restaurant," I asked.

Sam stopped playing with her toys and shot her hand in the air. No one else moved. She waved it around anxiously. Brian laughed and we all laughed with him. He stood up off the floor and shook my hand firmly. "I'm there for ya, I miss that old place," he said.

I nodded and smiled and my Mom gave us a hug. We were all excited about the future of our family. It would take a lot of work but it would be worth it in the end.

I didn't hire contractors, or construction crew, or even professional painters. I waited a week until the deal was closed and James had his money. He took one last look at the old place and shook my hand and he was gone. I told him he was always welcome back at the restaurant.

Brian, Sara, Mom, and I got out our old clothes on and started fixing up the place. We fixed the holes in the bar, and rewired the lighting, which caused a lot of sparks and a few shocks, but we did it. I bought new lamps for over the tables, and new chairs for the bar.

Sara and my Mom scrubbed and cleaned and painted from top to bottom. They made every inch of the place shine like it hadn't shined in years. There were layers of dust in the kitchen, but by the time they made their way through it, everything looked spotless. We had sore fingers from hammers, and cuts and bruises from wood and lumber.

Brian and I redid the walls, and the floors, all the while singing Michael's favourite songs. We had the best time of our lives fixing that old building up. I made sure everything was the way I remembered it, that very little changed, and everything had to be the same. Change in life was inevitable, and sometimes unwanted, at least we could make this one thing unchanged.

I think that restaurant, and the two months we spent in there fixing the place up, saved us all. For my Mom, it helped her do something other than think about my Dad. For Brian and I, it helped us come to grips with Michael's death, something we both had been avoiding. And for Sara, Sam and myself, it was our chance to build our family again.

By the time the four of us were able to stand back and look at a job well done it was mid-November. Sara and I had found the perfect house and coincidentally it was in Ryerson Neighbourhood. It didn't have a picket fence or gables like Sara wanted, but I promised her at the crack of spring we would renovate. We bought the house gladly and moved right in. Sam spent every day getting to know her Grandma and her Uncle Brian better, and we spent the long, cold winter evenings telling her and Sara all the great stories about Michael.

It was like a dream come true that day when we stepped back and looked at our restaurant. We had transformed it into the place I knew and loved. I closed my eyes and I could hear Sam humming to himself from behind the bar. "You did good son," he'd say.

"You okay?" Sara asked, leaning on my shoulders.

"Yeah I'm fine, it's just...perfect...," I said, giving her a kiss.

That night Sara and I spent the evening in the restaurant, alone, cooking the first meal. I cooked her up something simple, and then we ate while we discussed what we wanted in a chef. We would have to hire a few waiters and waitresses, and a full time cook, and a part time one for when the other wasn't there. Everything would take time to organize but it would be worth it when we were finally done. I think we all thought redoing the restaurant would never end. Snow fell from the sky outside and we looked out the windows and my mind once again went back to the summer when the four of us painted the fence outside. The fence was barely visible through the snow but it didn't matter, I could still see us out there, Kathy, Brian, Michael and I throwing paint on each other and having a great time.

Maybe those memories were gone but we had lots more ahead of us...Sara and I. High school seemed to go by in a blink, although at the time, it felt like it would go on forever. Looking back now, I have to struggle to remember a lot about it and yet some things you never forget. For instance I will never forget the writer who once said...*"So we beat on, boats against the current, borne back ceaselessly into the past."*

At the time when we all read *"The Great Gatsby"* in school, very little of it made sense, including that passage. However, years later, as Sara and I sat staring out the window of "Sam's Place," holding hands, and just dreaming about our futures and talking about our past, it all seemed to make sense. Not just Fitzgerald's writings, but everything, it just seemed to fall into place as we sat there.

My months of indecisiveness, and wondering, and confusion seems to finally make way to a clear vision of the future. That's not to say that at forty-one years old, my troubles were over. I had a daughter to raise, a new millennium just around the corner, and a new life to build in the town where, ironically, it all began. A person's hometown is almost like a second womb. It's where they're born into and some people spend their whole lives trying to get away from it...and yet for me...I realized that I had spent almost thirty years of my life trying to get back here. And now here I was...exactly where I should be.

My original point still stands true. Some people believe that a right of passage happens in adolescence or early adulthood, but I know the truth. A right of passage is just that moment when you accept your mortality, and take life by the throat and appreciate it till death. It can be horrible, gut wrenching experiences that forces you to this conclusion, or it can be beautiful, lovely moments. In my case, it was a combination of both. I still don't believe in the so-called mid-life crisis, I simply believe in a time of awakening. For me, my awakening came that late summer in Medford, with Michael and Brian by my side. I may have lost my Dad and Michael, two of the most important people in my life, but in some strange cosmic way that's what it took to make me realize what my life was really about.

On November 22, 1990...we opened Sam and Finn's...our perfect little diner. Old friends, new faces, family, and people from out of town, who had lived there twenty years ago, came to our grand opening. Sara and I stood at the door and welcomed everyone, and Brian showed them to their tables. It was like a dream come true, and I never would have thought that my future would be linked right into my past. I couldn't have wished it any other way. Well...that's not entirely true. I could wish that my father and Michael were there but in my heart, deep down, I knew that they were. *"Alone but never quite alone, I face an empty chair, and yet somehow in the silence, I know that they are there."*

"So we beat on, boats against the current, borne back ceaselessly into the past."